PRAISE FOR THE SC

CW00521535

"A book? Who's got time to read
play."

Beeromir son of Alehouse, Steward of Gonner

"We didn't run out the Trail of the Croaked 'screaming like little
girls.' It was more like excited yelling."

Lededgas son of T'Olive d'Oil

"I don't fall off that many barstools."

Gimmie son of Glowstick of the Kingdom
of the Dragon Mountain

"This book is fixated on tits. I mean, just because a girl is blond and
has big tits, it doesn't mean she isn't smart, too."

Elli Mae, Shieldmaiden of Rojo

"I liked the part about Arrowshaft's sword."

Argyle Evinrude, daughter of El Round

"I have a large sword. It was called Nasal and it was busted. Now the
elves have put it back together and I call it Narithil."

King Telecom, the king formerly known as
Arrowshaft son of Arrowhead, called Elixir the
Elfrock, Westhomey, the heir of Whiskeysour,
Ellendale's son of Gonner and bearer of
Narithil, the Sword that was Busted and
Remade

"Arrowshaft's other sword."

Argyle Evinrude, daughter of El Round

"Why don't you come up and see my mirror somctime?"

Glenda of Lostlorriland, Lady of the Woody

"I'm sure I would have loved this book, but I can't read."

Airtoground, the Great Windbreaker, first of the great eagles.

"This book is okay, but if you want to know what really happened, read *The Green Book of the Great War with the Great Schnoz* by Froyo Bagpants."

Grandkopf the Gray

"Yeah, go buy *my* book."

Froyo Bagpants, a halfbit of the Mire

THE SCHNOZ OF THE RINGS

The Schnoz of the Rings

A Parody
of J. R. R. Tolkien's
Lord of the Rings

John J. Osterhout

Clovendell Press
Central Oith

John J. Osterhout is a Professor of Chemistry at Angelo State University. He is an admirer of the works of J. R. R. Tolkien. He lives in San Angelo, Texas with his wife, Kathryn.

ISBN-13: 978-0-9962175-0-7 (Paper)
ISBN-10: 0-9962175-0-9 (Paper)

Published 2015
Version 1.B

This story is an unauthorized parody of J. R. R. Tolkien's magnificent work, *The Lord of the Rings*. This work has not been approved by any rights holders including, but not limited to, the MGM studios and the Tolkien estate. No endorsement is implied.

To my brother, David, and my friend, Cindy, whose books inspired me to put this story on paper. Many thanks to my editor, Lisa McNamara, who was a fount of great ideas. Special thanks to my wife, Kathryn, who was amused by the whole thing.

CONTENTS

CONTENTS

"War must be, while we defend our lives against a destroyer who would devour all; but I do not love the bright sword for its sharpness, nor the arrow for its swiftness, nor the warrior for his glory. I love only that which they defend…" –Faramir to Frodo, The Lord of the Rings, Book 4, Chapter V, The Window on the West

ONE

A Meeting in the Mire

I've had enough adventure for a while.
                                    –Froyo Bagpants, Halfbit of the Mire

Froyo Bagpants, a halfbit of the Mire, was standing in front of his icebox at ten o'clock on a Tuesday morning in July, hung over and wishing that there were at least one cold ale left. He was trying to remember what had happened the night before: he thought he'd been drinking Red Flagon Summer Ale with Sammy, Rosalie, and Primrose. He also thought he remembered that Primrose had flounced off in a huff over something he said, but he couldn't remember what it was. *Oh well,* he thought. *It isn't the first time something I said has caused Primrose to flounce off.*

While he was trying to decide if he cared about the current Primrose problem, there came a rhythmic pounding on his front door. He staggered to the door and pulled it slowly open, squinting against the bright sunlight.

"Grandkopf!" he said, recognizing, even in his mentally clouded state, the gray cloak and the long, white beard of the wizard. "I... I...

I'm surprised to see you. I didn't expect you back in the Mire until the fall."

"Greetings, Froyo," said Grandkopf, pushing his way through the door. "I finished my business in Minor Tetons much sooner than I expected," he said, "but that tale will have to wait. It has been a long and thirsty journey. Let us have a drink and smoke a pipe before we get down to business."

"Sure, Grandkopf, make yourself at home. I've got some Red Flagon Summer Ale in the cellar," he said, worried not so much about the ale as his supply of pipeweed. Grandkopf went through pipeweed like locusts through spring wheat. Returning from the cellar, he put four quarts of the Summer Ale in the icebox and brought two to the table.

Grandkopf grabbed a bottle, twisted the cork out with his teeth, and spat the cork into the fire, where it began to smolder sullenly. He took a long pull at his bottle.

"Taki, that's good stuff," he said. "Do you have any pipeweed?"

Froyo's heart sank. If this were a long stay, he'd have to hock the candlesticks again to keep Grandkopf in pipeweed. Then, much to Froyo's relief, Grandkopf continued.

"Because if you don't, I do." He reached into his sleeve, pulled out a tightly packed bag as big as a sack of sugar, plopped it on the table, and said, "This is Gonner Gold. Get your pipe."

Gonner Gold thought Froyo as he rushed to the living room to retrieve his pipe from the armchair. *I bet he had to pay dear for that!* Froyo had never had any Gonner Gold, but it had quite the reputation in the Mire. While it was nothing compared to Lostlorriland Silverleaf (generally acknowledged to be the best), Froyo was nevertheless anxious to try it. He'd had a little Rojo Red, imported from

Rojo through Brie, and lots of Southbog Leaf, grown in the Mire on the little solid ground found in the Southbog. Southbog Leaf was known mostly to the locals and those outsiders unfortunate enough to have business in the Mire. Froyo deemed it quite good. The rest of Central Oith had more discerning tastes, however, and called it "Mire taki," smoking it only if nothing else was available.

The pipes were soon loaded and lit and the two friends settled in for a long morning of drinking, smoking, and conversation. Froyo quickly noticed that the Gonner Gold was quite a bit more potent than he was used to, and soon it became difficult to open a fresh ale or form coherent thoughts. It didn't seem to bother Grandkopf, though. He kept smoking, drinking, and talking—especially talking.

Grandkopf regaled Froyo with stories of his travels, of all the easy elf girls he had encountered, of the twin elf sisters he met in Clovendell, of the ale he had swilled at the Red Flagon and the Dancing Donkey, and of his hopes for a vivacious redheaded barmaid he'd met at the Lazy Plowman in Minor Tetons.

Froyo, for his part, had little new to tell. He was still hanging out with his drinking buddies Sammy Gimchee, Marty Banksmuck, and Poupon Roak. He was still dating Sammy's cousin, Primrose Peachtree, and Sammy was still seeing Rosalie Clover. Marty and Poupon had a bet concerning the new barmaid at the Floating Frog in Frogbottom, but she seemed content to flirt with them both and keep her panties on.

The morning wore on: elevenses came and went, followed by lunch, snackies, and afternoon tea. Dinner was a cheese plate with crusty bread, roast lamb, and corned beef with cabbage, with apple and gooseberry pie for dessert. They drank all the rest of the Summer Ale, including the stash in the cellar, and switched to Goldenwasser, a liquor distilled from corn mash by the monks in Brie. Still Grandkopf kept quiet about his important business.

At three in the morning, Froyo went face down in the last slice of apple and gooseberry pie. Grandkopf smiled at the gentle halfbit, a friend for many years, and moved to the very comfortable human-sized chair in the living room. He settled in with his pipe and a last glass of Goldenwasser. He sat puffing his pipe, sipping his Golden-wasser, and considering the upheaval that his news would bring to his unsuspecting friend.

TWO

DARK PORTENTS

Let lying rings lie. –Bobo Bagpants

F royo couldn't decide which hurt more, his throbbing head or the morning light, which felt like daggers stabbing into eyes. *When did I get a canopy on my bed?* he thought. Then he realized he was looking at the underside of his breakfast table and that his arm was wrapped around a chair leg. *Note to self,* he thought, *never again try to stay up all night drinking with a wizard.* He tried to stand and made it as far as his hands and knees before it became too painful to continue. After a minute, he was able to use the chair and the table to lever himself into a vertical position. His face felt funny. He wiped it with his hand and his hand came away splotched with purple globs. He tasted one of the globs. *Gooseberry. It's the last of the pie,* he thought. He washed his face and staggered to his icebox. Empty. Not a single cold ale left. As he was staring remorsefully at the empty icebox, a crash and a stream of very imaginative, multilingual profanity came from the front hall.

Grandkopf had once again head-butted the chandelier. Froyo peered into the hallway. Grandkopf stood rubbing his forehead as the chandelier unremorsefully swung slowly to and fro in the morning light.

"Hey, you old fart, keep it quiet. My head is pounding." Froyo had started off yelling but tapered down into a whisper in deference to his head.

"Old fart, indeed! Your head wouldn't be pounding if you hadn't tried to drink a river of ale last night. And by the way, you're out of ale."

"You're the wizard—why don't you pull your staff out of your pants and conjure us up some?" retorted Froyo.

"I'm not *that* kind of wizard. I don't conjure *ale*. Which reminds me, we have important business today. So let's get some breakfast started."

Froyo rummaged through his liquor cabinet, stocked mostly with empty bottles, and found a half bottle of Yuck's Breath, a fiery liquor distilled by a family of squint-eyed men on the other side of Brie. Sentient beings shunned it because it tasted a lot like turpentine and produced hangovers that were likened to having oliphants playing dodge ball in one's head.

Beggars can't be choosers, thought Froyo, having a snort. And another. After the second had a moment to sink in, Froyo decided he might be able to manage breakfast. Second breakfast, actually, because they had slept through the first.

When they had finished their omelets, pancakes, bacon, eggs Benedict, fried breaded bog eels with white gravy, ham steaks, French toast, bagels, lox, and six pots of coffee, it was time for elevenses, and when they had finished that it was time for lunch. So in the early afternoon, with a two-hour break before four o'clock tea and with a good stock of cocktail peanuts for snackies, they settled down at the kitchen table to the business at hand. Grandkopf took a few minutes to get his long-stemmed pipe drawing to his satisfaction.

"After I left you in the spring," began Grandkopf, "I made my way down to Minor Tetons where I was able to study the old manuscripts and—"

"And drink good ale at the steward's expense and whore and generally make a nuisance of yourself," interjected Froyo.

"*Where* I was able to study the old manuscripts *and* learn some things that most particularly concern *you*, Froyo Bagpants, so put a sock in it and let me finish. There are many forgotten rooms in the bowels of Minor Tetons and some contain writings from the time of Whiskeysour. Some time ago, I began to suspect that your uncle Bobo's ring was a ring of power. The nine rings of men sustain the Schnozgoons who serve the Great Schnoz. The seven rings of the dwarves are lost or destroyed and the three of the elves are borne by the enemies of Schnozmon. The only ring of power unaccounted for is the Schnozring, the ring that Whiskeysour cut from the nose of the Great and Powerful Schnoz on the slopes of Mount Drool at the end of the Second Age."

"This *is* serious," said Froyo. "How can we know if this is truly the Schnozring?"

"There is a simple test. Throw the ring into the fire. If it is the Schnozring, the heat will reveal secret writing. If it is a cheap dwarf knockoff, it will just melt."

It took Froyo a half hour to find the ring. He finally remembered he had used it to make himself invisible while he watched Sammy and Rosalie on a "picnic" and it was in his green shorts in the laundry basket. He brought it back to the living room and placed it in the coals. After a few minutes, glowing red letters appeared on the ring. Grandkopf reached in with the tongs, plucked out the ring, and offered it to Froyo.

Holding the ring over Froyo's hand, he said, "If it is the Schnoz-ring, it won't be hot." *Of course*, he thought, *if it isn't, it is going to burn the snot out of you. Better you than me.* He let it drop into Froyo's hand.

"Grandkopf it *is* cool! I can see writing running along the outside. It says 'Property of the Great and Powerful Schnoz. If Found, Return to the Barn Adoor, One Rue-the-Day Avenue, Soredoor. Postage Paid.'"

"That tears it," exclaimed Grandkopf. "We are in some deep taki."

THREE

BEST LAID PLANS

The Great Schnoz has sent the Schnozgoons to thc Mire to get the Schnozring and whoever has it. That would be you.
–Grandkopf the Gray to Froyo

Grandkopf began puffing furiously. Froyo ran to his liquor cabinet and chugged the rest of the Yuck's Breath. He came back to the table, lit his pipe, and after a few minutes, felt sufficiently calm to speak.

"Grandkopf, shouldn't we take the Schnozring to Sorryman or at least go to him for advice? Isn't he the head of your order?"

After a moment Grandkopf said, "It is a pity, but no, we cannot go to Sorryman the Spumoni. It looks as if Sorryman is plotting with the Great Schnoz to enslave Central Oith. You see, on my way back from Minor Tetons, I stopped in to see Theobald…"

"Thcobald?"

"You know, Theobald son of Theodome, the King of Rojo. White beard, golden hall on a hill, lots of horses…"

"Oh, *that* Theobald. I thought you meant Marty's cousin, Theobald Reedbottom, the carpenter in Brie."

"No, Theobald King of Rojo. Why would I want to speak with Marty's cousin?"

"Maybe you wanted some carpentry?"

"I *went* to Rojo to speak with Theobald, the King of Rojo!" said Grandkopf. "When I arrived they were cleaning up the Ferret Face mess."

"Who the taki is Ferret Face?"

"Ferret Face was the nickname of the King's advisor. His official title was Grimpie Wormguts, His High Excellency, Chancellor, and Right Hand of the King, but behind his back everybody called him Grimpie Ferret Face or shortened it to Ferret Face."

"Was?" asked Froyo.

"Was. When I arrived in Rojo, Theobald's son, Theorug, and Theorug's cousins, Jethro, and Elli Mae had recently returned from the Westlands to report that yucks had been raiding, burning, killing, pillaging, raping, making taki in public, and generally running amok. The yucks bore shields emblazoned with a white fist, middle finger extended. The Rojoriders had taken prisoners who said that they came from Eisenfang and worked for Sorryman. Ferret Face called Elli Mae a liar to her face so she whipped out her sword and ran it through his chitlins. Then, while he was distracted by trying to put his intestines back in, she whacked off his head. Lots of blood. Hence the mess. Theobald was under some of Sorryman's enchantments, doubtless aided by Ferret Face. I was able to lift the enchantments and Theobald is himself again. Now Theobald is pissed. Theorug is pissed. Jethro and Elli Mae are pissed. The whole family is ready to ride to Eisenfang and shove that white finger up Sorryman's butt."

"What's stopping them?" asked Froyo.

"First there's the Yuck Corps, an army of twenty thousand yucks that Sorryman is keeping at Eisenfang. Treemoss the aughnt, or as you say in the Mire, tree-wrangler, has been watching Eisenfang. Treemoss says there are thousands of larger-than-normal yucks running around in the daylight, which is unusual for yucks. Furthermore, it looks like they are preparing for war. They have been busy digging, chopping trees, burning, melting iron, and forging weapons. Theobald doesn't have enough Rojoriders to go up against that many yucks. Then there is the fact that Sorryman is a Spumoni wizard. Even I would be hard pressed to go up against Sorryman *mano a mano*."

"So Rojo's frecked," said Froyo.

"Not necessarily. Treemoss is trying to rouse the aughnts. If he can, there's some hope. Theobald King lent me a cart and a swift horse, so I snuck through the Gap of Rojo under the cover of darkness and came straight here. I figure we'll head over to Clovendell to the Last House in the Crack of the Oith with the Schnozring and talk El Round into loaning us a few thousand elf warriors. With the elves, the aughnts, a bunch of pissed-off Rojoriders, and a little elven magic, wham, bam, end of Sorryman and his yucks."

"We," said Froyo. "I distinctly heard you say 'we'. Why did you say 'we'? I'm not going anywhere. I have a pleasant life. Plenty of pipeweed. Primrose. Good food, lots of parties."

"There is this one little thing," said Grandkopf, holding up his hand and making a small gap between his thumb and forefinger.

"One little thing?"

I ran into Badgrass the Brown on my way. He said that some of Schnozmon's scouts caught Gack in the Zombie Marshes. You remember Gack, the creature your uncle Bobo won the ring from on his adventure with the dwarves? Well, Gack spilled his guts about the ring. Now the Great Schnoz suspects that Bobo's ring might be the Schnozring, so he sent the Schnozgoons to the Mire to get the Schnozring and whoever has it. That would be you."

"Yuck taki!"

"Luckily, they made a right instead of a left at the Edwin Muir and headed out into the Nekked Lands south of Smirkwood.

"Then I'm safe!"

"Not exactly. Badgrass says that the Schnozgoons ran into a troll skinner and got directions. They should be here tomorrow or the day after. That's not all. Schnozmon put out wanted posters on you from Brie to South Gonner and in the southern countries, Del Mar, Ember, and Grim. By now there are hundreds of bounty hunters looking for you. To top things off, Sorryman decided that *he* might as well have the Schnozring as let Schnozmon get it. Treemoss sent word that there is a company of yucks of the White Finger on their way to the Mire."

"Holy yuck taki!" said Froyo.

"I think you better go with me to Clovendell tomorrow morning. In the meantime, let's smoke some pipeweed."

FOUR

A TASTE OF BRIE

What the fried yuck taki do you want?
                                    —Baldiman Butterbutt

Bright and early the next morning, after first and second breakfasts but before elevenses, Grandkopf and Froyo set out from Boggy End toward Halfbittowne on the road that wound through the Westbog. The rickety horse cart rattled and the wheels squeaked with every turn. Their gray, swaybacked horse, named Dobbin by the Rojoriders had, in a fit of optimism, been rechristened Blitzen by Grandkopf. Blitzen plodded along, his hoofs making sucking sounds in the mud with every step. Grandkopf smoked silently on the seat while Froyo sulked in the back under a tarp.

They passed through Halfbittowne and the Eastbog without incident. It was midafternoon before they left the bogs entirely and ascended three feet onto what was locally known as the high road to Brie. Blitzen found the drier dirt of the high road much more to his liking than the muck of the bog roads and was able to make better time. Their speed increased a notch, from plod to slow.

As they squeaked and rattled along the high road to Brie, they met nine riders clothed in black, riding black horses asking for Froyo Bagpants; a dozen yucks of Sorryman's Yuck Corps bearing black shields emblazoned with the white finger of Sorryman asking for Froyo Bagpants; twenty thugs from west of Brie carrying axes, scythes, and wanted posters asking for Froyo Bagpants; a dozen Haragrim—tall, grim, and dark-skinned—bearing long, devilishly sharp swords asking for Froyo Bagpants; a cool baker's dozen Corsairs of Ember wearing red head scarves and eye patches, carrying cutlasses and parrots, asking for Froyo Bagpants; Wimpy Webfoot of Wimpy's Wonderful Wine Emporium of Brie, carrying an unpaid bill for eleven silver pigs and nine bronze chickens (about US $750) asking for Froyo Bagpants; and Mrs. Daffodil Mudbottom and her pregnant daughter Tulip with murder in their eyes and a court order in their hands asking for Froyo Bagpants.

"I swear," said Froyo, when Grandkopf let him out from under the tarp after dark, "she was doing the whole bunch of us after the graduation dance last May. It could have been Marty, Poupon, Fatso, Sammy, Grumpy, Sneezy, Happy, Doc, or Fred."

"Fred?" said Grandkopf.

"You know, Sammy's pony, Fred. It was a real interesting party," said Froyo. "Did you get a load of that moustache on Mrs. Mudbottom? And those legs? Like an oliphant. I'll bet Tulip looks exactly like that in twenty years."

They rode in silence for a while, contemplating the cruelties of genetics. The night deepened. Soon the road was barely visible in the scant moonlight that filtered through the canopy of trees. When Froyo thought it could get no darker, they emerged from the woods into the moonlight of the open fields and so came at last to the west gate of Brie. Grandkopf was broke, as usual, so Froyo paid the night-time toll of one bronze chicken and they were granted admittance (seventeen bronze chickens equals one silver pig; nineteen silver pigs equals one golden goose). They wound through the town and finally arrived at the threshold of Brie's finest inn, the Dancing Donkey. On the third knock, the door flew open to reveal Baldiman Butter-butt, who held a meat cleaver that Froyo thought was large enough to use on trolls or maybe oliphants.

"What the fried yuck taki do you want?" shouted Butterbutt.

"The hospitality of your inn is much diminished these days, Baldiman!" said Grandkopf.

"Grandkopf, my word! Welcome! You must excuse me, there has been such a crowd of suspicious characters through Brie today—all looking for some idiot named Froyo Bagpants," he said as he ush-ered them into the parlor.

"Who's your little friend?" asked Baldiman, pointing a short plump finger toward Froyo.

"I'm Fro…, er, Freddy Undermud from the Mire, Mr. Butterbutt. I'm with him," said Froyo, flipping a thumb at Grandkopf.

Grandkopf cleared his throat and intoned, "I seek Arrowshaft son of Arrowhead, called Elixir the Elfrock, Westhomey, the heir of Whiskeysour, Ellendale's son of Gonner, and bearer of Nasal, the Sword that was Busted."

"Nope, never heard of him," said Baldiman.

"Tall, skinny guy, stringy black hair, nice ass, probably drunk," whispered Grandkopf.

"Oh him! String Bean we call him, or Deadbeat. He's passed out on the back table by the fire on the right hand side. By the way, he's broke, so you are out of luck if he owes you money."

They walked back to the fire. Sure enough, there was a skinny guy with long, unkempt, black hair face down on the back table. Grandkopf walked up to the table and hooked his staff under the leg of Arrowshaft's chair. He whipped his staff back and Arrowshaft went sprawling on the floor.

Arrowshaft shook his head and squinted upward. "Grandkopf!" he said. "That was harsh." He rubbed his jaw. "Sit down and buy me an ale."

"Not now, Arrowshaft. We must confer about the road ahead."

"We're going somewhere?"

"We are going to Clovendell to seek the aid of El Round, to lift the threat of Sorryman and Schnozmon and save Central Oith!"

"Wha?" said Arrowshaft.

"Argyle will be there," said Grandkopf.

"I'm in, let's go," said Arrowshaft. It had been a few months since he was last in Clovendell and had last seen his lover, the beautiful half-elven daughter of El Round, Argyle, known as the Evinrude of her people. Suddenly enthusiastic, Arrowshaft struggled to pull himself to his feet, rolled under the table, banged his head as he attempted to stand, and wound up unconscious on the floor.

"What's wrong with him?" asked Froyo.

"Girl trouble," said Grandkopf, thinking *at least he will fit in the back of the horse cart.*

FIVE

WHITHERTOP

Being a wizard isn't all about fireworks and parlor tricks, you know.

–Grandkopf the Gray

As the sun came over the eastern hills, Grandkopf and Froyo were on the seats of the rickety horse cart, eating their first breakfast as they jounced down the road. Arrowshaft was in the back, still unconscious.

"Now what?" mumbled Froyo, through a mouthful of a fried bog eel muffin with egg and cheese.

"I suspect we were recognized in Brie. It won't be long before our pursuers discover that you are not at Boggy End and are hot on our trail again. We need to get off the road. We will head for Whithertop. It is the highest point around. I will use the Sight of the Ouestari to find the safest route to Clovendell. Perhaps we can shake our pursuers.

They soon came to a cart trail, barely visible in the high grass. Grandkopf steered the broken-down horse up the trail and in a few seconds they were invisible to travelers on the road.

A half hour after they turned, up the road came the nine riders in black, the Yuck Corps, the thugs from Brie, the Haragrim, the Corsairs of Ember, Wimpy Webfoot and Mrs. Daffodil Mudbottom and her pregnant daughter, Tulip, with murder in their eyes, still carrying a court order but now riding a pony they had purchased in Brie.

The travelers arrived at Whithertop shortly before dusk and proceeded directly to the summit. They had to go the last hundred feet on foot since Blitzen couldn't negotiate the steep path. The top was ringed in stones and there were empty ale bottles, pizza boxes, and used rubbers strewn over the ground, evidence of past ranger camps and frat parties.

Grandkopf reached into the sleeve of his robe and brought out a tube covered with mysterious runes, which he extended.

"I will now use the sight of the Ouestari to peer into the misty distance and divine our path," said Grandkopf.

"That looks like a cheap dwarf telescope, Grandkopf. What do you hope to see with that?" asked Froyo.

"This is an *enchanted* cheap dwarf telescope, upon which are woven spells known only to the Ouestari, spells devised when the forests were young and before the coming of men out of the west. So hold your tongue and let me look," said Grandkopf, raising the instrument to his eye and gazing off into the distance toward the south.

"Well, what do you see?" asked Froyo.

"Patience, impertinent halfbit! These things take time. The mysteries of far-seeing are not to be hurried," replied Grandkopf.

He fell quiet for a few moments, gazing intently into his enchanted instrument. "I see columns of dust arising from the main road to the south and west of us. Our pursuit is moving east along the road. If they continue to the bridge of the Makewater tomorrow it might be trouble. But that is for tomorrow," he said. "Those black riders we saw on the road today were certainly the nine Schnozgoons. The Schnozgoons were kings and queens of men who were seduced into taking one of the nine rings of power that the Great Schnoz forged in the fire pit of Mount Drool in Soredoor. Wearing the rings caused them to fade over the centuries until they are almost ghosts. The capes they wear give them physical form and their swords are real. Their powers are strongest at night. If they can smell the Schnozring from the road, then we may have visitors."

They built a tiny fire and had a frugal but warming supper. Afterwards, they drank up their supply of ale and started in on their pipeweed. Froyo passed out at midnight and Arrowshaft soon after.

Lightweights! thought Grandkopf. *I guess I'll stand the first watch.*

At around three o'clock, Grandkopf jerked awake. Something was coming up the hill. He jumped up and piled wood on the fire. Grandkopf kicked Arrowshaft in the ribs until he rolled over groggily.

"The Schnozgoons are upon us!" Grandkopf whispered. Next, he grabbed Froyo and shook him.

"Primrose?" Froyo said, his eyes still closed.

"No you silly halfbit, the Schnozgoons are here! Get a weapon if you have one and put your back to a stone," Grandkopf hissed.

Froyo scrambled backwards until he was sitting with his back against a stone. He pulled his backpack to him and fumbled inside until he found a large carving knife. He tried to imagine what he could do against the Schnozgoons, failed, shut his eyes, and began to despair. He tightened his grip on his carving knife; the heft of the ancient kitchen implement was strangely comforting.

Four Schnozgoons appeared at the edge of the firelight. They wore black capes and held their swords in gloved hands. The sword blades shone in the light of the campfire. One of the Schnozgoons pulled back its hood to reveal the face of a woman, a haunting beauty. A silvery crown rested on her brow. Her eyes flashed neon blue. She held a long double-edged sword.

"Give us the halfbit," she said. "Or die."

Froyo almost wet himself. *If I could only hide,* he thought. *This would be a great time to be invisible.* Then he remembered the Schnozring.

He moved swiftly to slip the ring on his finger. When he did, the world changed. He was used to everything getting fuzzy when he wore the Schnozring; it was a real nuisance when he followed Sammy and Rosalie on their "picnics".

Although the world was fuzzy, the four Schnozgoons were suddenly alarmingly clear. Simultaneously, they turned toward Froyo and began to advance.

Arrowshaft jumped in front of the Schnozgoons with a flaming branch in one hand and the stump of Nasal in the other.

The Schnozgoons attacked Arrowshaft, who danced around them, brandishing fire and fending off sword thrusts with the hilt of Nasal.

Froyo had two strangely disconnected thoughts: *Those Schnozgoons fight pretty good for dead guys,* and *Arrowshaft is doing surprisingly well with the stump of Nasal.*

"Everybody down!" yelled Grandkopf, and Arrowshaft immediately dropped face down into the dirt. Grandkopf drew himself up and lifted his arms.

"Nárë alta Anar! Nárë vanya Isil! Tul quárë degi coth!" he cried. (*Flame of the great sun! Flame of the beautiful moon. Come to my fist and slay my enemies.*) He slammed his staff to the ground. Four shafts of fire streaked from his staff to the Schnozgoons. They burst into flames with a deafening roar. Four fireballs rose into the night and vanished.

"Taki!" said Froyo, taking off the Schnozring and becoming visible to his friends.

"Yuck taki!" agreed Arrowshaft, who stood and gave Grandkopf an appraising look. Froyo was wide-eyed with amazement.

"Being a wizard isn't *all* about fireworks and parlor tricks, you know," said Grandkopf. "We dodged an arrow just now. The Schnozgoon that spoke was the Bitch Queen of Del Mar. She is a powerful witch. If she had started blasting from the shadows she could have fried us all. Perhaps she didn't expect us to put up a fight or maybe the Great Schnoz wants Froyo alive and she was afraid to blast indiscriminately. Either way, we were lucky."

"Did you kill them?" asked Froyo.

"No, you can't kill a Schnozgoon; they are already dead. Well, almost dead anyway, the verdict is still out on that one. I merely burned up all their clothes, slagged their swords, and severed the magical connection between them and the physical world. Without the connection they can't interact with physical objects. After all, they are all but ghosts. They will have to return to Schnozmon to get reconnected.

"What about their rings?" asked Arrowshaft.

"Schnozmon holds their physical rings. The power of the rings holds their essence together. I cannot destroy the Schnozgoons or their rings. Only the destruction of the Schnozring can undo the Schnozgoons and their power," said Grandkopf.

"There is the prophecy," said Arrowshaft.

"Yes, a prophecy made in the second age by Barnabas, the blind seer of Grim, says that no man can kill the Bitch Queen of Del Mar."

"So a woman could?" asked Froyo.

"It is not clear if the prophecy implies a woman. Perhaps it means an elf, a dwarf or even a halfbit. If it were a woman she would have to be a mighty warrior and there aren't many of those." said Grandkopf.

"I know two such women, Argyle daughter of El Round and Elli Mae, shieldmaiden of Rojo and niece of Theobald King," said Arrowshaft.

"Your two girlfriends," said Grandkopf.

"Technically, Elli Mae is my ex-girlfriend," said Arrowshaft.

"Point taken," said Grandkopf. "At least we don't have to worry about the Bitch Queen for a while. It will take some days for her and her fellow Schnozgoons to make their way back to Barn Adoor and get reconnected by the Great Schnoz."

"All this Schnozgoon fighting makes my stomach rumble. Is it time for breakfast?" asked Froyo.

"Count on a halfbit to be hungry," said Grandkopf.

Six

ON THE ROAD

Yucks are seriously misunderstood. All we want is what we
have… and what you have.
                    –Gornast the Merciless, Long Tooth Clan,
                                     Musty Mountain Yucks

At first light, the company ate a meager first breakfast and
Grandkopf used the sight of the Ouestari to examine the
road to the south. What he saw disturbed him greatly.
"I perceive seven columns of dust moving east along the road,"
said Grandkopf. "They will beat us to the bridge of the Makewater.
It will be held against us unless the elves get there first and defend
it. Eventually we must get back on the road again in order to cross
the bridge, but we must be careful. The enemy could be anywhere."

On that ominous note, they packed up their cart and set out for
the bridge of the Makewater, hoping that they would live to see the
ford of the Brandyspring.

For hours they traveled on barely visible cart paths until they
could no longer avoid the road. Knowing full well that it would be a
disaster to be seen by their enemies, they stopped to discuss strategy.

"I say we send Froyo ahead to scout the road," said Grandkopf.

"I second the motion," said Arrowshaft quickly. They both raised their hands as if voting and turned to look at Froyo.

"What the freck? You've got the famous sword, why don't you go?" he said to Arrowshaft, "Or you, mister big wizard, fry the Schnozgoons, save the day. Why don't you haul your staff down there and check it out yourself?"

"Well," said Arrowshaft, looking sheepish, "you *are* a halfbit, you know, small and sneaky, right? All the better to spy out the road."

"Freckin' stereotypes. Small and sneaky, my ass. Well, you can take that sword and that staff, and shove them up your collective…" The rest was lost as he crashed off into the brush toward the road.

After a few yards, he thought better of the ranting and decided he'd better be careful in his approach to the road. After all, halfbits *could* be sneaky when they wanted.

He found a likely bush, crawled underneath it, and peered out through the leaves. What he saw coming down the road was not what he had expected.

He saw Mrs. Daffodil Mudbottom and her pregnant daughter, Tulip, carrying a court order, riding a pony, and traveling west with murder in their eyes.

After that initial shock, he settled in to watch the road, and twenty minutes later he couldn't see anything on the road to the east, and Mrs. Mudbottom, Tulip, and their laboring pony had disappeared around a bend to the west.

Froyo returned to his friends and found them shooting dice on a blanket behind the horse cart. Neither paid him the least attention as he approached.

"What the chocolate-covered yuck taki, Grandkopf, that's the sixth eleven in a row," Arrowshaft said, so loudly that Froyo was sure he could be heard from the road. "I've had it with these dice. I'm never gambling with you again. I'm never gambling with any wizard again, you white-bearded bas—"

"If I could interrupt this little party, I think the road is clear. We can go on now," said Froyo.

Grandkopf slipped the dice into his sleeve. Arrowshaft threw the blanket into the back of the horse cart and jumped in after it. Grandkopf and Froyo took their positions on the bench seat and in a few minutes they were on the road heading for the bridge of the Makewater. Grandkopf reached into the sleeve of his robe and pulled out a buggy whip, which he cracked loudly over Blitzen's withers. Blitzen raised his head in surprise and broke into a lackadaisical trot.

The trotting horse soon brought them to the bridge of the Makewater. When they were a hundred yards away from the start of the span, they stopped and looked around suspiciously. They didn't see anything suspicious.

"I say we send the ranger to read the signs on the bridge," said Froyo, raising his hand.

"Second the motion!" said Grandkopf, who raised his hand, too. They both looked at Arrowshaft.

"Wait! Wait! This could be an ambush," said Arrowshaft. He hunched his shoulders and his eyes darted left and right, looking for enemies. He leaned toward his companions and spoke quietly. "There could be Schnozgoons down there or Corsairs of Ember or giant raccoons of Fingold or—"

"Oh, put a cork in it," interrupted Froyo, "For sneaking, a halfbit; for scouting, a ranger. So get on with it." He stood on the seat of the cart and extended his arm toward the bridge.

Arrowshaft sulked off the cart and ambled toward the bridge. He slowed as he got to the beginning of the span, looked around carefully, then continued to the center. He paused a moment, gazing down, then knelt, examining something on the bridge.

When he got back to his friends, he said,

"Goldfinger of the House of El Round was here with a company of fifty mounted elves. They chased some Black Riders off the bridge. They will wait for us at the ford of the Brandyspring and escort us to Clovendell."

"Wow," said Froyo. "You can tell all that from the tracks on the bridge? I am seriously impressed with your ranger skills."

Arrowshaft looked off into the distance for a second, then down at his shoes. He raised his head. "Goldfinger left a note under a rock." He held up a small piece of paper.

"We better get going," said Grandkopf. "It would be best to get to the ford before nightfall in case the other Schnozgoons are about."

SEVEN

FRACAS AT THE FORD

We called the Yuck Corps churlish Neanderthal poopy
heads. Then they wanted to fight.
                    –Goldfinger of the House of El Round

In a few short hours Blitzen managed to drag the horse cart within
sight of the ford of the Brandyspring. A rider bore down on them
swiftly from the direction of the ford. Fearing the worst, they all
jumped off the cart and hid in the bushes, forgetting that the horse
cart parked in the center of the road might actually give them away.

Sure enough, the rider pulled up beside the cart and called out,
"Grandkopf you old fart, where in the sautéed yuck taki are you?"

"Close enough to sauté *you* to a yuck-lovin' crisp, you overdressed
girly-boy elf," said Grandkopf, stepping out from the bushes.

"Greetings Grandkopf! I was beginning to fear that the yucks
killed you along the road," said Goldfinger.

"Well met, Goldfinger! The note you left us on the bridge gave us
hope that we may yet make our way to the Last Crack House."

Arrowshaft and Froyo stepped out of the bushes.

"Goldfinger! Am I ever glad to see you," said Arrowshaft.

"It is I who am glad to see you, alive at any rate. There was a dangerous pursuit following you from Brie. We feared you might have been waylaid on the road and killed—or worse," said Goldfinger. As he spoke he stared intently at Froyo.

"Who's the midget?"

"Midget? Midget?" said Froyo. "I am no midget. I am a halfbit of the Mire and have traveled far on a dangerous mission. Midget! I should have stayed home." He threw up his hands in frustration.

Goldfinger looked perceptively at Froyo. "So this is the bearer of the you-know-what?"

"Yes," said Grandkopf. "That is his fate. This is Froyo son of Dodo, a halfbit of the Mire, but it is best not to speak of this in the open. Let us make haste to the ford."

Goldfinger remounted and the others took their places in the horse cart. Grandkopf reached into his sleeve, retrieved his buggy whip, and once again cracked it over the withers of Blitzen. Blitzen flicked his ears and cast a disdainful glance over his shoulder but accelerated into a begrudging trot. Soon, Goldfinger had galloped out of sight. The horse cart followed after, its occupants bouncing down the road like jumping beans in a little red wagon.

Bumping and bouncing, they looked around with some trepidation, fearing that some of their enemies might still be lurking in the shadows of the great trees beside the road. After three nervous hours they arrived at the ford and were met by Goldfinger.

As they crossed the ford, Goldfinger began, "You guys are real popular. Everybody has been at the ford looking for you. It's like you won the Minor Tetons lottery and all your relatives came out to cash in. First these five riders all in black came down the road and started asking for Froyo Bagpants. We knew they were Schnozgoons so we taunted them until they rode into the river and then we called up the waters. They all washed down the Brandyspring with their horses." He circled his hands in imitation of the Schnozgoons tumbling down the river. "It will take them a little while to pull themselves back together.

"About twenty minutes after that, a dozen of Sorryman's Yuck Corps showed up with that stupid white *freck you* finger on their shields and demanded we turn over Froyo Bagpants. We said you weren't here. They called us liars. We said we weren't. They called us faggy tighty-pants elven prissy boys and we called them churlish Neanderthal poopy heads. Then they wanted to fight."

"That sounds dangerous," said Froyo, quaking at the thought of fighting Sorryman's Yuck Corps.

"Well, there were twenty of them with swords and spears, and I had two hundred elves in the trees across the river with longbows. In about one minute the fighting Yuck Corps looked like the porcupine yuck corpses.

"Then these dudes from Brie walked up looking for Froyo Bagpants. We were busy cleaning up the Yuck Corps and there were a hundred of us milling around in the open. We pointed out that we were friends of Froyo Bagpants, that we were already pissed off, and that they should find something more profitable to do, like perhaps travel south along the river to Inn of the Roaring Falls on the west fork of the Noisywater and get stinking drunk. That, or die right here, right now. They thought that the drinking option seemed like the deal. So they all set out south.

We made them leave their hardware and gave them a couple of gallons of Silverfire (a liquor distilled by the elves to 190 proof) to get them started. They'll be lucky to be conscious by nightfall.

"Next, a dozen Haragrim arrived with their war paint and those long curvy swords they like so much. We hate those sons of wags so we didn't bother to talk. We shot them all."

"Everybody hates those sons of wags!" said Arrowshaft.

"We thought we were done but then these pirate guys turned up."

"Did you shoot them, too?" asked Froyo.

"Shoot the pirates? No way." Goldfinger shook his head. "They're cool guys. Earrings and sashes. Cutlasses, high boots, and parrots. I mean how cool are parrots? What's not to like about pirates?"

"So you ran them off?" asked Arrowshaft.

"No, we have a camp back in the woods about half a league. The pirates are all there smoking pipeweed, drinking Silverfire, and eating roast venison. They've been on the road for a month and they were really excited about the venison. They're fixed to party all night long. By the time they sleep it off, we will all be in El Round's house." Goldfinger glanced around as if looking to see if anyone could overhear him and leaned toward the others.

"But that's not the end of it. As the pirates were going back to camp, this old dude rides up with a bill for a passel of pigs. He was real feisty. He wanted his silver or Bagpants' head on a spike and he wouldn't take no for an answer. We offered him some Silverfire, just to be sociable you know, and after a few hits we got down to bargaining. He finally traded us his watch and the bill for a sack of Silverleaf and a quart of Silverfire. He started off down the road but fell off his horse after about a hundred yards. So we threw him in the back of a cart and shipped him off to camp to party with the pirates."

Goldfinger paused. "And then the worst..." His voice dropped and he looked around at the faces of his small audience.

"More black riders?" interjected Froyo.

"More Haragrim?" asked Arrowshaft.

"Sorryman?" queried Grandkopf.

"No. This old biddy and her pregnant daughter. She was madder than a balfrog with hemorrhoids!"

"Did you get a load of that moustache?" asked Froyo.

"Yuck taki! Are you kidding me? And those legs! It took us the better part of an hour to convince Mrs. Moustache that we hadn't seen you. She wouldn't take a drink with us so she finally set off on the road east, stone cold sober and still mad enough to bite the head off a basilisk. But enough! Let's make haste. We are expected tonight at the Last Crack House and there are miles to go," said Goldfinger.

Soon, the horse cart, escorted by fifty mounted elves, was making its way down the winding road to Clovendell. Froyo and Arrowshaft were in the back of the cart with a couple of pints of Silverfire. After a few hits Froyo began to feel fuzzy and warm. After a few more, Arrowshaft's jokes started to seem funny. After that he had a hard time remembering his name.

EIGHT

CLOVENDELL

You gotta love a place where Silverfire is a breakfast drink.
—Bobo Bagpants

Froyo knew he was alive because his head was pounding. The last things he remembered were being in the horse cart and Arrowshaft starting a story about a wizard, a dwarf, a penguin, and a bottle of ketchup. Now he seemed to be in a bed with clean sheets. He opened his eyes. It was dark. Then he realized there was a pillow on his head. He sat up, which caused the room to spin, but he could see that it was morning.

He sat until the room stopped spinning then resigned himself to getting out of bed. He had to confront the only thing that could possibly motivate a halfbit to get out of his nice soft bed with a pounding head: he was hungry. He got dressed and staggered out into the hall where he nearly crashed into someone. It was a moment before he realized it was Bobo.

"Bobo!" he shouted. He cringed as the sound of his own voice echoed in his throbbing head. He noticed that Bobo looked a little under the weather as well. Nevertheless, they embraced with much halfbitly back pounding.

"Froyo! They told me you were in the Gillybreath room, but this place is huge and I get confused in this part. Let's hurry, we've almost missed second breakfast and if we don't eat now we'll have to wait until lunch, because the cafeteria doesn't serve elevenses."

At second breakfast, Froyo found out that Grandkopf had called a council for the next day to decide a course of action for the you-know-what, that Elves like to mix some weird taki in their eggs, and that Silverfire was considered a breakfast drink in Clovendell. After a light halfbit breakfast of a half-dozen scrambled eggs with weird taki, twelve strips of bacon, six pancakes, four slices of thick toast slathered with butter and topped with genuine bog-fruit jam from the Mire, a bagel and lox, a cheese Danish, a quart of strong coffee, and a couple of shots of Silverfire, he thought he might be able to face the day.

Later that day, after a very satisfying lunch on a terrace high above the river that clove the dell, Arrowshaft, Froyo, and Bobo were talking in Bobo's room. Arrowshaft and Froyo were regaling Bobo with tales of the trip from the Mire and only embellishing things a little when there came a knock at the door.

Arrowshaft opened the door to a tall, silver-haired elf woman with startling green eyes, a beauty that mirrored starlight and dreams, and a mischievous smile that suggested she already knew your secret desires. Behind her were two elven girls, twins, who were an inch or two taller than Froyo, except that both were wearing platform shoes with four-inch heels. Both girls looked to be about fifteen years old, and wore star-shaped earrings. They had on short-shorts that covered very little and exposed long, shapely legs. Their tank tops concealed breasts for which the term perky would be a feeble and inadequate description. They had identical eyes of impossibly deep emerald green and pointed elf ears.

"Argyle!" exclaimed Arrowshaft.

"Hello, Arrowshaft. I just returned from visiting my cousin Wendolyn's and they told me you were up here with Bobo."

She motioned to the two girls behind her.

"These are my friends, Ela and Niphre."

"Hi!" said Ela and Niphre simultaneously.

The twins seemed to know Bobo, and the introduction of everyone was quickly completed. Froyo's status as the bearer of the you-know-what was exclaimed over. Ela attached herself to Bobo, and Niphre to Froyo.

Argyle lowered her eyes and said softly to Arrowshaft, "So, do you want to come up to my room, smoke some pipeweed and..." She bit his earlobe.

Arrowshaft suddenly looked a little unfocused. He nodded, and set off with Argyle without even looking back.

"Not a single word," said Froyo. "Not a 'see you later,' or an 'I'll be back,' or anything. Just up and gone. Some people have no manners."

Ela giggled and Niphre whispered in Froyo's ear, "So, do you want to go back to your room, smoke some pipeweed and..." Then she bit *his* earlobe.

Froyo looked over at Bobo, who was laughing so hard that he fell off his chair and lay on the floor holding his sides. Ela giggled again. Niphre took Froyo's hand and led him through the doorway. Froyo looked back. As Bobo was closing the door, he saw Ela pull her tank top over her head.

NINE

WAKE-UP CALL

The elves have very strict rules about that sort of thing and the penalty is death or dismemberment and by 'member' I mean...

—Bobo Bagpants

Froyo woke up with his head pounding, again. He sat up and, after the room stopped spinning, looked around. He saw carnage. He glanced across the bed and saw a single silver, star-shaped earring on the pillow. Vaguely, he remembered that earring dangling in his face while something else was going on. He took a few seconds to work that out and then remembered how he had spent most of the afternoon and the part of the evening before he passed out. The evening's activities accounted for his lack of pajamas, his clothes scattered around the room, the empty pizza box, the pipeweed ashes, and the empty Silverfire bottles. His crotch started to stir a little at his memories of the other activities of the evening but his equipment was too tired to care much. He got up quietly in deference to his pounding head and sought out Bobo at breakfast. Froyo had a couple of purely medicinal shots of Silverfire before broaching the question that was on his mind.

"Is some elf lord going to come gut me because I slept with his teenage daughter? Do the elves have laws about this? Do they have jails or do they feed halfbits to dragons?" asked Froyo.

"Well, the elves have very strict rules about that sort of thing and the penalty is death or dismemberment and by 'member' I mean..." started Bobo.

"Death! Oh, taki! I like my member where it is. Do you think I can sneak out the back door before the meeting?"

"Don't worry, they're both of age!" said Bobo.

"What's *the age* then, fifteen? They can't be a day over fifteen," said Froyo.

"Elves don't age like men or halfbits. The twins are a little over three hundred years old, three hundred six, I think. Their birthday was last month," said Bobo.

"Yuck taki!" said Froyo, flabbergasted. He didn't know whether he should be relieved that he wasn't going to have his member removed by some elf lord or aghast that he had slept with a three-hundred-year-old woman.

He settled for having another shot of liquid breakfast, a dozen biscuits, a half-pound of bacon, and three cinnamon rolls. Then he went back to his room to nap and recover until second breakfast.

CHAPTER TEN

THE COUNCIL WITHOUT EL ROUND

It shall be the nine Schnozgoons of Soredoor against the Six Pack of Central Oith.
                              -Goldfinger of the House of El Round

After lunch, Bobo and Froyo were summoned to the main council room for the council of the you-know-what. When they arrived they found that halfbit-sized chairs had been prepared for them. As they took their seats, Froyo examined the other council members. Grandkopf was there, of course, as was Arrowshaft, along with a man dressed in green and silver who looked like he had traveled many weary miles before arriving. As Froyo was eyeing the finger sandwiches, two others approached—an elf and a dwarf. The elf had on tights and was either very well endowed or there had been a sale on the extra large at Berenthall's Codpiece Emporium in southern Clovendell. The elf and dwarf were holding hands as they got to the door but disengaged and stepped away from each other before they came into the conference room.

"Gimmie, Lededgas. Good to see you," said Grandkopf. "Let me introduce you while we wait for the wisdom of El Round. This is

Arrowshaft son of Arrowhead, called Elixir the Elfrock, Westhomey the heir of Whiskeysour, Ellendale's son of Gonner, and bearer of Nasal, the Sword that was Busted. This is Beeromir son of Alehouse, son of Brewpub, heir to the stewardship of Gonner. These are half-bits of the Mire, Bobo son of Nobo, of whom you may have heard, and his nephew, Froyo son of Dodo, who is the current bearer of the you-know-what. Meet Gimmie son of Glowstick of the Kingdom of the Dragon Mountain, and Lededgas son of T'Olive d'Oil of the Woodland Elves. All have gathered to represent their kingdoms and races in the matter of the you-know-what and the doom of the third age," he said.

Six elf women appeared with sparkling spiced Silverfire in tall flutes, spiced meats, and various other delicacies. Goldfinger came in to announce that El Round was feeling a little under the weather and that perhaps the group should get started on the back story while El Round composed himself.

Grandkopf began the tale. "From my studies in Minor Tetons and the waterboarding of Gack last spring, I have determined that the you-know-what passed from the hand of Whiskeysour into the Old Man River where it lay for centuries before being discovered by Sack, a creature kin to the halfbits and friend of Gack. Gack envied the you-know-what and strangled Sack for it. Eventually, Gack took the you-know-what into the caverns under the Dragon Mountain to escape the light of the sun and the eyes of men. Gack stayed under the mountain for decades; all the while the Schnozring ate away at his sanity and extended his life well beyond the normal span of his race. Then, on Bobo's trip to the Dragon Mountain with the dwarves, Bobo found it in the bowels of the mountain and brought it with him back to the Mire."

Bobo took up the story. "I may not have been entirely truthful before about how I 'found' the you-know-what. You see, I was lost under the mountain when I ran into Gack. I wanted to get out and he wanted to eat me. I had my sword, Sticker, so he couldn't eat me, but I didn't know the way out and he wouldn't tell me, so we were at an impasse. To kill time we decided to shoot some dice. He never caught on that I was using loaded dice and pretty soon I had everything he owned except his loincloth and the you-know-what. Then we played for the you-know-what, only if I won, he also had to show me the way out. I won and he went ballistic. He lunged for me and I kicked him in the nuts. When I kicked him, the you-know-what popped out of his loincloth. I snatched it up and ran up the first tunnel I saw. Gack came after me as soon as he recovered a little. I slipped the you-know-what on my finger so as not to drop it and when Gack ran past without seeing me, I realized that it made me invisible. I followed Gack to the surface. When I got away from him, I found the camp by following the smell of the stinking roadkill stew that the dwarves liked so much and the rest is history." Bobo nodded as if satisfied with his story and snagged a flute of spiced Silverfire from a passing service elf before resuming his seat.

Then it was Froyo's turn. He told of the revelation of the writing on the you-know-what, the flight from the Mire, the fight on Whithertop, the fracas at the ford of the Brandyspring, the hideous moustache of Mrs. Mudbottom, and the present condition of Tulip. All agreed he had dodged an arrow on that last one.

Then Beeromir stood. "I have come, despite much hardship, hundreds of leagues to ask this council about the words of an omen," said Beeromir. "As I was walking through the Minor Tetons county fair and stock show, I happened onto a fortune teller's booth. The crone within beckoned to me with gnarled fingers and when I approached, whispered 'I know what you seek.' For the low, low price of two bronze chickens she used her magic ball to see my future. 'The ball is hazy,' she said. 'Wait! I see words, beware the ring in midget's hand, a broken sword, an oath too far, Able, Baker, Charlie, enter key code.' She shook her magic ball, slapped it, peered into its little window, and slammed it back down on the table. 'Damn, I think this thing's on the fritz again. That'll be two chickens, honey.'

"Now I see the sense of the riddle. Here is the ring, the midget, and the sword," said Beeromir.

"Enough with the midget taki already," whispered Froyo to Bobo.

"But friends," Beeromir continued. "We have among us lords of strength and lineage, worthy of power. Why not seize this gift and wield it against our enemy? This talisman of power has come to us in our time of need. It is a sign."

"Nay," said Grandkopf. "It is perilous to wield the you-know-what. Gack, Bobo, and now Froyo have borne the you-know-what for years, but none has ever tried to control its full power. Besides all three are *ot-nay oo-tay ight-bray*, if you know what I mean. Everyone nodded and looked at Bobo and Froyo.

"I hate it when he talks Elvish," whispered Bobo.

"Right now, Schnozmon only *suspects* that Froyo has the you-know-what, and the Schnozgoons are abroad on that suspicion. They can sense the you-know-what dimly if no one wears it. If one of the mighty among us were to claim the full power of the you-know-what, the Great Schnoz would know immediately, the Schnozgoons would be upon him like trolls on a sick sheep, and the full power of the Tower of Barn Adoor would hunt him to the ends of the Oith."

"Ack," said Froyo.

"So we're frecked," said Arrowshaft.

"Big time," said Beeromir.

"No kidding," said Lededgas.

"Up the butt," said Gimmie.

"Taki," said Froyo.

"Double fried yuck taki," said Bobo.

"Do not abandon hope," said Grandkopf. "The power of the West has not entirely faded. Gonner and Rojo still stand. The three rings of the elves are still free. There is hope if we are wise. We are here to seek the wisdom of El Round, the wisest among us. By the way, where the taki *is* El Round?"

When Grandkopf mentioned El Round, Goldfinger motioned toward the door and the six elf women hurried out bearing more flutes of sparkling spiced Silverfire and trays of hors d'oeuvres. Grandkopf, Arrowshaft, Beeromir, Gimmie, Lededgas, and Bobo each grabbed a Silverfire, knocked it back, and reached for another. Froyo choked on his and coughed it all over his pants.

"Smooth," he said, reaching for a fresh one.

After half an hour with the Silverfire and munchies, the company was feeling much better about everything. Grandkopf looked to Goldfinger and said, "It is time. Summon El Round. He is needed."

Goldfinger seemed preoccupied with his pointy shoes. Finally he said, "Well, there is a little problem with that. Three days ago, a mushroom vendor came to Clovendell with some new merchandise. He gave El Round a sack of samples and while they were having polite conversation about the weather and the price of wheat, El Round ate five or six. Nothing happened, so after a couple of shots of Silverfire, he ate five or six more. He still didn't feel anything, so he finished the bag. Then he turned to the mushroom seller and asked how many he should eat. The mushroom seller said that strong men had been known to eat four and survive."

"So El Round is—indisposed?" asked Grandkopf.

"Majorly."

"How *indisposed* would you say he is?"

"He thinks he is having a conversation with an oliphant about the socioeconomic conditions of Rojo. The oliphant seems to be quite the authority."

"So we're frecked?" asked Arrowshaft.

"Completely," said Grandkopf.

"Well, you *could* go to Lostlorriland and consult the lord and lady of the woody," said Goldfinger.

"Butter-braised yuck taki, why didn't I think of that," exclaimed Grandkopf as he slapped himself on the forehead.

"Consult who?" said Froyo.

"Celrreybran sand Glena, they rif in Frostlorrilan', they're the mos' powful elvers in central rarth. If anny yon can pull our rat outta da fire it's dem," said Bobo, who had been enjoying his Silverfire.

"But what of the you-know-what?" asked Beeromir. "If we cannot wield it, what should we do with it?"

"We could toss it in the river and let it wash out to sea," said Lededgas.

"We could take it to Gonner and lock it in the deepest dungeon," said Beeromir, thinking that if he could get it to Minor Tetons, his dad would know what to do.

"We could give it to Thom Bombardier," said Arrowshaft.

"None of these strategies will suffice," said Grandkopf. "The you-know-what will call someone to it. If that person truly claims it then the corruption will begin. The you-know-what would create another monster among us. We cannot hide it. We cannot wield it. We *must* destroy it."

"Okay," said Gimmie. "Bring me a hammer, I'll have it flatter than a bronze chicken with a few quick whacks."

"You can't destroy it with any force. It can only be unmade in the fire pit of Mount Drool. We destroy the you-know-what, the Schnozgoons fail, Schnozmon's tower, Barn Adoor, falls, Schnozmon is undone, the war is over, and we all go drink ale," said Grandkopf. "The only problems are the 200,000 yucks and men the Great Schnoz has on the Plateau of Googolplex around Mount Drool and the 20,000 of the Yuck Corps that Sorryman has at Eisenfang. If Rojo rides to help Gonner, Sorryman sends his Yuck Corps in the back door and that's the end of Rojo. If Gonner goes to help Rojo with Sorryman, the Great Schnoz pounces, sacks the city, and we are undone."

"So what you're saying," said Arrowshaft, "is that we're frecked."

"Are you listening? Hello? Destroying the you-know-what is our get-out-of-jail-free card. Destroy the you-know-what and we are saved," said Grandkopf.

Bobo couldn't stand it any longer. Wobbling up from his seat he said, "You pushees, ish nod a you-no-wha ish the fleckin' Schnozaling. Ruck faki! *I'll* take the fleckin' ling to Moont Droo'. Shum one bling me my schord," and went face down on the tiles in a drunken faint.

Everyone briefly stared at Bobo on the floor, then switched their gaze to Froyo.

"I...I...but...oh, taki!" he said, and stomped out.

"Froyo's in," said Arrowshaft.

"Gimmie's in," said Lededgas. Gimmie punched Lededgas in the stomach. Lededgas doubled over and tried to suck air.

"Pointy shoes is in," said Gimmie.

"Beeromir is in," said Arrowshaft.

"Busted Sword is in," said Beeromir, looking pointedly at Arrowshaft. They all turned and stared at Grandkopf.

"But…I have a meeting. Someone has to guard the…" stammered Grandkopf.

Suddenly everyone was holding cutlery except Lededgas, who had an arrow notched to his war bow.

"Well, when you put it that way," agreed Grandkopf.

"Damn right we put it that way," said Gimmie.

"And so it is decided," intoned Goldfinger, pompously and with a straight face, in what would become one of the worst movie lines in the history of cinema. "It shall be the nine Schnozgoons of Soredoor against the Six Pack of Central Oith."

CHAPTER ELEVEN

THE SIX PACK

Out of my way conceited, fatheaded, monkey boy.
                    –Argyle to Arrowshaft at the ford
                              of the Brandyspring

Out of *my* way prissy, spoiled, elf bitch.
                    –Arrowshaft to Argyle at the ford
                              of the Brandyspring

Froyo woke up, hung over and disgusted that he was expected to haul the stupid, frecking Schnozring to stupid, frecking Mount Drool. He hadn't the vaguest idea where Mount Drool was, or how to get there. He was about to get into a good snit when he noticed the pile of clothes on the floor. Cork-soled platform shoes, aqua short-shorts, a tee shirt that read "Visit Minor Tetons" and an aqua thong. Then he remembered: one of the twins was consoling him last night.

He heard a flush and either Ela or Niphre (no one could tell them apart except Bobo) came out of the bathroom wearing a "The Last Crack House" souvenir robe. Her face lit up in a smile.

"You're awake!" she said. Elves don't sleep like men and halfbits; they let their minds wander into a meditative state that relaxes and refreshes. She had clearly hung around while Froyo was sleeping. She sat on the bed.

"I think you are so brave to take the Schnozring to Mount Drool," she said. She took his hand and intertwined her fingers with his. "Everybody's talking about the Six Pack and how you have to fight a million yucks before you can even get there. You are so very brave." Her eyes were moist as she spoke. Then she stood.

"Of course, if you are going off to your doom, you'd want to have as much fun as you could before you left." The robe slid to the floor and she crawled on top of Froyo.

She kissed his neck. Then his chest. Then his stomach. Then Froyo gasped. After a second he felt he could speak.

"By the way," he said, his voice almost cracking, "Which twin are you?"

Froyo heard a soft pop.

"Do you care?" she said.

"No, I guess not," he said.

Pop. "Then neither do I."

A satisfying hour later, he found Grandkopf and Bobo at breakfast. They had a map, a half-consumed bottle of Silverfire, and a stack of empty plates. Froyo went to the buffet and got a light first breakfast: a plate of scrambled eggs with weird taki, a dozen slices of bacon, a stack of pancakes, a couple of bagels with cream cheese, six breakfast sausages, and two blueberry muffins.

He accepted a shot of Silverfire, knocked it back, got another, knocked it back, got a third, took a deep breath, and began to think he might make it until second breakfast.

"Since Sorryman and his 20,000 yucks are blocking the Gap of Rojo," said Grandkopf, "our choices are to go over the pass of Cowhideras or through the mines of Mordia. The pass of Cowhideras is high and cold, and we could freeze our nuts off. The mines of

Mordia would at least be warmer and flatter. The drawback is that we don't know for sure what's down there. Legend has it that the dwarves of Mordia woke something ancient and evil. The dwarf lord, Baleen, set out years ago to recolonize Mordia and hasn't been heard from since."

"Do you think yucks live there now?" asked Froyo.

"Or worse," said Grandkopf.

"What's worse than yucks?"

"There are many things worse than yucks; mountain trolls, for one. There are many unspeakable things that live deep in the Oith and lurk in the dark. Things that are strong and evil. Things we do not name in the light," said Grandkopf.

"Let's take the pass," said Froyo.

"Good thought," said Grandkopf.

"Where is everyone?" said Froyo.

"The Six Pack? Arrowshaft left the party last night with Argyle and no one's seen him since. Beeromir left with three of El Round's serving elves, three sisters, and we haven't seen him, either. Gimmie and Lededgas were here a minute ago but they are off in some corner having a quickie."

"So they're..." started Froyo.

"A couple," said Grandkopf.

"Lededgas is a typical elf," said Bobo. "He is horny all of the time and he doesn't much care where he sticks his sausage—boys, girls, or whatever. Gimmie, on the other hand, is the jealous type so Lededgas has to be careful that Gimmie doesn't have reason to take his axe after Lededgas's sausage!"

"They're both very handy in a fight, though," said Grandkopf.

"What's up with Arrowshaft and Argyle?" asked Froyo.

"It wasn't love at first sight, I'll tell you," began Grandkopf. "They met a few years ago at the ford of the Brandyspring. They had an argument about who had the right of way. Argyle called Arrowshaft a conceited, fat-headed, monkey boy, and Arrowshaft called Argyle a prissy, spoiled, elf bitch. Well, Argyle may be the best being with a sword in Central Oith so she whipped it out and went after Arrowshaft. He doesn't look like much, our Arrowshaft, but he may be the second-best being with a sword in Central Oith. Argyle hadn't met anyone who could stay with her for more then ten minutes in a fight for half a thousand years. Imagine her surprise when Arrowshaft took it to her for nearly three hours. In the end she beat him but mostly she wore him out. When it was over they were both exhausted, bloody, and in love. It hasn't been an easy relationship, though. El Round doesn't approve, but the worst of it is that if Arrowshaft hangs around The Last Crack House too long, Argyle, being half elf, tries to love him to death. He has to go ranging to recover from the lovemaking.

"Thus accounting for his condition in Brie," said Froyo.

"He always comes back, though, like a moth to a flame. When he's in Clovendell, he spends most of his time with the elf warriors practicing his swordplay. They find him amusing. Even so, he can beat them all despite the fact that many of them have had over three thousand years to practice," said Grandkopf. He was using a pencil to figure in the margins of the map he had spread in front of him. He sat back in his chair and tucked the pencil behind his ear. "Well, I figure fifty leagues down to the pass, three days over the pass, and two more down the Silverwash to Lostlorriland. Call it eleven days if we ride steadily and don't run into trouble." Grandkopf rolled up the map and tied it with a ribbon. He tucked the map into his sleeve.

"El Round is still in his room talking to the oliphant. Now they're discussing the history and politics of Gonner. The oliphant isn't clear about the reasons for the decline of Gonner during the reign of Antlerhead and his sons. El Round is trying to explain it to him. It doesn't look like their conversation is going to end soon, so Goldfinger is organizing things. He's lining up horses, reforging Nasal, and getting us provisioned for the journey. I've got to go talk with him now, so, good halfbits, if you will excuse me..." Grandkopf stood, knocked back a last shot of Silverfire, walked out puffing his pipe, and left a trail of smoke rings all the way to the door.

Froyo had a burning question on his mind.

"Bobo, were you with one of the twins last night?" asked Froyo.

"Yeah, Ela. I thought Niphre was with you."

"Well one of them was but I can't tell them apart."

"If you can get them apart you can tell that their personalities are different. They like to confound everyone so they do almost everything together and dress alike. You can also tell them apart when they are naked. They both have tiny heart-shaped birthmarks on their butts: Ela left, Niphre right. The twins are some minor nobility from northern Smirkwood. The tree elves there are smaller than some of their kin, the better to live in the trees, I guess. The twins say that they aren't considered short at home. Their parents sent them away for their education. They spent a few decades in Lostlorriland and now they are here for a while. They say it's more fun here, not so stuffy."

Gimmie and Lededgas joined them and helped themselves to some Silverfire.

"Bobo, Froyo," said Lededgas, nodding to each. Gimmie nodded but said nothing.

"Grandkopf tells me that the Six Pack is leaving in the morning," said Lededgas.

"I wish I were going," said Bobo.

"Yeah, you are going to miss all the fun," said Gimmie.

"Fun?" said Froyo.

"First we get to freeze our butts off on Cowhideras," said Gimmie. "That, or fight yucks and trolls through Mordia. Then we have to make it through Lostlorriland without being fried to grease spots by crazy Glenda, the Lady of the Woody (who is supposed to be on *our* side), find our way through the Edwin Muir, survive the Zombie Marshes, slip past the guards of the Towers of the Fangs and make our way down the Valley of the Undone."

"Then the fun part," said Lededgas. "We get to fight 200,000 yucks and men on the Plateau of Googolplex to get to Mount Drool."

"That's 40,000 apiece, counting Grandkopf," said Gimmie.

"Counting Grandkopf?" said Lededgas

"Okay, 50,000. Unless you want some?" said Gimmie, looking at Froyo.

"Ulp," said Froyo, eyes bulging. "Then what?"

"Then we walk up the side of Mount Drool and you toss the taki-licking Schnozring into the fire pit. End of story," said Gimmie. "Piece of cake."

"Cake," said Bobo.

"No problemo," said Lededgas.

Froyo, unable to form a more poignant sentiment, gulped and shakily reached for more Silverfire.

—

Arrowshaft stood on a secluded balcony overlooking the river. He came to the balcony often to soak up the peace that permeated

everything. Although Central Oith was besieged by the evil of the
Great Schnoz, it was peaceful in Clovendell. The magic of the elves
still held all evil at bay. Here, overlooking the perfect world of the
elves, he could forget his cares for a moment. This day though, he
would have his reverie interrupted. Argyle came to him bearing a
sword. She approached him and stood very close. She looked up
into his eyes.

"I bring you Nasal, my lord Elixir," she said. "Forged by the dwarf
smith Telechat of the Flamingbeards in the First Age and shattered
on the slopes of Mount Drool, it has been reforged by the elven
smiths of Clovendell." She lowered her head in a slight bow and offered the sword on open palms to Arrowshaft. Arrowshaft took the
sword.

"Forevermore it shall be called Narithil, the flame of the moon,
in honor of the light and beauty of the moon that is in your eyes."

"I thank you, Lord Elixir," she said. "But perhaps we should now
go practice with your other sword?"

"My other sword?"

"You know," she said, glancing downward, "your little sword."

"Oh! You meant to say, I presume, my large, kingly sword."

"As you wish, m'lord."

TWELVE

PARTING SHOTS

I fear the worst. –Grandkopf the Gray

Dawn was barely getting underway when Froyo woke, hung over, to banging on his bedroom door. He staggered up and opened it to find the twins with their pipes, a bag of Silverleaf, and a bottle of Silverfire.

"We're here to say goodbye," said Ela.

"Get your pipe," said Niphre, as they pushed past him.

Two hours later, Froyo limped down to first breakfast with his head spinning from the effects of the Silverfire and Silverleaf to find the rest of the Six Pack debating the merits of the pass of Cowhideras versus the Mines of Mordia.

Froyo was ravenous. He helped himself to a couple of ham steaks, a dozen pancakes with maple syrup and butter, some cinnamon rolls, a gooseberry and dewberry blintz, a quart of orange juice, a mug of coffee, and some French toast. He missed the traditional Mire breakfast dish of fried breaded bog eels in white gravy. Froyo sat down with the others. Thanks to his earlier recreational activities, he was having a little trouble focusing on his fork and the conversation at the same time.

"I don't want to freeze my butt off in the pass," said Gimmie. "The chance of dying in a yuck-lovin' snow storm is every bit as dangerous as anything you are imagining in the mines."

"Still, we don't know what happened to Baleen in Mordia. He was a stout dwarf, very dangerous in a fight," said Grandkopf. "I fear the worst."

"Mountain trolls?" mumbled Froyo, his mouth full of French toast.

"Worse," said Grandkopf, "A balfrog."

"We'd be toast," said Beeromir.

"Frelled," said Lededgas.

"Fried," said Gimmie.

"Frecked," said Arrowshaft.

"What's a balfrog?" said Froyo.

"Larger and stronger than a mountain troll," said Gimmie.

"Meaner," said Beeromir

"Covered in flames," said Arrowshaft.

"Powerfully magical," said Grandkopf.

"Pissed off *all* the time," said Lededgas.

"Let's take the pass," said Froyo.

Everyone nodded and looked at their plates.

An hour later, Froyo was mounted on a pony, freezing his butt off and wishing that his underwear weren't riding up. He was wearing the practically indestructible *vargentum* (true silver) mail vest that Bobo had acquired on his expedition to the Dragon Mountain. It was reassuring to have such a garment in light of the dangerous nature of their expedition, but in the cold of the morning it felt like he was wearing a shirt made of sheet ice. Froyo also had Bobo's old sword, Sticker, buckled to his hip. Although he had absolutely no sword fighting skills, its weight was comforting. He took solace in the fact that it really was a much better weapon than his old kitchen knife.

Froyo looked back at the balconies of the Last House in the Crack of the Oith. Argyle, Goldfinger, three tearful service elves, Bobo, and the twins were there, waving goodbye. Argyle held a dainty handkerchief to her eye. The twins looked forlorn. Goldfinger looked relieved. Froyo was fairly sure that Bobo was smirking.

Thirteen

To Cowhideras and Beyond!

Our little group has a surprising capacity for mayhem.
–Arrowshaft to Froyo, referring to the Six Pack

Six days later, Froyo was sure his butt couldn't get any sorer. He felt he should have gotten at least a little acclimated to the saddle. He felt that the saddle should have been constructed a little less like a knife so he would have felt a little less like he was being split in half. He felt the pony should have been able to walk with a smoother gait, that the weather could have been a little less cold, and that the clouds, which had produced dampness that was more than a mist but less than a rain, were taking personal exception to his comfort. In short, he was cold, damp, sore, miserable and, most annoyingly, sober. He was definitely feeling sorry for himself. He kept wishing he were back at El Round's house with one, either, or preferably both of the twins, smoking pipeweed, sipping Silverfire and having his feet rubbed. He got so caught up in that last thought that he almost fell off his pony.

Arrowshaft rode along in the shadow of the towering gray peaks of the Musty Mountains in stony silence. He was long accustomed to the rigors of travel in the wild. *Majesty and grandeur, grandeur and majesty,* he thought, *if I never see another mountain it will be too soon.* His thoughts would ever stray to the soft, white peaks of Argyle who had given him a very personal and thorough goodbye. Which, he thought, might have been his last, given the obstacles that lay ahead.

Grandkopf's saddlebags were mostly full of Silverleaf and he kept his pipe lit as he traveled. Enchantments woven into his flowing robes kept him a little warmer than the others. Through a pipeweed-induced haze he was thinking about the elf girl he had been with the last night in El Round's house. She was thin and sweet and had a very long tongue. A very long, talented tongue. A very long, talented tongue that she put to excellent use. Grandkopf sighed and took a long pull on his pipe. If they made it to Lostlorriland, Celerybrains and Glenda threw some great parties with lots of horny elf girls. He blew out a smoke ring that grew larger and larger until it could have encircled his horse. He sighed.

Beeromir was a doughty man descended from a long line of noble forbears. He, too, was much accustomed to hard travel and short rations. He rode in a stoic silence. He thought of the glory and majesty of the white town, of the grandeur of Gonner, of the midget who was selfishly hogging the Schnozring, of the three elf sisters at El Round's. He, too, hoped there would be more horny elf girls in Lostlorriland. It seemed to him that the elves were completely infatuated with pipeweed, booze, and sex—especially sex. Not at all becoming of a man of Gonner. Still, those sisters...

Gimmie was the only one not thinking about sex. He and Led-edgas had had a quickie in the bushes beside the trail and he was relaxed and thinking of gold. Piles and piles of gold. Gold in candle-sticks, gold in coins, gold in bricks, a bed made of gold, and a throne of gold. He was also thinking of glory, but mostly he was thinking of gold. He smiled. Thinking of gold always made him happy.

Lededgas *was* thinking about sex. He was wondering if he could get Gimmie back into the bushes, if Beeromir went both ways, if Arrowshaft had a fight with Argyle and needed some sympathy, if Froyo would prove too small for his elven equipment, if Grandkopf was as good with his mouth as some of the elven girls claimed, if there was anyone new to play with in Lostlorriland, and if he could have a short interlude with the ponies after dinner. He was wishing he had some Silverfire and that he hadn't already smoked up his sup-ply of Silverleaf. Mostly, though, he was thinking about sex. In short, he was being an elf.

They made an early camp so they could have extra time to repack much of the gear. In the morning, the company would begin the assault on the pass and the horses could only navigate the bottom parts of the trail. After that, the company would have to continue on foot. The packing was accomplished with much swearing as articles lost were searched for and found. Much gear and a goodly supply of food were to be abandoned. Froyo glared at his pack, sure that he wasn't carrying enough food to keep a halfbit satisfied for three days. He suspected that Grandkopf was only carrying pipeweed and wizard knickknacks. He resigned himself to tightening his belt a bit more.

Late that night, Froyo woke suddenly. He lay in his sleeping bag listening. He could hear howling off in the distance. He staggered up and found Grandkopf and Arrowshaft by the fire.

"Wags, likely sent from Eisenfang," said Grandkopf.

"Lots of wags, judging from the howling," said Arrowshaft.

"What's a wag?" asked Froyo.

"A large dog-like creature, black coat, big fangs. Sorryman keeps them for his yucks to ride and uses the riders as scouts and shock troops."

"Are they dangerous?"

"Very. Particularly if they are carrying yucks," said Grandkopf.

"I'd expect less howling if they had yucks with them. I think they are talking to each other," said Arrowshaft.

"Do you think they're talking about us, like they know where we are?" said Froyo.

"We haven't bathed for six days, we have horses that smell, like, well, horses, and we have this bloody great campfire that anyone could see for a mile. Wags have a very keen sense of smell. Between the campfire and the stink, I'd say they know right where we are. I suppose they could be reminiscing about hunting deer back on the old home range, but I'd expect them here before morning," said Arrowshaft

"H…h…here?" said Froyo.

"It's just as well. Gimmie hasn't gotten to whack the head off of anything since before he came to Clovendell. He's begun to finger his ax every time Beeromir starts blathering about Gonner, the honor of Gonner, the shining white walls of Gonner, the tall white tower of Gonner and the milky white cleavage of the Gonner girls. Gimmie will get a chance to do some chopping before morning. He'll be happier for it," said Arrowshaft.

"Can we beat them?" asked Froyo.

"We have a very good group of fighters. I've not seen Beeromir in action but he talks like he's been in real fights. I've seen Gimmie and

Lededgas fight and it's impressive. You saw Grandkopf at Whither-top. Our little group has a surprising capacity for mayhem. But it will depend on a number of factors: if they have yuck riders for one. If there are less than a hundred and if they come at us in groups or rush us all at once. I think it will get interesting before morning," said Arrowshaft.

"Go back to your bag and try to sleep. Keep Sticker beside you," said Grandkopf.

Froyo trudged back to his bag and went to sleep with his fingers wrapped around Sticker's hilt. He was having a very pleasant dream, in which Ela was rubbing his feet, Niphre was loading his pipe, both of them were naked, and he could tell them apart because of the little hearts on their butt cheeks, when the wags came.

"Wags! Wags!" cried Grandkopf. "Awake!"

Froyo jerked awake and staggered toward the fire with Sticker. His companions were already arrayed around it. He took a place behind Lededgas and Gimmie and looked toward the trees. He saw eyes glowing in the dark, lots and lots of eyes.

A dark form coalesced at the edge of the campfire light, a huge wag. It had a black coat with puffy balls of hair around its feet and at the tip of its tail. Gleaming white fangs the size of machetes thrust down from its upper jaw and dripped saliva. *A saber-tooth poodle,* thought Froyo, quaking. As the wag stepped into the light, Froyo could see that it wore a collar set with rhinestones that spelled "Butch". A second wag appeared. It's collar read "Spike". Now a third, "Fang". Froyo shook his head to clear the sleep, set his feet apart and gripped Sticker with both hands. He tried not to be afraid but failed horribly. The largest wag howled and this set the others off. Soon the woods were a cacophony of howling and snarling.

"Twenty," said Gimmie. "I can do for twenty of these."

"Twenty-five, easy," said Lededgas.

"Twenty-five in your dreams, you conceited sissy elf," retorted Gimmie.

"I'll beat you whatever you get, you bandy-legged dwarf retard," Lededgas shot back.

"Lededgas, if you please, kill the big one for me," said Grandkopf.

Lededgas's bow thrummed and the lead wag fell, thrashing, with an arrow in the throat.

"One," said Lededgas.

"Taki," said Gimmie. Grandkopf shot a bolt of flame at the wag on the right and it disappeared in a fireball. Arrowshaft's knife came tumbling out of the night and caught the third wag in the throat. It fell as well. Then things got a little exciting.

Lededgas managed to shoot three more before the wags were upon him. His two long knives flashed out of their scabbards. He slashed the first wag across the muzzle and when it jerked its head away he cut its throat with his other knife.

"Five," said Lededgas.

"You, you…" Gimmie started, but the rest was lost to the howling and snarling. A wag bore down on Gimmie. Gimmie waited until the last instant before he sidestepped the wag and took its head cleanly with his axe.

Froyo was quaking. He cowered behind Lededgas and Gimmie, who were calmly and methodically killing wags. Froyo tried to look invisible.

A wag jumped over the fire and landed on Lededgas, pushing him down. Froyo hesitated for a moment, then sprang forward and dealt the hind leg of the wag a mighty halfbit blow. The wag whirled on Froyo, growled menacingly, and began to advance with its head lowered and its fangs dripping. Gimmie's ax came down on its neck.

"Quick, help Lededgas up," gasped Gimmie.

Froyo ran to Lededgas and grabbed his shoulder in an effort to haul him onto his feet. A wag bore down on them. Froyo charged it, screaming and waving Sticker. He took a tremendous swing at the wag's muzzle and missed. The wag was so taken aback by this tiny screaming warrior with a shining blade in its hands that it paused. An instant later, a blast of fire from Grandkopf turned it into a cloud of smoke and flames rising into the advancing dawn.

Lededgas was back on his feet. A wag jumped at him. He ducked and disemboweled it. Gimmie took the head of another and turned slowly, looking for another foe. There were none. The wags were finished.

The companions looked toward each other. They were clawed and bloody, but still standing. They were all smiling. Wag bodies were everywhere.

The piles of wags around Grandkopf, Arrowshaft, and Beeromir were at least as large as that at the feet of Gimmie and Lededgas.

"Ten," said Gimmie. "I ran out."

"Fourteen," said Lededgas, smirking.

"No fair shooting! Those first four shouldn't count!" said Gimmie.

"So get a bow, shorty," said Lededgas.

"Dwarves don't use bows, you skinny elf taki!" yelled Gimmie. "We use axes!" He brandished his ax to emphasize his point.

"Fifty at least," said Arrowshaft. "Maybe a few more."

"Yes, a whole battle pack," said Grandkopf. "Let's clean the blood off and patch up any wounds. We need to get moving in case there is a second pack around."

"Where's Lededgas?" said Arrowshaft.

"For that matter, where's Gimmie?" said Grandkopf.

"There's nothing like a fight to get the juices flowing," said Beeromir.

"Those fools! There may be more wags around," exclaimed Grandkopf.

Arrowshaft gestured to piles of dead wags where Gimmie and Lededgas had been fighting. "I think it's the wags that might want to watch out for Gimmie and Lededgas."

FOURTEEN

DECISION IN THE FOOTHILLS

Chicken and we go over Cowhideras, egg and we go through Mordia.

                                        —Froyo Bagpants

As the sun came up, the Six Pack decided to have a hot breakfast before the next leg of the journey. Froyo, as usual, did his fair share with fork and knife, especially since he suspected that second breakfast, elevenses, and lunch might not be on the schedule. After a breakfast limited in its variety but adequate in its quantity, he felt the need to spend some time communing with nature. What with the fighting, the lack of sleep, and the high-protein diet, he took a rather long time to finish his business. When he finally did, he arrived back in camp to find the rest of the team arguing over their next step.

Froyo thought that they had decided on the pass of Cowhideras but apparently this was still a matter of debate. Looking up at the pass, he saw that it was completely covered with snow. Gimmie and Grandkopf wanted to chance the mines of Mordia. Gimmie wanted to see his cousin Baleen and the wonders of the mines. Grandkopf feared that the group couldn't make it through the snow pack and preferred warm feet for a few days through the mountain. Arrowshaft and Lededgas were in favor of the pass of Cowhideras. Arrowshaft wanted nothing to do with whatever the dwarves had stirred up from the bowels of the Oith and Lededgas wasn't bothered by the thought of a little snow. Beeromir still wanted to go through the gap of Rojo because he thought he might be able to sidetrack the whole quest to Gonner and save the White Town.

They continued to argue and Froyo listened attentively. Finally Grandkopf boomed out, "Enough! We make no progress. Let the Bearer of the Schnozring decide." Silence fell. Everyone turned to Froyo.

"Flip a coin," said Froyo

This proved to be difficult. Arrowshaft, being a ranger, spent most of his time ranging. He moved from place to place, fighting evil and living off the land. Unless he wanted to eat something that he didn't kill himself, or drink himself into a stupor, he had little use for money. Of course, he was heir to the throne of Gonner, but that did not actually come with any monetary advantages until he declared himself at the gates of Minor Tetons and kicked out the current steward. Arrowshaft was broke. He had not a bronze chicken to his name.

Beeromir, on the other hand, was stinking rich. His family had ruled Gonner for generations and profited immeasurably thereby. Unfortunately, he lost all his cash playing dice with the elves. It is never wise to gamble with elves. Or, for that matter, with dwarves. Or wizards. Or goblins. At any rate, Beeromir was now wiser but also coinless. He carried letters of credit that would get him cash in any bank in Central Oith. Unfortunately, the closest bank was a branch of the First Elven Bank of Smirkwood back in Clovendell.

Gimmie had a pouch full of gold coins. The problem was that they were dwarf coins. Dwarf coins carried the visage of some previous king or hero: Darren the Great was popular. The coins had the weight stamped on the face but since both sides were the same, they were not particularly useful for decision making.

Grandkopf wandered around Central Oith doing wizard work. Most innkeepers were happy enough to give him food and lodging in exchange for minor spells. Then they sent the bills to their city councils, who filed the expenses under civic improvement. It was always handy to have a wizard around when the taki hit the windmill. For instance, in the brutal winter of '07, Grandkopf had single-handedly staved off a wolf attack on Brie.

Grandkopf rummaged around in his sleeves and came up with three dwarf coins of dubious authenticity, three Central Oith bronze chickens with a chicken on both sides, one with two eggs, and a coin from the coast of Ember that had a hole in the middle and said "Visit Ember, the Seaside Paradise" on both sides.

Lededgas did not carry money. The elves used an elaborate system of credit. He could sign for whatever he wanted and infuse the signature with a little elf magic that was unmistakably verifiable by his bank. Anyone who faked a signature or spent money he didn't have received a visit from an elf squad made up of very serious elves with very sharp swords. Discussions were short and outcomes were permanent. No one had tried to cheat the system in nearly 500 years. Since Lededgas was the son of the king of the Smirkwood elves, he was heir to the kingdom. Besides that, thanks to the wonders of compound interest and the fact that he was 1143 years old, he was rich beyond the wildest dreams of the others. No one knew it but the First Elven Bank of Smirkwood. Gimmie was aware that Lededgas wasn't hurting for money and, being a dwarf, was more than happy to let Lededgas pay for everything. Unbeknownst to the others, Lededgas was footing the bill for the current expedition. Goldfinger had kicked in some incidentals, but the horses, food, and equipment had been paid for by Lededgas. The effect on his bottom line was negligible. Most elves were content to stay at home drinking Silverfire, smoking Silverleaf, and having sex. Lededgas liked adventure, so he traveled around with Gimmie essentially doing ranger work, though in much greater comfort than Arrowshaft. Lededgas had no coin, either.

Froyo rummaged around in his pockets and found a legitimate bronze chicken. It had a chicken on the front and an egg on the back. Both sides were optimistically marked *1C.*

"Okay, chicken and we go over Cowhideras, egg and we go through the mines."

He flipped the coin high into the air. It seemed to hang there, frozen in the moment, heavy with portent. Finally, it came back to Oith, landed in the dirt of the Land of Holly, and decided the fate of them all.

"Egg," said Froyo.

"Two out of three," said Lededgas and Arrowshaft simultaneously.

"No!" said Froyo. "Fate has chosen our path. It shall be Mordia." He picked up his coin and checked it to be sure it still had a chicken on the other side. When you traveled with a wizard, you could never be too sure about these things.

Everyone started packing up. They bickered the whole time about the decision.

They were still bickering hours later as they approached the western gates of Mordia. The path they rode wound through evergreen trees and became narrower as it rose. The trees disappeared before the gates, which were set into a sheer rock face. A lagoon of murky water lay separated from the gates by a space of twenty yards. The area before the gates was strewn with boulders. A picture of a city gate with ornate posts, lintel, and two doors was carved into the rock. Dwarvish characters covered the posts and lintel. The writing said: No salesmen! Post no bills! Beware of wag! If the gates are closed, don't bother knocking!

"How do we open the gates?" said Froyo.

"The gates are locked by elven magic," said Grandkopf. "Years ago, when the elves and the dwarves were still friendly, the dwarves crafted the gates to be perfectly fitted and finely balanced. The elves provided the magic to lock and open them. In those days, the gates stood open all day and were guarded by dwarf warriors. They were only closed at night, if at all. In the morning, they were easily pushed open from the inside. Since the dwarves all lived inside, the password was rarely needed and was probably forgotten by both the elves and dwarves in the long years since Mordia was abandoned. From the outside the gates are impossible to open unless one knows the password."

"So you know the password?" asked Froyo.

"No, but it should be easy enough to guess. These gates were not meant to be locked permanently. Now be quiet while I guess the password."

"Ahem," said Grandkopf, intoning, "Melon."

"Lededgas might know the password," said Arrowshaft. "Where is he?"

Everyone looked around. No Lededgas. No Gimmie. They exchanged eye rolls.

"Cantaloupe, honeydew," intoned Grandkopf and then, "Anar! Isil!"

Thirty minutes later, he was still at it.

"Fahrvergnügen," said Grandkopf, stretching our the *aaaaahr* while rising to his toes and spreading his arms wide, his staff held in his right hand and his head tilted back.

Beeromir looked at Arrowshaft, mouthed *fahrvergnügen*, and rolled his eyes.

Arrowshaft smiled, shook his head very slightly from side to side, and shrugged.

"Taki, double taki, yuck taki, oliphant taki, horse taki, owl taki, and taki taki!" Grandkopf flopped onto a nearby rock, threw down his staff and added, "Taki."

"Are those secret passwords?" asked Froyo.

"No, that's just how I feel about it," said Grandkopf, who sat fuming and mumbling under his breath for a few minutes until Lededgas and Gimmie came strolling up the trail.

"Lededgas, do you remember the password to the western gate?" said Arrowshaft. Grandkopf looked up expectantly.

"I might," he said, and walked up to the gate. He looked the gate up and down then stood silently. After a moment he spoke in Elvish:

> *Elves are hot.*
> *Dwarves are not.*
> *Elves are smart.*
> *Dwarves just fart.*
> *Elves are cool.*
> *Dwarves, they drool.*
> *Elves take the cup.*
> *So open up!*

The gates swung slowly open.

Grandkopf and Arrowshaft, who both spoke fluent Elvish, laughed aloud. The others were mystified.

"It must have been amusing to hear the dwarves chant that," said Grandkopf.

"It did make for some chuckles," said Lededgas.

"What?" said Gimmie.

"It's better you don't know," said Grandkopf. "Words of power are not to be used lightly."

"Sheesh, sorry I asked," said Gimmie.

From behind them came the sucking sound of something large and disgusting extricating itself from the muddy bottom of the lagoon. The Six Pack turned to see a kraken the size of a cottage rising from the water. Its tentacles shot out, grasping for Froyo and knocking the others out of the way. A tentacle wrapped around Froyo's ankle and began hauling him toward the gaping maw of the kraken. The rest of the Six Pack grabbed their weapons and hacked frantically at the tentacles.

"Into the mines!" shouted Grandkopf.

"Gimmie ring! Gimmie ring!" burbled the kraken in the voice of Sorryman.

"Up yours, Sorryman!" cried Arrowshaft, severing the tentacle that was holding Froyo, and giving the kraken the finger. They chopped at the tentacles while they retreated toward the gates of Mordia. They ran through the gates, snatching up backpacks and equipment. The tentacles followed them for a bit but soon withdrew.

"Good luck, Grandkopf. Eat balfrog and die!" came the voice of Sorryman again. The doors of the western gate slammed shut and absolute darkness fell around the Six Pack.

Chapter Fifteen

The Long Dark of Mordia

You cannot pass, Toad of Hell.
                    –Grandkopf on the bridge of Krazi-dumb.

W*hat the freck was that?*" shouted Froyo in the pitch black. "*That* was a kraken," said Grandkopf. "They usually live in the sea. I'm guessing that the one outside was not entirely natural."

"Since it was 300 leagues from the sea," said Beeromir.

"Since it was talking," said Lededgas.

"Since it was talking with the voice of Sorryman," clarified Arrowshaft.

"Exactly," said Grandkopf.

"Do you think it was serious about the balfrog?" asked Gimmie.

"It has been rumored that Darren's folk mined too deeply and awakened an ancient evil. Since it sounded like there was a lot of rock falling around the gate out there, we will have little choice but to find out," said Grandkopf. He reached into his sleeve and pulled out a crystal in a metal cage. When he breathed on it, the crystal began to glow—faintly at first, but it soon gained strength. Grandkopf gave the crystal to Froyo to hold while he twisted the end of his staff, which popped off, revealing a quick-change attachment. He took the crystal from Froyo and clicked it into place.

"Quick-change wizard staff. Five pigs sixteen chickens at Willie's Wicked-Wild Wizard Warehouse in Minor Tetons. Worth every chicken," said Grandkopf. Grandkopf's staff now gave off enough light for the Six Pack to see that they were standing at the bottom of a steep stairway whose top disappeared into the darkness above.

"Forty miles to the other end. Let's get moving," said Grandkopf, starting up the stairs.

Two days and many long miles later, they saw, in the seemingly interminable darkness, a glimmer of light coming from a chamber beside the main hall. The light came from a skylight set into the solid rock ceiling. Grandkopf knew they were far underground. The light was coming from the outside, where it must have been the afternoon of the second day since they met the kraken. The dwarves had crafted a shaft from the outside that reflected light into the room. A sarcophagus made of white stone and intricately carved with scenes of dwarves in battle rested on a raised pedestal in the center of the chamber. To the right of the sarcophagus, a low wall surrounded a circular hole in the floor. Littering the chamber were the bones of dwarves and yucks, many of which had sharp objects jutting out from between their ribs. Grandkopf crossed to the sarcophagus carefully. He could see that there was dwarvish writing carved into the lid. Grandkopf translated for the Six Pack.

"Here lies Baleen, son of Fondue, King of Mordia."

Gimmie wailed. Lededgas walked over to him and put a consoling arm around his shoulders.

"It is as I feared. The colonization of Mordia is kaput," said Grandkopf.

"What happened?" asked Froyo.

"Judging from the condition of the carcasses, I'd say they were all wiped out by yucks. A freckin' wagon-load of taki-lickin' yucks," said Beeromir.

"Taki!" said Froyo.

"You got that right," said Beeromir.

Froyo peered over the edge of the low wall. The wall surrounded a shaft that went deep into the mountain and might once have been a well. The skylight illuminated the sides of the shaft for a few yards, but beyond that there was only darkness. A draft of foul air wafted up from the depths and assaulted Froyo's nostrils. He neither heard nor saw anything that suggested where the bottom might lie. He was tempted to throw a stone in, but after a moment thought better of it.

Gimmie came over and sat on the wall beside Froyo. Froyo patted him on the leg in sympathy and Gimmie caught his hand and squeezed it.

Grandkopf found a book that was slashed and torn. Although many pages were missing, it was still readable in parts. "This is a journal of Baleen's attempt to reclaim Mordia. It says here that a yuck chieftain put an arrow in Baleen's back while he was squatting to take a taki on a pilgrimage to Mudomirror. This was in the third year of the colony. So Baleen's reign was short. It goes on to say that they slew the yuck chieftain but there was a great host of yucks that drove them back to the gate. They apparently held out for another year fighting closer and closer to this hall. At the end there is written 'the drums, the drums. They are coming. It is the end.'"

Phoooooot. Gimmie let go a fart that reverberated off the stone walls of the chamber. Lededgas and Froyo stepped away from him and waved their hands before their noses. Then came the echoes. *Phoooooot. Phoooooot. Phoooooot. Phoooooot.* Everyone looked at Gimmie.

"It's the beans! We've had beans for every meal for three days!"

Boom. The sound came from deep within the heart of the mountain. Then another: *Boom...* A second drum: *Doom.*

The drummer began to pound out a rhythm.

Doom, boom, boom, boom. Doom, boom, boom, boom.

Soon, other drummers joined in. They played off of each other, the beat weaving in and out with a strange syncopation, as if produced by a tribe of aboriginal drummers.

"I don't think we are alone," said Froyo.

"Get ready to move," said Grandkopf.

"There are yucks coming down the corridor. Lots of yucks," reported Lededgas.

They barred the door with spear shafts and fallen beams. Lededgas notched an arrow. Arrowshaft and Beeromir faced the doorway on the right of the sarcophagus, Grandkopf and Lededgas on the left. Gimmie clambered up onto Baleen's tomb.

"Come on, you sorry yuck takis," shouted Gimmie, brandishing his axe.

The yucks used a timber as a ram and attacked the door with gusto. Lededgas shot four of them through cracks in the door before the doors burst open. The yucks sprang forward as if the Six Pack were the seafood buffet at the Ember Golden Nuggie™ Seaside Resort and Casino. The eager yucks had not expected to meet five true warriors of Central Oith with cold steel in their hands.

Two more died by Lededgas's bow before the yucks were upon the Six Pack. Grandkopf whirled and slashed, and a yuck died. Then another. Beeromir and Arrowshaft were methodically working their way through the yucks. Lededgas had his long knives out and was making short work of any yuck that appeared before him. Gimmie stood on the tomb. No yucks were getting through. Frustrated, he took a running start and hurdled over the others. Screaming, he landed smack in the middle of the group of yucks. His blood was up and he laid into the yucks with abandon. They recoiled from his axe but fell onto the blades of the others. In the end, there was no escape for the yucks. At the last, three decided to run. Lededgas shot them all and it was over.

"Ten," said Lededgas.

"Up yours," said Gimmie.

"A scouting party," said Arrowshaft.

"Yes, let's get out of here before they are missed," said Grandkopf. "I know where we are now. This is the chamber of Marzipan. It is two levels above the bridge. The door at the back of the chamber opens onto stairs that lead down to the bedchamber of Darren's mistress, the guard barracks, and assorted bureaucratic offices before winding up in the kitchens, which are one level above the bridge. We have to go now."

Grandkopf led the way with his glowing staff. It seemed much dimmer after the light in the chamber of Marzipan, but soon their eyes began to adjust to the darkness. They passed many chambers along the way but none was lit or occupied. Finally, they made their way through the kitchens and emerged into a vast chamber with towering stone columns. Row upon row of columns marched off into the distance.

"We are almost done," said Grandkopf. "We must cross a few hundred yards of this chamber. On the right, two-thirds of the way down the hall, a stairway leads down to the bridge of Krazi-dumb. Once we cross the bridge, it is only a few score yards to the eastern door. We must make haste. Quickly!"

They trotted through the huge chamber. The stone columns about them receded upward into the looming darkness of Mordia. In the distance, they spotted a glimmer of green light. Some titanic force had split the stone floor of the hall, creating a gaping chasm out of which green flames rose. As they drew close they could make out tiny figures swarming on the opposite side of the chasm.

"Yucks!" said Grandkopf. "Thousands of them. It is fortunate for us they are on the far side."

The yucks were jumping up and down and waving their weapons. A creature covered in green flames hurtled out of the chasm and landed with a splat that reverberated off the walls and echoed through the empty halls. Its legs thrashed spastically as it gathered its limbs under its bulk. It hoisted itself onto its hind legs. It was thirty feet tall. Red, burning eyes were set in its black skull. It roared its ancient cry and the very bones of Mordia shook.

RIIIIIIIIIBIT! Through its open mouth you could see the sulfurous furnace blazing inside, an orange-red fire hot enough to melt steel and reduce rock. It dropped onto all fours and took a hop toward them that covered a hundred feet. The Six Pack stood, mesmerized by the sight of the behemoth, until that first hop snapped Grandkopf out of his trance.

"It's a balfrog! Run! Run for the bridge!" he cried. Everyone sprinted toward the opening to their right. The balfrog roared again and hopped after them.

The Six Pack reached the stairs and hurtled down them. At the bottom they could see the bridge of Krazi-dumb, a thin arc of stone fifty feet across that spanned a chasm so deep and so still that it seemed to swallow both light and sound. Designed as an ancient defense, attackers were forced to cross in single file, making them easy pickings for the archers who would line the inner ramparts.

"Gimmie, lead the way, if you please," said Grandkopf. The sure-footed dwarf ran confidently across the bridge, followed by Beeromir, who gestured for Froyo to follow. Froyo stepped onto the bridge hesitantly, but managed to make slow progress, doggedly putting one foot in front of the other until he was across. Arrowshaft, Lededgas, and Grandkopf remained.

"Go!" said Grandkopf. "This foe is beyond you. The others will need you both if I fall. Go!" He clasped Arrowshaft's shoulder and nodded to them both.

Arrowshaft nodded back, turned, and sprinted across the bridge. Lededgas followed, crossing the narrow bridge as nonchalantly as if he were running down a country lane in the Mire. Grandkopf paused, then began to cross the bridge slowly. Halfway across, he halted.

The balfrog unfolded itself through the entryway, drew itself to its full height and moved to the foot of the bridge. *RIIIIIIIIIIIBBIT!* Its roar echoed from the walls and its breath reeked of rancid meat and sulfur. It set a foot deliberately on the span. Grandkopf drew himself up.

"You cannot pass, Toad of Hell. Your halitosis will not avail you here. Go back to the shadows."

The balfrog roared again and stepped forward onto the bridge. A flaming sword appeared in its claws and descended on Grandkopf. Glambake, the gray wizard's legendary elven sword, flashed in Grandkopf's hand. The elven blade met the balfrog's sword and, for seconds, the two blades strained against each other. Finally, the flaming blade of the balfrog shattered. The balfrog gazed in puzzlement at its empty foreleg. Its eyes flashed red and it slowly turned its gaze back to Grandkopf.

A faint nimbus of light formed an outline around Grandkopf's staff. Lededgas and Arrowshaft watched from the outer door. Lededgas tapped Arrowshaft on the shoulder and pointed.

"See his staff?" said Lededgas. "He's drawing in his power for a major stroke."

The balfrog pulled back its head as if it were going to roar. Instead, it shot out a thirty-foot long tongue that was covered in green flames. The tongue stuck at Grandkopf's feet. Grandkopf looked down at the tip of the tongue stuck to the stone of the bridge of Krazi-dumb. He took a step back. He raised Glambake to chop at the tongue but thought better of it. The balfrog was jerking its head left and right. Its tongue was stuck. The balfrog grabbed its tongue with its forelegs, leaned back and strained to pull itself free of the bridge.

"I wield the light of the sun and the moon. I am the keeper of the secret password. You cannot pass," cried Grandkopf. He raised his staff and shot a bolt of power at the bridge beneath the balfrog. The bolt blazed white against the darkness of the cavern. It writhed and arced like lightning. The bridge beneath the balfrog's feet crumbled. The balfrog fell into the abyss kicking and windmilling its forelegs. It roared as it fell. Its tongue held. The balfrog swung to and fro underneath the bridge. Grandkopf looked down at it and began to chop at its tongue with Glambake. The balfrog roared in pain, but the tongue proved tougher than Grandkopf expected. His elven sword was just annoying the balfrog. Grandkopf stepped back. He took a deep breath and his staff glowed even brighter.

The balfrog used its small forelegs to climb up his tongue. In a few seconds it was able to crawl up onto the remains of the bridge. It hunched over, grasped the tongue with its forelegs, pressed up with its legs and strained against the obstinate tongue. Its back was to Grandkopf. Grandkopf didn't hesitate. He shot the balfrog in the ass with another bolt. The balfrog jumped and tried to grab its butt with its forelegs, but they were too short. It turned its head, glowered, and used a talon to shoot Grandkopf a very creditable bird. It turned back to its tongue and strained. The flames covering its body flared emerald in the darkness; the tongue popped loose. The balfrog pitched over backwards and its back slammed into the stone of the bridge. The rock shook under Grandkopf's feet. Grandkopf found himself looking down onto the gigantic head of the flaming creature. The balfrog looked up at him.

"I am seriously displeased," it said. Grandkopf's eyes widened.

"It talks," said Lededgas. "Who knew?"

The balfrog lurched to its feet. The bridge was narrow and the balfrog was wide, so it took a moment to regain its balance. It drew itself to its full height and roared its defiance.

RIIIIIIIIIIIIIIIBBIT!

"Look at his staff! Grandkopf is getting ready for another shot. He's really going all out this time," said Lededgas.

Grandkopf's staff was a searing light in the darkness. He mumbled a spell. Grandkopf extended his staff toward the balfrog and a shaft of pure energy shot out and smashed into the balfrog's chest. It blazed red, purple, then white. It writhed and crackled for three long seconds. When the shaft of energy winked out, the balfrog remained standing in the center of the span. The balfrog looked at its chest. It tilted its head and scratched the spot where the bolt had hit it. Then it looked at Grandkopf and roared again. Grandkopf drew himself up and raised his staff.

"Holy twice-baked yuck taki!" he said, turned on his heels, and sprinted for the outer door.

"He's going to be a long time getting to be Grandkopf the Spumoni at this rate," said Lededgas.

"Run you sons of wags!" cried Grandkopf as he sped past. Arrowshaft and Lededgas bolted after him, Beeromir, Gimmie and Froyo joined them, and the Six Pack dashed down the corridor toward the east gate of Mordia.

Meanwhile, back on the bridge of Krazi-dumb, the balfrog, surprised at the sudden retreat of his foe, made a desperate leap for Grandkopf, but it was an instant too slow. Grandkopf scurried through the far door, which was too small for the balfrog by half. The balfrog slid the last ten feet on its stomach and slammed its head into the archway. Dazed, it slid off the narrow landing and fell into the abyss. Its *ribbits* grew ever fainter as its flames faded into the depths.

None of the Six Pack saw the balfrog fall. They were too busy fleeing down the passageway toward the east gate. Lededgas was the fastest and led the way. He stopped beside an outcrop of rock and held up his hand. The others came up slowly.

"The gate is guarded," said Lededgas. "Two dozen at least."

"Two dozen. I'll do it myself!" cried Gimmie and took off, screaming down on the surprised yucks. Lededgas looked at Arrowshaft and shrugged. Arrowshaft grinned at Beeromir who nodded. Screaming, they ran after Gimmie. Gimmie charged the first yuck and Lededgas shot it in the throat. Gimmie charged the second and Lededgas shot that one through the throat, too. Gimmie turned and gave Lededgas the universal dwarf hand sign for disapproval, which was strikingly similar to the white finger of Sorryman. Lededgas tilted his head back and laughed as he placed his hand over his heart and bowed to Gimmie. Gimmie repeated his hand gesture and lopped the head neatly off the third yuck. Soon they were all busy fighting yucks. The engagement was short. The yucks were not the fighting Yuck Corps but the smaller yucks of the Musty Mountains. The yucks had been eating lunch and had not expected hell to descend upon them. They dived for their weapons but to little avail, for the Six Pack slew them all.

Grandkopf and Froyo had lagged behind. Grandkopf was exhausted by his efforts on the bridge. He leaned against the wall of the cave breathing heavily. Froyo, who was more suited to a workout with a knife and fork, wasn't in much better shape. He was panting like a basset hound a marathon.

When the last of the yucks were dispatched, Grandkopf and Froyo rejoined the rest of the Six Pack and they made their escape through the east gate of Mordia. They rested in the sunlight only five minutes before Arrowshaft had them on their feet again.

"Unlike the Yuck Corps, these Musty Mountain yucks don't like to move about by daylight, but come nightfall the hills will be swarming with them. It is best if we are in the woods of Lostlorril-and before dark," said Arrowshaft.

Despite their exhaustion and hunger, they rose and set off determinedly toward the relative safety of Lostlorriland. After a few miles, Gimmie spotted a small obelisk of black, polished stone that marked a narrow trail winding downward through tall grass.

"Stop! Stop!" he cried. "This is the path to Mudomirror and Darren's Rock. There the first dwarf king, Darren, saw the Seven Stars, which became the emblem of the dwarf kingdom of Krazi-dumb. I cannot come this close without seeing it. Come, Froyo, come see one of the wonders of the dwarves." Tired though he was, Froyo arose and followed Gimmie down the path. At the bottom he beheld a huge mud flat, speckled with puddles and occasional piles of animal droppings.

"It doesn't look like much now, but in the spring, when the rains come, the flats are covered by a thin layer of water that reflects the sky. Those with the sight can see fantastic scenes of palm trees, hump-backed horses, and such."

"So Darren first saw the Seven Stars of the dwarves reflected in the night sky?" asked Froyo.

"No, it gets slick down here by the edge. Darren slipped and hit his head on that rock there. Not that one, the big one with the D rune carved in it. *Then* he saw the stars," said Gimmie, lifting his boot, which was now covered with black muck that smelled like fresh yuck taki mixed with fermented cabbage. He sighed. "It has always been my dream to see Mudomirror. I have lived long and have seen the place of inspiration of the dwarves of Krazi-dumb at last. I am happy."

When they turned to rejoin the others, Froyo was happy to get away from the stench.

CHAPTER SIXTEEN

THE LOFT OF LOSTLORRILAND

Is there no other way? It is said that the woods are ruled by an evil queen.

–Beeromir son of Alehouse

At dusk, they reached the boundary of Lostlorriland, which was marked by the beginning of a dense forest. Beeromir's eyes darted back and forth as if he were imagining enemies behind every tree.

"Is there no other way?" he asked. "It is said that the woods are ruled by an evil queen and that few who enter the wood emerge with their wits about them."

"Aye, and the dwarves say that crazy Glenda would as soon fry visitors as look at them," said Gimmie.

"There is but small truth in these legends," said Arrowshaft. "Glenda, the Lady of the Woody, once had an accident with some magic, but I believe that no one was fried. It is true that in the elves of Lostlorriland do not happily welcome visitors, but I am known to the lord and lady of the Woody. We share the same enemy and our cause is known. We should fear no harm from them."

Arrowshaft noticed that no one was listening to him and that everyone seemed to be staring wide-eyed at something behind him. He turned and beheld fifty elves bearing long bows with arrows at the ready.

"Er, hi," he said. He paused. "I'm Arrowshaft son of Arrowhead? I am a friend of the lord and lady of the Woody?"

"So *you* say," said a large elf with a serious visage. "How do we know you are who you say? If you are a friend of the lord and lady why do you travel with this rabble? A wizard, a man, a midget..."

"*A halfbit!*" Froyo yelled. "*I'm a halfbit* and I'm really, really tired of this midget taki."

"What...ever," said the leader. "A half-baked and *oh taki*, is that a dwarf? You guys are in deep, deep yuck taki. We don't let dwarves in here. The lady of the Woody will fry me to a greasy lump if I bring back a dwarf." He paused. "Maybe we can kill him here and bury him nice and deep. We can all pretend that he never existed, hmm?" At this point, Gimmie gave Lededgas an elbow in the ribs and shoved him forward.

"We are the Six Pack, a group of allies on a mission to save Central Oith. Our cause is sanctioned by Lord Celerybrains of the elves of Lostlorriland. This dwarf is Gimmie son of Glowstick of the kingdom of Dragon Mountain. He is a dwarf prince and a founding member of the Six Pack. He has killed many yucks in defense of our party. He is stalwart, brave, and no enemy of Lostlorriland. I am Lededgas son of T'Olive d'Oil of the Woodland realm and I will vouch for this dwarf," said Lededgas.

"As will I," said Arrowshaft.

"And I," said Froyo.

"And I," said Grandkopf.

"Well..." said Beeromir, and Froyo kicked him in the shin.

"And I," said Beeromir.

"This *is* a quandary. Grandkopf the Gray and sons of kings walking in the daylight with a half-baked."

"*Halfbit!*" asserted Froyo.

"What-*ever!* I will send a swift messenger to the lord and lady to learn their will. In the meantime, I will hold you, Lededgas, a kindred elf, responsible for the dwarf. If he gets out of line, we will kill the whole bunch of you and bury you in shallow graves.

"We had best get into the trees. If the yucks pursue you from Krazi-dumb, we may not have numbers enough to fight them off."

The members of the Six Pack were paired up and sent to separate trees: Arrowshaft with Froyo, Gimmie with Lededgas, and Beeromir with Grandkopf. Strong, thin rope ladders were let down and the parties climbed to spacious platforms set in the upper branches of the trees.

A bit later, as the sun was going down, Froyo sat with his legs dangling over the edge, watching the changing colors of the sky through the golden leaves of the trees. Arrowshaft came and sat beside him.

"How can you be so brave?" asked Froyo.

"I simply fear dishonor more than death," said Arrowshaft. "Honor is duty. If I die doing my duty then I have died well. If I ignore my duty and live, I could not stand the shame."

"You ran from the Balfrog today," said Froyo.

"Yes, my duty is to see the Schnozring pitched into the fires of Mount Drool and to protect you as long as you are its bearer. My duty today was not to kill the balfrog, which is fortunate, because I would have certainly died in the attempt. It was a foe beyond even the magic of Grandkopf," said Arrowshaft.

"Still, I wish I were not so afraid," said Froyo.

"We are all afraid. We do our duty despite our fears. *That* is what makes us brave. You are brave, too," said Arrowshaft.

"How can you say that?" said Froyo.

"The Schnozring came to you and became your burden without your knowing its power or peril. Back at the Last Crack House you could have put it aside and let someone else take it onward. You did not. Yes, I think you are very brave."

They sat silently for a while, watching the colors in the sky fade to grays.

"I saw some eyes earlier," said Froyo. "They were shining in the next tree over."

"I saw them too. It is Gack. He has been following us since we left the eastern gate of Mordia. He must have been lurking around the yucks looking for food. He has followed us from Mordia to the edge of Lostlorriland. It is the Schnozring. It calls to him. He will follow you to the very end of the Oith as long as you have it," said Arrowshaft. "Do not worry. The elves will watch over us tonight. They will not let Gack come near."

In the wee hours of the morning Froyo was awakened by a strange elf who stuck his head through the opening in the floor of the platform.

"Yucks! Be very quiet. We will lead them deep into the woods. More of our kin will arrive in the morning. The yucks will find it much harder to leave Lostlorriland than to enter!" he said and was gone. After that, Froyo could not sleep and remained awake until his companions were rousted out at dawn.

"Messages have come," said the elf leader. "The yucks that were pursuing you last night have been dealt with. None survives. The lord and lady send word that the Six Pack and their quest are known and that all may pass unhindered, even the dwarf. They command that you be brought to the loft of Lostlorriland as soon as may be so as to have council with them."

He turned to Gimmie and bowed. "I am Halfwidth son of Halfheight and I make my apologies, master dwarf. It is many long years since a dwarf has been welcomed to Lostlorriland."

"Well it's a fine thing—" Gimmie was cut off by a whack in the back of the helmet from Lededgas. Gimmie glowered at Lededgas for a moment, then started again.

"I mean, you cannot speak any fairer. Many thanks for your welcome, Halfdick." Whack. "I mean, Halfwidth."

Though they set a swift pace, it was near dusk when they arrived at the gate of Lostlorriland. Passwords were exchanged and the Six Pack were led through a forest of magnificent trees towering hundreds of feet into the air. Finally, they arrived at the largest tree. There was a narrow stairway winding around the trunk of the tree that led to platforms that were set high up in the branches. A slender elf greeted them.

"I am Lorland son of Lorfald. The lord and lady have sent me to guide you to the Loft of Lostlorriland. Please follow me single file. Feel free to rest at the platforms—we have a long climb ahead."

An hour later they were still climbing. Froyo's legs were wobbly, his lungs burned, his head was swimming. Grandkopf was pulling himself along with the hand rail; Gimmie was looking down at his feet as though commanding each one to move in turn. Arrowshaft's hair, never completely tamed, was plastered to his head by sweat, and his knees wobbled. Manly Beeromir was breathing heavily; sweat dripped from his nose, and his armor was showing signs of rust around the armpits. Lorland and Lededgas looked as if they were out for an amusing stroll on a pleasant evening.

"How much farther?" gasped Froyo.

"Only a few hundred more steps," said Lorland. "We are almost there."

"Yuck taki!" exclaimed Froyo. Lorland scowled at him.

"I mean, oh good, let's be off then," said Froyo, rolling his eyes as soon as Lorland looked away.

A few hundred steps later, they arrived at the largest, most magnificent platform yet. Lorland led them through several rooms until they were finally ushered into what looked like a kitchen.

Sitting at a table was a stately elf wearing a bathrobe. His silver hair was messed up; he looked as if he had climbed out of bed only moments earlier. He had a bottle of Silverfire and a shot glass in front of him and he was loading pipeweed into a calabash that had a bowl the size of a grapefruit. He looked up in surprise to see the Six Pack panting at the end of his kitchen table. He crooked a finger at Lorland. Quietly but with obvious purpose he said, "Lorland, did our guests just climb the stairs, all 3,743 of them?"

"Yes, my lord Celerybrains."

"And *why* did our guests not use the cage lift?" said Celerybrains.

Beeromir gasped; his eyes were unfocused. Arrowshaft sagged against the wall and beat the back of his head against it several times. Froyo sucked in a hard breath and Grandkopf rolled his eyes. Gimmie mumbled, "I'll kill him. I'll kill him, but first I'll slice off his balls. I'll stew, no, I'll fry them up and feed them to a fire lizard while he watches. Then I'll kill him. I'll do it slow…"

"Er, the lift crew was at dinner and I didn't want to disturb them," said Lorland.

"Lorland, listen carefully: you are my personal assistant. If you go to them and say that Lord Celerybrains wants the cage lift working *right now,* then I expect them to haul their sorry butts up from the table and get it working, understand?"

"Yes, my Lord Celerybrains."

"A second thing. Lorland, what room is this?"

"Your private kitchen, m'lord."

"And where do we *usually* receive honored guests?"

"In the council room? M'lord."

"That is correct, Lorland. Let's try to remember that in the future, okay? Now go to your room and contemplate your transgressions. On your way down, please ask Elanor to attend us."

When Lorland was gone, Celerybrains turned to his guests.

"Sorry, that was my sister's husband's cousin's daughter's son. He is a little green, but *my manners*! Welcome all. Please have a seat. He gestured at the chairs with a sweep of his arm. I had planned to be rather more formally dressed when I received you, but no need to stand on formality. I know of the Six Pack and your mission. Arrowshaft and Grandkopf are known to me. This must be Lededgas son of T'Olive d'Oil of the Woodland realm, Gimmie son of Glowstick of the kingdom of the Dragon Mountain, and Beeromir, son of Alehouse of Gonner." He nodded to each in turn.

"Finally, this must be Froyo son of Dodo, halfbit of the Mire and bearer of the Schnozring," said Celerybrains. Elanor, maidservant to the lord and lady of the Woody, was coming through the door as Celerybrains spoke. She gasped at the mention of the Schnozring.

"Elanor, my dear, you did not hear that."

"I never hear, understand, or remember anything that is said in this room," said Elanor.

"Good girl. Elanor, four ales, one mead, and a shot glass for Led-edgas. Bring two bottles of Silverfire and keep the mugs filled. Tell the cook to send up an extra large antipasto plate, cold cuts, bread, and hot stew. Have him send lots because we have a halfbit with us and he looks particularly hungry."

Froyo had begun to think well of Celerybrains when he called Froyo a halfbit instead of a midget, but the thought of a real meal! This sealed the deal. Celerybrains was his new best friend forever.

"Taki! Where's my ring? Freck! I can't find my ring! *Where in the fried yuck taki is my freckin' ring?*" An excited voice came from the bedroom behind Celerybrains.

"Glenda? Glenda, dear," called Celerybrains.

"Taki! Taki! Taki! What?"

"Glenda, it's in your shoe. You always put it in your shoe when you...," he glanced around, then continued, "It's in your shoe."

"Taki! *Oh!* Here it is! It was in my shoe! I'm good!" A few seconds later, Glenda appeared in the doorway. She leaned back against the frame, eyes closed. She raised her arms over her head, stretched and sighed. The effect was spectacular. She was tall, beautiful almost beyond imagination, voluptuous in a manner approached only in wet dreams, and wearing nothing but a wispy red baby doll nightie and matching thong. She hadn't noticed the visitors.

"Glenda dear, we have guests. You might want to put on a robe," said Celerybrains. Glenda looked up with wide green eyes and darted back into the bedroom. "Glenda is sometimes a little scattered after she...uh, after her nap," said Celerybrains.

Glenda returned a few seconds later wearing a fluffy white bathrobe with an ornate "G" embroidered on the left breast. She sat beside Celerybrains. As she was saying hello to the Six Pack she gazed deeply into the eyes of each. Arrowshaft, Grandkopf, and Lededgas were able to hold her gaze but Beeromir and Gimmie quickly looked away. When Froyo's turn came, it seemed as if the universe unfolded into a cornucopia of carnal possibilities. Carnal possibilities with Glenda. He felt as though he was being offered a chance to pull away the robe and the nightie. To caress her impossibly smooth skin. To put his face in... His halfbit package stirred and he quickly looked away. Glenda smirked.

"Halfbits do it like rabbits, you know," said Glenda, stealing a drag off Celerybrains' pipe.

"How would you know that?" said Celerybrains. Glenda sat back in her chair, lowered her chin, and gave him a frank look through her eyelashes.

"Oh. And rabbits?"

"Rabbits are tricky. They have these tiny little peckers and they hump very fast. It's all over in a minute and they go eat carrots."

"Out of curiosity, is there, in fact, any creature that walks in Central Oith that you haven't done it with?" asked Celerybrains.

"Well, I haven't done it with an oliphant. Oliphants are hard. By hard, I mean difficult. Imagine. Here's this big oliphant and he can't see you. You start fooling around with his sensitive parts and he doesn't know what's going on. He only knows that something is messing with him *down there* and he doesn't like that so he stamps around and it gets dangerous. Trolls are difficult, too. Mostly, they'd just want to eat you. Literally eat you. You'd have to distract them from wanting to eat you until they got interested in the other thing, and as soon as they finished they'd try to eat you again. It wouldn't be worth the trouble. Now, yucks. They're so ugly and smell so bad, I mean, who would want to, really?"

Celerybrains rolled his eyes. Glenda was concentrating on pouring Silverfire into a small silver cup and didn't notice. The others became very interested in the wall hangings. Glenda knocked back a shot of Silverfire and took an enormous drag off of Celerybrains's pipe. "I'm famished. Let's eat. Where's Elanor?"

—

Three hours later, Froyo was still eating. The others had finished long before and were nibbling, sipping their drinks, puffing on their pipes, and enjoying a few minutes of quiet conversation.

Beeeerrrraaaaaaaaaaaahahahahahahpppppp. Froyo, who had not had what any self-respecting halfbit would consider a real meal since leaving the Last Crack House, forgot he wasn't in the Mire and let go a very appreciative multitoned burp. All conversation stopped and everyone turned to look at Froyo. Froyo glanced around the table.

"Sorry," said Froyo, looking contrite. "It's impolite *not* to burp in the Mire." He hung his head and gazed down at the half-eaten sandwich on his plate.

"We must forgive our friend for feeling at home," said Celerybrains, smiling. "After all your trials, the Six Pack may relax in Lostlorriland. I know of your quest. There is much to discuss. Tomorrow at midday we will hold our council. Tonight, go and sleep easy. No evil will befall you in Lostlorriland." The Six Pack all took their leave.

As they left, Glenda said, "That Arrowshaft has a fine ass. I'd like to sink my teeth into that."

"You do know that Arrowshaft is our granddaughter's lover?"

"Yeah. What's your point?"

"I think you haven't had sex in nearly four hours. You'd better put your ring in your shoe."

SEVENTEEN

THE COUNCIL OF THE SCHNOZRING

There's nothing like a case of good cigars to focus the mind.
–Grandkopf the Gray

After lunch the next day, the Six Pack gathered in the kitchen with the lord and lady of the Woody. Elanor and Lorland were in attendance and both had been sworn to secrecy. Elanor and Lorland distributed ale, mead, Silverfire, Silverleaf, and an assortment of cigars. When everyone was comfortable, Celerybrains began.

"I must impress upon everyone here the utmost confidentiality of this meeting," he said. "Our success hangs by a thread. If the Great Schnoz smells our plans then we are undone." He paused to let this sink in. "We have several problems. First, Sorryman has twenty thousand yucks at Eisenfang ready to make war on Rojo. He wants the Schnozring because he thinks he can supplant Schnozmon. Second, the Great Schnoz has 200,000 yucks and men on the Plateau of Googolplex in Soredoor waiting to conquer Gonner. Third, the Bitch Queen of Del Mar is leading the forces of Schnozmon. She is a powerful witch and an ancient prophecy says that no man can kill her. Fourth, if the Great Schnoz gets hold of the Schnozring, we are all toast."

"So what's the plan?" asked Arrowshaft.

"The basic plan is to take care of Sorryman then get the great eagles to fly Froyo to Mount Drool. Froyo tosses the Schnozring in the fire pit of Mount Drool and it's goodbye to the Bitch Queen and the Great Schnoz."

"Why Froyo?" asked Gimmie.

"The Schnozring doesn't sing to halfbits like it does to the other races of Central Oith," said Celerybrains. Gack, who is related to the halfbits, Bobo, and Froyo are the only beings of Central Oith who have been able to posses the ring without it corrupting them, and to occasionally wear the ring without attracting the notice of the Great Schnoz. Some scholars think that when the great rings were forged, the halfbits were little more than pigs, grubbing around in the Mire. So Schnozmon discounted them."

"Can we get the great eagles?" asked Grandkopf, his head wreathed in smoke from his fat cigar. "They don't work cheap."

"Tell me about it. I've been talking with the Great Windbreaker, Airtoground, and he says it's a flight of twelve eagles or nothing."

"That's a lot of birdseed," said Grandkopf.

"Birdseed my ass," said Celerybrains. "He wants a thousand cattle."

"That doesn't seem so bad," said Arrowshaft.

"Each."

"Yuck taki!" exclaimed Gimmie.

"He knows he has us over a barrel. Save the world and all that," said Celerybrains.

"I thought there were only ten male adult great eagles left in Central Oith," said Lededgas.

"Airtoground has a couple of young ones he wants to break in. Basically, it's the whole clan or nothing," said Celerybrains.

"How are we going to round up all the cattle?" asked Lededgas.

"That's the beauty—we don't have to," said Celerybrains. "The eagles would rather swoop down and *harvest* their cattle when they feel like it. That way they can pretend they are hunting. We have a treaty about this or they would have carried off half the cattle in Central Oith already. We will just reimburse the farmers for any cattle they lose. If we save the world it will be cheap in the long run and if we fail we won't have to worry about paying up."

"I can help with the payments," said Lededgas.

"You are doing enough already," said Celerybrains. "When El Round stops talking to his oliphant, I'll send him a bill for half and make sure he pays it."

"So we have aerial transport," said Grandkopf. "But I'm worried about Sorryman. We don't have the troops to counter his Yuck Corps and he is a powerful Spumoni wizard."

"I have received messages from Rojo. Treemoss has been able to rouse the aughnts and they are preparing to assault Eisenfang. The aughnts will herd the smartaspens into a ring around Eisenfang in the dark. At dawn, the aughnts will attack. Theobald King and his Rojoriders will be there to mop up any escapees. The aughnts will be ready in a week. Grandkopf, you will need to get there as soon as possible to take care of Sorryman," said Celerybrains.

"Sorryman inside of Eisenfang will be tough," said Grandkopf.

"I sent a messenger to Old Thom Bombardier. He will come help with Sorryman."

"Good, we can use Old Thom. I hope he doesn't forget."

"He won't. I promised him a case of good cigars."

"Nothing like a case of good cigars to focus the mind," said Grandkopf, holding his own cigar up to the light and admiring the uniformity of its wrapper.

"As soon as you take care of Sorryman, everyone must ride to Minor Tetons. Goldfinger and I will round up some elf warriors. With six or seven thousand Rojoriders and the 20,000 defenders of Gonner it will give us in the neighborhood of 30,000 troops," said Celerybrains.

"It's not enough," said Arrowshaft.

"No, even if you fort up in Minor Tetons and make them pay three or four to one, Schnozmon can afford the losses," said Celerybrains. "He will prevail in the end. The defense of Minor Tetons is a ruse. We must make him think that one of us is going to claim the Schnozring and use it against him. We want him to attack Minor Tetons and commit the Schnozgoons to the battle."

"Why are we worried about the Schnozgoons? Didn't Grandkopf and Goldfinger destroy all of them?" asked Gimmie.

"The Great Schnoz has the Schnozgoons put back together again and, to make matters worse, they are mounted on giant flying monkeys," said Celerybrains.

"Flying monkeys? Where the taki did Schnozmon get flying monkeys?" asked Gimmie.

"Our spies say that the flying monkeys heard that the great and powerful Schnoz was hiring. They thought that their old buddy, Oz, was getting back into the wizard business and they showed up looking for a new gig. The Bitch Queen captured some and bred them for size," said Celerybrains.

"This is bad," said Grandkopf. "The Schnozgoons' greatest weapon is their ability to project fear. Now they can fly over the battlefields and sow panic in our troops."

"Not only that," said Celerybrains, "Their new mobility makes them a threat to our plan to destroy the ring. If the Schnozgoons defend the Door of Drool, it will be difficult for any living warrior to pass. If the Bitch Queen is there, then even a wizard as accomplished as Grandkopf would have a difficult time.

"We must get the Great Schnoz to commit the Schnozgoons and their flying monkeys to the battle before the gates of Minor Tetons. Then they won't be able to interfere with our destruction of the ring.

"Grandkopf will go with Froyo to Mount Drool. He is the only one who stands a chance against the Bitch Queen if things go awry. Froyo and Grandkopf will fly to the eastern side of the Shady Mountains on the southwestern edge of the Plain of Googolplex under cover of darkness to await the signal from Minor Tetons. When the Schnozgoons are committed, Arrowshaft will light a beacon and the eagles will fly Grandkopf and Froyo to Mount Drool from the southwest. You will be revealed to the Great Schnoz as soon as you fly around to the Door of Drool. By then it will be too late. The Schnozgoons won't be able to get there in time to stop you. When the Schnozring is destroyed the Schnozgoons will be undone. Without the Bitch Queen of Del Mar and the will of the Great Schnoz I expect the forces of Soredoor will lose focus and either fight among themselves or wander off."

"There's a lot that can go wrong with this plan," said Grandkopf.

"The most important thing is to get the Great Schnoz to commit the Schnozgoons, particularly the Bitch Queen of Del Mar, to the battle so they don't notice Grandkopf, Froyo, and the great eagles approaching Mount Drool. If the Bitch Queen of Del Mar gets wind of this, Grandkopf will have to fight his way into Mount Drool," said Celerybrains.

"That could get interesting," said Lededgas. Gimmie snorted.

"We must keep up the impression that we are going to use the Schnozring," continued Celerybrains. "If the Great Schnoz thinks we are going to destroy it, then he can surround Mount Drool with yucks and archers, overfly with the Schnozgoons and the Bitch Queen, and we will never be able to fight our way through."

Lorland slipped into the room and whispered to Celerybrains for a few seconds. Celerybrains nodded and whispered back. Lorland left quietly and Celerybrains turned to his companions.

"Friends, please follow me to the council room. There is something you must see."

Froyo came through the door to the main room and saw four elves standing against the far wall. In the center of the room was a cage lashed together out of stout branches. Inside the cage was Gack.

"They found him passed out on a landing about three-quarters of the way up. He might have been avoiding the stairs by climbing straight up the trunk. It is possible that he slipped and knocked himself unconscious," said Lorland.

Or passed out from hunger, thought Froyo, remembering his own hungry journey up the stairs. The Six Pack started toward the cage.

"Careful! They say he spits," said Lorland, prudently remaining in the doorway. The elves standing against the wall nodded vigorously.

"Gack, gack, hack, ptooie," said Gack as he hawked a loogie at Froyo. The glob of phlegm squelched against Froyo's pants leg.

"Twenty feet. Good distance," said Gimmie. Lededgas winced and offered Froyo a handkerchief.

"What shall we do with him?" asked Celerybrains.

"Fry him now and be done," said Gimmie. The four elves standing against the wall nodded vigorously. Froyo's heart sank at the thought of killing one so emaciated and helpless, even though the being in question had just slimed his pants leg.

"No, let us not kill him. He may still have a role to play in the story," said Grandkopf.

Or not, thought Froyo.

EIGHTEEN

THE MIRROR OF GLENDA

My mirror. The mirror that shows all things—only not in any particular order.

—Glenda, the lady of the Woody

That night Froyo was happy that the elves had prepared a very comfortable pallet of leaves and woven reeds and placed it safely on the ground. He was slumbering peacefully when he was awakened by the gentle pressure of a six-inch spiked heel against his throat. It was Lady Glenda. She held a finger to her lips.

"Shhhh. Come with me. If you wish, you may look into the mirror."

"What mirror?"

"My mirror. The mirror of the lady of the Woody. The mirror that shows all things— only not in any particular order."

"What will I see?"

"Who knows? But come. The mirror awaits."

Froyo arose and followed Glenda past the trunks of many great trees to some mossy steps. The shallow steps led down to a hidden alcove that contained some low stone benches, a bubbling spring, a silver pitcher, and a concrete birdbath. Lady Glenda had trouble descending the mossy steps in her spiked heels, so she pulled them off and continued barefoot. Froyo followed her down, mesmerized by her thinly covered hips swaying at eye level.

Lady Glenda filled the silver pitcher at the spring and poured the clear spring water into the birdbath. When there was an inch of water in the birdbath, she replaced the pitcher, turned toward Froyo, and extended her arm.

"Behold! The Mirror of Glenda. Will you look, young halfbit?"

"I will."

"Then step up on that rock and gaze deeply into the waters. Do not disturb the surface."

Froyo took a deep breath and stepped up onto the rock. He leaned over the birdbath and gazed into the water. He wasn't sure how to gaze deeply into an inch of water so he just stared at the bottom.

"Do you see anything?" asked Glenda.

"Nope, nothing."

"Well, give it a minute. It sometimes takes a bit before the visions start."

Froyo gazed deeply into the birdbath.

"How about now?"

"I think I see some bird taki on the bottom there.," he said, pointing at a white glob.

"Give it another minute."

Froyo gazed deeply, very deeply into the birdbath and thought he saw some scratches on the bottom, but didn't think that would count.

"Are you seeing anything now?" asked Glenda.

"Nope, just the bird taki."

"Yuck taki! It usually works." She walked over to the birdbath and leaned over, her low-cut gown giving Froyo a startling view of an elf bodice at its best.

"Yup, it's working for me, I'm seeing all kinds of taki. Let's see, did you lean way over?" asked Glenda. "

"Yes."

"Did you disturb the surface of the water?"

"No"

"Did you gaze deeply?"

"Yes."

"Did you eat the mushrooms?"

"What mushrooms?"

"Oh, taki! You didn't eat the mushrooms." Glenda picked a few of the tiny brown mushrooms that were growing in the moist soil beside the spring.

"Here, eat these." Froyo, who hadn't eaten *anything* in nearly five hours, went for her hand.

"No!" Glenda pulled her hand back quickly, wondering if he would have eaten it, too. She hadn't much experience with hungry halfbits.

"Only eat three," said Glenda.

Froyo took three small, nondescript mushrooms and popped them into his mouth. "These things taste like dried yuck taki," he mumbled.

"Yuck taki might actually taste better. Just swallow them." She sat down on the stone bench and patted the spot beside her.

"Sit here with me for a few minutes," she said, pulling a small flask of Silverfire from her cleavage. She took a slug and proffered the flask to Froyo. "Better have a shot of this to wash the taste away." He took a deep drink and almost choked on the fiery liquid.

"Are you enjoying Lostlorriland?" Glenda asked.

"Yes, it's been great."

"Here, have another hit." Froyo took another shot and burped daintily, at least daintily for a halfbit.

"Glenda, may I ask you a question?"

"Sure. Fire away," she said, helping herself to another snort of Silverfire.

"Why do you put your ring in your shoe when… you know."

"When I have sex?"

"Yes," he said, taking another hit on the bottle.

"Well, Celerybrains is, you know, a really good lover. After all, he's had three thousand years to practice and he's got a big sausage, if you know what I mean." Her eyes unfocused as she gazed into the distance and a wistful smile appeared on her lips. "A *really* good lover," she repeated. "One time, we had been at it for a while and I had this whole-body, rock-and-roll orgasm that made me lose control for a second. When I lost it, my control of the ring slipped and I blew a hole in the roof ten feet wide. If I hadn't been flat on my back with a grip on Celerybrains's ass and the ring pointed at the ceiling, I might have killed somebody." She shrugged. "So now I put it in my shoe."

"Is that a miniature oliphant coming down the stairs?" asked Froyo.

"I think you are ready for the mirror now," said Glenda. She stood and extended a hand to Froyo.

Froyo wobbled to his feet; the Silverfire and the mushrooms made it difficult to navigate up the rock. With Glenda's help he positioned himself over the mirror and stared deeply into the bird taki at the bottom. The surface of the mirror began to roil. In a few seconds, the water calmed and an image began to form.

"I… I see Primrose. She's wearing a pink nightie. She's undoing the buttons…."

Glenda slapped him on the back of the head. "New channel," she said.

"Now I see the Mire. It's been drained. Someone is building condos. Those look pretty comfy."

Slap.

"I see a dead tree. Grandkopf is there. He's shooting bolts of power at a Schnozgoon on a flying monkey. The city is burning around him."

Slap.

"I see myself. I'm fighting someone, something," said Froyo. "It's *Gack*. We're fighting for the Schnozring!"

Slap.

"There is a mountain with smoke coming out the top. I see a dead eagle. Grandkopf is running down a tunnel and flames are rising from a cavern."

Slap.

"I see these two elves. They're naked. Yuck taki, look at the size of his—"

"Taki! I see it, too," said Glenda, peering into the birdbath. "Look at them go. I wish— "

Suddenly the view was replaced with a great hooked nose glowing orange and surrounded by a flashing orange neon light. The nose was snuffling and…*nosing* about. The snuffling grew louder until it seemed to form actual words.

"I smell you there. I seek the Schnozring. The Schnozring."

Froyo and Glenda fell back from the birdbath, landing together on the damp ground.

"I hate it when he interrupts the good parts," said Glenda, putting her ring into her shoe.

"You'd better take out your little halfbit," she said.

—

Several hours later, dawn came to the alcove. Froyo lay beside the birdbath naked but for the Schnozring hanging from its chain around his neck. His clothes were scattered around the alcove. He awoke, hung over, to the toe of a black leather boot prodding him in the left buttock.

"Wake up, sleepyhead," said Arrowshaft. "We have been looking all over for you. There has been quite a panic."

"Wha?" said Froyo.

"Looks like you got the elf sex channel on the mirror. Happened to me once," said Arrowshaft. "Better get dressed, and make it snappy."

Froyo found his shirt and pants nearby, but his underwear was soaking in the birdbath so he decided to go commando. "What's the panic?"

"We have word from Treemoss," said Arrowshaft. "The aughnts are on the move. We have to get to Eisenfang as soon as we can. We ride after breakfast, which, by the way, they stop serving in ten minutes." Arrowshaft picked up Froyo's vargentum vest and tossed it to him.

"Why didn't you say so in the first place?" Froyo snatched his vest out of the air and set off at a halfbitly sprint without buttoning either his pants or his shirt. He was *not* going to ride off to Eisenfang, or any other yuck-infested place on a taki-licking empty stomach.

CHAPTER NINETEEN

PARLAY AT EISENFANG

A good cigar is a more reliable source of contentment than
a woman.
> —Thom Bombardier, Free Thinker

After a week of hard riding, the Six Pack approached the southern edge of Eisenfang. As they rode up the Eisen River, instead of the great wall of Eisenfang they saw a forest shrouded in shadow. Above the forest they could see a bit of Eisenfang as it rose above the plain and disappeared into a low-hanging cloud of gray smoke. As they rode toward what should have been the southern gate, Treemoss strode out to meet them.

"Welcome young Grandkopf! We have had a morning to remember. We have torn down most of the wall, broken the dam of Sorryman and drowned most of the yucks." He briefly told the story of the battle of Eisenfang. The smartaspens had moved in under the cover of night. When the dawn came, the aughnts attacked the walls and tore them to bits. They diverted the Eisen River into the pits around Eisenfang and drowned most of the yucks. Many of the survivors tried to escape by running into the smartaspens. None of these returned. A few escaped by climbing the cliffs and making their way over the ring of smartaspens. These were now being hunted by Theobald King and his Rojoriders.

"Naught remains but the wizard locked in his tower," said Treemoss, shaking his branches in the direction of the tower.

"This is good news indeed," said Grandkopf. "I have come from Lostlorriland with the Six Pack on a mission to save Central Oith from the Great and Powerful Schnoz." He gestured toward his companions.

"Word has come to me of your quest. I do not know your companions: two men, an elf, a dwarf, and what form of creature is that—a beardless dwarf?" said Treemoss.

"*Taki!*" said Froyo.

"Taki, hmmmmm, that is strange name for a creature that walks under the sun. I thought that was the man-talk word for..."

"*Halfbit!* I'm a *halfbit,*" cried Froyo.

"He's a little sensitive about the halfbit thing," said Grandkopf. "This is Froyo son of Dodo, a halfbit of the Mire. He is the bearer of the Schnozring."

"A halfbit, from the Mire, eh? Is that far? You haven't perhaps seen any aughnt-mates have you? I haven't done the hoochie-coochie for five or six thousand years."

"Treemoss, please," said Grandkopf. "Focus."

"Well, it's been a long time."

The introductions were quickly finished. Although the yucks had been mostly annihilated and their engines of war destroyed, Sorryman the Spumoni was holding out in Eisenfang and occasionally shooting bolts of energy down at the invaders.

"That sounds dangerous," said Froyo.

"His bolts merely annoy the aughnts, but earlier he almost fried Theobald King. Some of the younger aughnts now watch for him and hurl stones when he appears. He has to shoot quickly and his aim isn't very good from the upper windows. He seems to be making fewer appearances now."

"There are riders coming," said Lededgas, looking toward the west. "It is Theobald King and some Rojoriders."

Theobald King soon arrived with Theorug, Jethro, Elli Mae, and forty or fifty assorted pages and Rojoriders. Before anyone could speak, Elli Mae jumped off her horse and strode toward the party. She was dressed for battle: two long yellow ponytails hung from beneath her helm and she wore a steel breastplate that was significantly augmented to hold her quite significant breasts. She was dripping yuck blood. Her sword rattled in its scabbard as she walked. Elli Mae stopped in front of Arrowshaft, who looked around as if he were looking for somewhere to hide. Her hands were on her hips and she looked him in the eye without smiling.

"Ah, Elli Mae," said Grandkopf. "I believe you've met Arrowshaft son of Arrowhead?"

She pulled back a gloved hand and punched Arrowshaft in the nose. He fell back on the ground and grabbed his nose, which was now bleeding profusely.

"Apparently, she hasn't gotten over the last meeting," said Lededgas, offering his handkerchief to Arrowshaft who pressed it to his face. Arrowshaft gave a nod of thanks.

Elli Mae stomped over to Beeromir. She looked him up and down, her eyes lingering for a moment on his crotch. "You look like a real man," she said. "Want to come kill some yucks?" Beeromir nodded and they walked to the horses.

Gimmie smiled up at Lededgas. "Can we go, too?" he said. Lededgas nodded and they set off after Elli Mae and Beeromir, who were mounting up with the Rojoriders.

"Ah, youth," said Theobald, as the Rojoriders and friends thundered off to hunt the remaining yucks. Treemoss, Froyo, and Grandkopf stood near Arrowshaft, who was still sitting on the ground and trying to stanch the flow of blood with Lededgas's handkerchief. Theobald walked over to Arrowshaft and offered him a hand.

"How's your nose?"

"Id wib be beda id a biddit," said Arrowshaft, regaining his feet.

"Theobald King," said Grandkopf, "This is Froyo son of Dodo, a halfbit of the Mire and bearer of the Schnozring." Theobald extended his hand.

"Well met, little master," he said, "You have assumed a heavy burden. May the luck of the hills be with you."

"May your horse never tire and may your ride be long and end in song," said Froyo. It was a blessing he had read in an old book back in Boggy End. Theobald smiled to hear this blessing of the Rojoriders come from the lips of this tiny stranger from beyond the hills. He turned to say something to Grandkopf, but Grandkopf was gazing intently at the tower of Eisenfang.

"I suppose we should see if we can do something about Sorryman," said Grandkopf.

"Come, I will make a path through the smartaspens," said Treemoss, and began to move slowly into the misty forest. Without seeming to move, the trees parted and the mist cleared, revealing a broad, smooth path for the horses. They mounted and followed Treemoss through the smartaspens. When they emerged from the ring of trees a few minutes later, they beheld the plain of the Eisen

River, which was a steaming mess. Vapor rose from a multitude of holes and there were puddles everywhere.

"The water from the Eisen has quenched the fires of Eisenfang and drowned most of the yucks," said Treemoss. "It will take a long time to fix the damage of these yucks and this crazy wizard."

Grandkopf looked to the tower of Eisenfang for a long time and finally said, "Theobald, may I borrow a page?"

"Certainly, pick any you favor."

Grandkopf looked at the crew of pages, who were dressed uniformly in green tunics except for a single page wearing red. Grandkopf crooked a finger at the page in red, who dutifully walked over.

"In a minute, all who want to be near when I treat with Sorryman are going to ride to the base of the tower and gather by the door. You will go with us, understand?" said Grandkopf.

"Yes my lord wizard," said the page. Soon everyone who was willing to risk death to see the parlay at the tower was mounted and thundering the two hundred yards to the tower's door. The ride was uneventful. Sorryman apparently didn't want to risk the stones of the aughnts to take pot shots at the advancing party. They dismounted, and flattened themselves in a line to the left of the steps leading up to the door. Grandkopf motioned the page forward.

"Why are you wearing a red tunic today?" asked Grandkopf.

"My green tunic was in the wash. Why?"

"No reason. I was just curious. So, here's what you do. Go up to the door and knock. When Sorryman answers, tell him we'd like him to come out and chat with us, okay?"

"Okay. Whom shall I say is calling?"

"Say it's his old buddy Grandkopf the Gray and some friends."

"Okay."

The red-tunic-clad page walked up the short flight of stairs to the door. The others flattened themselves against the cool stone of Eisenfang. The page knocked three times and the door swung slowly open, without apparent help, to reveal a small alcove and a set of stairs receding upward into darkness. No one was visible.

"Er, hello?" said the page.

Silence.

"Mr. Sorryman, my lord?"

Silence.

"Mr. Sorryman, my lord, it's my lord Grandkopf the Gray to see you?"

Silence. The page glanced over at the cowering observers and Grandkopf motioned for him to continue.

"Er, Mr. Sorryman, my lord, sir, your, er, buddy, my lord Grandkopf the Gray wants to know if you will come down and … well, chat."

Zaaaaap! A two-foot wide shaft of energy came down the stairs and hit the page in the chest. When the spots cleared from everyone's eyes, there was nothing left of the page but a seared feathered cap and two boots from which protruded stumps of legs cauterized to carbon on the tops.

"Taki," said Grandkopf.

"Yuck taki," said Arrowshaft.

"Horse taki," said Theobald.

"I think I taki my pants," said Froyo.

"I guess he doesn't feel like chatting," said Theobald King.

"Theobald, when do you expect Old Thom Bombardier?" said Grandkopf.

"At noon tomorrow."

"Let's all come back tomorrow at noon." Grandkopf looked over at the others, who nodded and began inching away from the door. They scrambled up on their horses and rode like madmen back to the opening in the smartaspens.

The next day, as the king's cooks were putting the finishing touches on lunch, reports came in that Old Thom was riding up the valley. A half hour later he arrived. Thom Bombardier was on a yellow horse named Buttercup that was so large that Thom looked like he was riding a round hay bale with legs. Buttercup plodded along placidly. Thom himself was about five feet six inches tall and weighed nearly three hundred pounds. He was wearing a white long-sleeved shirt that was ruffled in the front and only a little splotched with the remnants of breakfast. Two armpit stains were spreading down his sides, doubtless the result of the quickly warming morning. His bright green lederhosen were held up with matching leather suspenders, and he wore white socks that came past mid-calf with his Elfenstock™ sandals. Atop his head sat a battered brown fedora with a scraggly blue feather tucked into the band. In Thom's mouth was the stump of a fat cigar that glowed ominously as he puffed. As he rode up to the small group that had gathered to meet him, he removed the butt of his cigar.

"Grandkopf. 'Moss," said Thom.

"Thom," said Grandkopf. Treemoss bobbed forward slightly.

Thom jabbed the unlit end of his cigar toward Froyo while raising his eyebrows.

"Froyo, Schnozring," said Grandkopf. "A halfbit," he added.

"Charmed." Thom nodded and tossed the butt of the cigar into a puddle, where it sizzled briefly. He pulled another fat cigar out of his pocket and bit off the end, spitting it near where the old butt lay,

Thom scratched a match on his lederhosen, and took his time lighting the new cigar to his satisfaction. He finally looked at Grandkopf.

"Problem?"

"Sorryman," said Grandkopf, jerking his thumb toward Eisenfang.

"On it," said Thom, and put heels to his mighty yellow steed, who let out a surprised fart and started plodding determinedly toward Eisenfang. The others were caught off guard and had to scramble to saddle up and follow. Soon a small crowd was thundering after Thom with Treemoss striding along behind them.

Everyone dismounted. The Six Pack, Theobald, Theorug, Elli Mae, Jethro, and Treemoss were all flattened against the cruel obsidian of Eisenfang. Thom mounted the steps and kicked the remnants of the unfortunate red-tunic-clad page out of the way.

He pounded on the front door. "Sorryman!" he yelled.

The door swung slowly open, revealing the empty alcove and the stairs as it had the day before.

"Sorryman, you son of a cross-eyed salamander, get down here and take your medicine."

Zaaaaap! A shaft of red and orange flames three feet across roared down the stairs and struck Thom full in the chest. When the spots cleared from everyone's eyes, Thom stood on the steps of Eisenfang wearing only his feathered fedora, white socks singed at the tops and still smoking, and unharmed Elfenstock™ sandals, proof that their slogan "All-natural materials and elven magic for happy feet and a pleasant day" constituted truth in advertising. Thom spat out the remaining tip of his cigar.

"Son of a wag! You fried my cigar!" he cried, He charged up the stairs. His Elfenstocks slapped on the stone as he ascended.

"Wow!" said Gimmie.

"No kidding," said Lededgas.

"That thing came down to his knees," said Elli Mae. "No wonder Boysenberry is always smiling."

Zaaap! They heard electricity crackle from somewhere within the tower.

"Ouch!"

Zaaap!

"Ouch. Son of a wag. Stop that."

Zaaap!

The group heard loud scuffling sounds followed by a crash. More scuffling, another crash, and then a huge crack, as if a tree trunk had been snapped in two. The halves of Sorryman's staff came clattering down the stairs. The scuffling continued, though in a more subdued fashion. A door slammed and Thom came down the stairs dragging an unconscious Sorryman by the collar of his tricolor robe. Thom was wearing a fluffy pink bathrobe that was very much too small for him. His arms bulged out of the sleeves, and although he had managed to tie the belt under his ale gut so the robe partially covered his manhood, his chest, belly, and a lot of body hair remained exposed. He tossed Grandkopf a ring of keys and held up Sorryman by the collar of his green, white, and pink-striped robe.

"Sorryman," said Thom, giving the hapless Sorryman a shake for emphasis.

"Treemoss, will you do the honors?" said Grandkopf. Treemoss took two strides, plucked Sorryman from Thom's grasp, and held him aloft.

"Make it a challenge," said Grandkopf. Treemoss tossed Sorryman thirty feet into air. At the apex of his flight, Grandkopf fired a bolt of energy from his staff. When it struck Sorryman, an intense sphere of fire blossomed briefly and the flames floated upward as they faded, finally resolving into tendrils of black smoke. Sorryman's boots thudded to the ground, and charred, tricolored tatters of his robe fluttered to the Oith through the smoky air.

"Good riddance," said Thom, rubbing his chest. He looked at Grandkopf. "We done?"

Grandkopf nodded. Thom walked over to Buttercup, reached into a saddlebag, and pulled out a fresh cigar. He bit the end off it and lit a match by dragging his thumbnail across the tip. He took his time lighting the cigar, rolling it in his fingers until he had established an even red glow at the end. He rummaged in his other saddlebag and pulled out a pair of bright yellow lederhosen with matching suspenders, which he proceeded to don in front of everyone. When he was done, his privates were covered but he was still wearing the fluffy pink bathrobe. He mounted his faithful Buttercup and stopped in front of Grandkopf.

"Grandkopf, 'Moss, Froyo halfbit," he said, nodding to each. Then he put heels to his yellow mount, which plodded ponderously back to the opening in the smartaspens.

"You gotta love Old Thom," said Grandkopf to no one in particular.

Twenty

Gwendolyn of Eisenfang

There were once seven seestones that the kings of Gonner used to communicate with different parts of the kingdom. I did not know that any still existed.

–Grandkopf the Gray

Later that day, Grandkopf and Froyo began exploring Eisenfang. Grandkopf had often visited Sorryman in more peaceful times, but he had only seen a few of the thousands of rooms within. Mostly, he had spent time in Sorryman's office near the top of the tower. Grandkopf wanted to search that office. He hoped the lift was working because he didn't want to climb the stairs forty stories to the highest rooms. The lift door opened and Grandkopf pulled out the stop for the top floor. Slowly they ascended. When they finally reached the top, Grandkopf and Froyo stepped out into an atrium with windows at both ends and doors set at intervals around the walls. Grandkopf remembered the atrium from previous trips, and he and Froyo began to open doors and peek inside. Behind one set of doors Froyo found what looked like a living room. It had a fireplace, two comfortable-looking upholstered chairs, a long couch, and a low table upon which sat something about eight inches high covered by a dark cloth. The walls were lined with bookshelves, which were overflowing with books. Froyo saw many books in the writing of men, including several popular novels. There were books in Elvish and Dwarvish, and other books whose titles were in writing that he did not recognize. Grandkopf recognized many wizarding books in the collection: most of the old standards and one that he knew only by rumor.

Froyo found a bathroom and went in to do his business. Grandkopf turned to the bookcases. He ran his fingers over the spines of several of the older books, thinking how much he would like to rest from his travels and have time to study the old manuscripts.

"Hello." The voice came from behind him.

Grandkopf whirled, staff ready to blast the intruder. He saw a slender elf-woman perhaps five-and-a-half feet tall, barefoot, wearing a short white dress hemmed to about mid-thigh. She had long, light-brown hair and a heart-shaped face. Her eyes were the blue of the deep ocean, her nose small and upturned, her lips not full but not thin, either. She twirled a strand of hair and leaned against the back of the couch.

"You're the wizard, Grandkopf the Gray," she said. "I saw you when you came to visit Lord Sorryman."

"Who the backside of Schnozmon are you?"

"I'm Gwendolyn. I'm Lord Sorryman's assistant. Was Lord Sorryman's assistant." She looked sad.

"How come I never saw you before?"

"Lord Sorryman didn't want anyone to see me. I don't know why. I had to hide whenever visitors came. It isn't hard to hide here; there are 3,573 rooms." She climbed onto the couch and perched on the back, feet buried in the cushions.

"Are you going to be my new master?" she asked, squeezing her clasped hands between her legs.

"I don't know. Eisenfang rightfully belongs to the king of Gonner. I suppose Arrowshaft will decide, if he survives."

"Arrowshaft. Lord Sorryman hated him. He hated you, too. He hated everybody. Especially everybody who was out to get him, but that seemed like everybody in Central Oith since the Schnoz came." She had risen from the couch and was walking along a wall, idly touching knickknacks and books.

"The Great Schnoz has been here?"

"No, we see him in the seestone." She pointed to the covered object on the table. "We used to get three channels on it. Then the Schnoz came. Sorryman used to sit in front of the stone and stare at the Schnoz. He said the Schnoz talked to him in his head. I tried to look once but it scared me so I never did it again." She flopped in a chair, head and shoulders on one arm, shins and feet dangling over the other. She stretched, arching her back as she settled in.

"Sorryman changed after the Schnoz came. He got mean. Then he brought in all the yucks. It was terrible. I think he was planning bad things. I was afraid of what he might do next."

"Why didn't you leave?"

"Sorryman cursed me. I can't leave Eisenfang or I'll die." She was up again. She twirled in a circle and leaned against a bookcase.

Froyo came out of the bathroom. "Grandkopf are you talking to yourself again?" He stopped short when he saw Gwendolyn. "Who's this?"

"Froyo, this is Gwendolyn of Eisenfang. She was Sorryman's assistant before the recent unpleasantness. Gwendolyn, meet Froyo, a halfbit of the Mire."

Gwendolyn's face lit up and she clapped her hands. "Oh! I know the Mire. We get ale from the Mire, from the Red Flagon Inn. We still have two casks in the eighth room in the third basement. Lord Sorryman said that blessing the Red Flagon ale was the least bone-headed thing you ever did." She smiled at Grandkopf and the room seemed to grow brighter.

"What's that?" Froyo gestured at the cloth on the table.

"Apparently, *that* is a seestone. There were once seven seestones that the kings of Gonner used to communicate with different parts of the kingdom. I did not know that any still existed," said Grandkopf.

"We get four channels," said Gwendolyn, now on the arm of the couch. "The geezer channel, the elf-sex channel, the locker room channel, and the Schnoz channel."

"What do you see?" asked Grandkopf.

Gwendolyn moved off the couch and knelt beside the low table. She tilted her head as she ran her hands over the cloth that covered the seestone. "The geezer channel shows a room with a table, chair, and wall hangings. Some old dude is sometimes there. Sorryman used to stare at him. He said they were talking but they never said anything. Sorryman hated him. The second channel has elves having sex. We used to watch that one a lot before the Schnoz came. Sorryman was fun then. The third channel is a girl's locker room. You can watch them change clothes but they never look into the stone. The last channel is the Schnoz. The Schnoz is always there. The seestone shows a nose that fills the view and glows orange, like it is made of hot iron. It is always surrounded by an orange neon light that flashes. Sorryman spent a lot of time staring at the Schnoz. We didn't watch the elves much after the Schnoz came," she repeated, pouting.

"Well, let's check it out," said Grandkopf and motioned for Gwendolyn to remove the cloth. Gwendolyn pulled the cloth away to reveal a squarish piece of white quartz.

"How does it work?" asked Froyo.

"You can tap it on the top to start it up or to go forward a channel. Two-taps is backwards and three is off," she said, "but Lord Sorryman didn't like to get up so he enchanted it so you can work it from the couch." She sat on the couch and patted a spot beside her. "Sit here and I'll show you." Grandkopf and Froyo sat down on either side of Gwendolyn. She looked at Grandkopf, then Froyo. She rocked back and forth a little in preparation and sat up very straight. "Ready?" They nodded.

She clapped her hands. *Clap, clap.* "Clap on, clap off," she said. The seestone made a sound like a fairy striking a tiny glass bell. *Ding.* The rock dissolved in a nimbus of colors that seemed to explode, leaving an irregular, roughly circular window that was so clear it felt as if you could stick an arm through it to the other side. The window revealed an empty room and a high-backed chair. The seestone appeared to be sitting on a table in front of the chair. A tapestry was barely visible in the corner.

"I think I know this room," said Grandkopf. "I hope I'm wrong. Let's move on."

"You give it a thumbs up to get it to go to the next channel," said Gwendolyn. "Watch." She gave the thumbs up sign and pushed her arm toward the seestone. When her arm was fully extended, the seestone made its ding and the view became cloudy before clearing to reveal a group of naked elves enthusiastically performing various lascivious acts on each other. She sighed. "I don't suppose you'd want to smoke some pipeweed and watch this for a while?" she asked.

"Not now. We'd better see the rest." Reluctantly, Gwendolyn gave the seestone the thumbs up again, they heard the ding, and when the view cleared there was an empty locker room.

"There are not usually any girls in the locker room at this time of day. They get dressed before gym and shower afterward. We think it's a girl's school in Minor Tetons, but we're not sure," said Gwendolyn.

"Okay, Gwendolyn, let's see the Schnoz channel," said Grandkopf, holding her wrist before she could move her arm again. "But be ready to change it as soon as we see the Schnoz."

"Okay. It's thumbs down to go back," said Gwendolyn. She gave the stone the thumbs up, the stone gave its ding, and when the view cleared the window was dark. A speck of light appeared in the center of the window. It expanded from the center outward to reveal a glowing orange nose surrounded by an oval orange neon light that flashed slowly with the word "Schnoz" shining in an arc at the bottom of the neon circle. A narration started in their heads. "Need a vacation? Come to Barn Adoor Hotel and Casino tucked away in the corner of beautiful Soredoor…"

"What the taki?" said Grandkopf.

"The ads started about six months ago. The Schnoz comes on right after the ad," said Gwendolyn.

The view in the seestone pulled back to show that the Schnoz sign was mounted on a low building flanked by two towers that dwarfed the sign. The narration continued, "Ten thousand deluxe rooms in the twin towers of Barn Adoor. Fifty-thousand square feet of gaming in the casino. We have all your favorite games: Wag Races, Gladiator Fights, Roll Seven Dice, Dwarf Toss, Fire Lizard Fights, or the favorite, Twenty-Two! Appearing nightly, the Great Schnoz and the Schnozettes. 'Take my mother-in-law... Please!' Come to the Barn Adoor Hotel and Casino, free rooms, easy credit, and we never close!" The view faded to black. The seestone became cloudy. An orange neon oval appeared. In a few seconds, the glowing Schnoz appeared in the center of the oval.

"What? Is that Sorryman? You don't smell right! Who *is* this?" the words appeared in their minds.

"Back," said Grandkopf. "Turn it back now!"

Gwendolyn quickly extended her arm with the thumbs down. *Ding.* They were back to the locker room.

"That was scary," she said.

"I smell Slick's Mentho Rub," said Froyo. "It must be horrible to have a cold when you're all schnoz." Froyo had been sickly as a baby 'bit.

"Let's go back to the first channel," said Grandkopf. Gwendolyn gave a thumbs down to get back to the elf channel and another to return to the geezer channel.

"Holy taki! Turn it off!" cried Grandkopf. *Clap, clap, ding!* The view collapsed upon itself, there was a soft pop, and the quartz chunk reappeared. Grandkopf snatched up the cloth and threw it over the stone.

"I thought I recognized the room. The geezer channel is Alehouse's private office in the palace on the seventh level of Minor Tetons. I saw Alehouse son of Brewpub, the steward of Gonner, come into the room right before we turned off the stone. The stone started humming. *Hm, hm, hmmmmm. Hm, hm, hmmmmm. Hm, hm, hmmmmm.*"

"That's the geezer calling. It does two short and one long when the geezer wants to talk," said Gwendolyn.

Hmmmmm, hm, hm. Hmmmmm, hm, hm. Hmmmmm, hm, hm. Hmmmmm, hm, hm.

"One long and two short—that's what it does when the Schnoz is calling. The elves never call." She looked wistfully at her feet and scratched a toe.

"We learned some valuable things today," said Grandkopf as the seestone continued its humming. Sorryman and Alehouse both have seestones. I fear the Great and Powerful Schnoz has brainwashed Alehouse as well as Sorryman. All the more reason to get to Minor Tetons quickly. Gwendolyn, can we put forty or fifty Rojoriders up for the night?"

"Forty or fifty?" She clapped her hands and hopped up and down. "We have thousands of guest rooms on the middle levels. It will be fun! I'll tell Cookie."

"Who's Cookie?"

"Cookie's the cook. He's a dwarf. He won't tell anybody his dwarf name, but he's sweet and he cooks, so I call him Cookie. He is the only one besides me that stayed after the yucks came."

"Can he cook for fifty?"

"Fifty! He used to cook for hundreds. He'll be thrilled."

"Where *is* Cookie?"

Gwendolyn paused and stared at the ceiling for a second. "He's in the basement, level two, room six. The one with the barrels of flour."

"How do you know that?"

"I just know. I know what's in all the rooms at Eisenfang. It pops into my head. I can find anything or anyone anywhere in Eisenfang if I concentrate for a second. That's how I knew you were here. I could feel you as soon as you stepped on the stairs."

"I'd like to hold a dinner for Theobald King and few special guests in the dining room tonight," said Grandkopf.

"Theobald! He's so cute!" She spun in place. "I love his beard. I haven't seen him for years. Sorryman hated him and the others, too. I love Elli Mae. She's so tough. I wish I could be like her. And Theorug, he's so handsome. He has a girlfriend, though, I heard, not that I care of course but…"

"Gwendolyn?"

"Yes?" She stopped spinning, scratched the back of her left leg with the toes of her right foot and pushed her brown hair on top of her head with her left hand. Her right arm was wrapped around her waist. She cocked her head.

"Better go find Cookie."

"Yes!" She exploded out of the room in a flash of legs and skirts and disappeared down the hall.

TWENTY-ONE

THE COUNCIL OF EISENFANG

The Great Schnoz fears that one of us will claim the
Schnozring and use it against him.

–Grandkopf the Gray

At six o'clock, preparations for the dinner were well underway.
Theobald and his party would eat in the highest dining
room while the Rojoriders and the pages would eat in the
lower dining rooms. Cookie had organized some of the pages as
servers and assistant cooks.

Gwendolyn and Grandkopf were in the seestone room. Gwendolyn was worried about the seating. She stood behind the couch
and held up drawing of a table for Grandkopf to consider. Grandkopf bent over slightly and pointed to the drawing.

"Theobald King will be at the head of the table. Lord Arrowshaft
will be on his right. I'll be on his left," said Grandkopf.

"Then Lord Theorug next to Lord Arrowshaft and Lord Beeromir
next to you?" asked Gwendolyn.

"No, put Lord Beeromir next to Lord Arrowshaft and you will sit
next to me."

Gwendolyn sat down hard on the back of the couch and dropped her drawing. Her mouth popped open and she stared blankly at the opposite wall.

"I... I... Lord Sorryman never let me sit with real people. Only with Cookie or the servants."

"This evening, you are the hostess. You *must* sit at the head table."

"I... I... I don't know what to say." She looked up at Grandkopf. Her eyes were wet.

"There's one thing," Grandkopf said. "Well, two, really."

"Yes?"

"You do have some shoes don't you? And maybe another dress?"

"I have lots of shoes. Lots and lots of shoes. But I never wear them in Eisenfang. I like the feel of the stone on my feet."

"And you never leave Eisenfang?"

"No."

"So you never wear shoes?"

"No."

"So why do you have lots of shoes?"

"I like shoes. They're pretty. I just never wear them."

"A dress?"

"I have lots of dresses, too." She hopped up and circled the room. "Sorryman sometimes wanted me to wear a fancy dress to dinner. *Those* dinners were always private and I had to wear shoes, too, but he only liked the kind with the big spiky heels. They weren't very comfortable."

"Well tonight, pick a nice dress and some pretty shoes and sit with me."

"Okay." She stopped in the corner and stretched. She was up on her toes. She bent her right arm behind her head and grabbed her upstretched left arm. She laid her head in the crook of her bent arm and smiled. "It will be fun?"

"Loads of fun."

—

Gwendolyn wore a light blue dress with puffed sleeves and a high waist. She went to the treasure room and found a string of pearls. She had dark blue pumps with a modest heel. She had tied a beaded band around her head and it helped tame her light brown mane. Grandkopf was wearing his gray wizard robe. It was his only robe. Occasionally, when he was in Minor Tetons and had a little cash, he would get a new one at Willie's Wicked-Wild Wizard Warehouse, but he'd had neither time nor cash during his last visit. Theobald and the guests from Rojo had come away from King Theobald's hall, Metamucil, to kill yucks, not to attend state dinners, so mostly they were wearing their fighting clothes without the armor. Fortunately, the corps of pages that traveled with the king's party had been able to remove most of the blood and gore so the dinner guests looked (and smelled) almost civilized. Gwendolyn had directed Lededgas to a room full of odds and ends of clothing that had been left behind over the years and Lededgas looked good. No, Lededgas looked very good indeed. Of course, he always did. Gimmie wore a blood-stained leather shirt that even a small army of pages could not get clean under his mail vest, which the pages were able to polish to a fantastic shine and which hid most of the bloodstains on his shirt. Mail is the perfect accessory for the well-dressed dwarf.

The dinner came off splendidly. In his earlier days, Cookie had been a chef to one of the dwarf kings. He was caught in a compromising position with one of the ladies of the dwarf court, which necessitated him taking it on the lam. Employment at Eisenfang provided a comfortable existence far away from the dwarf courts. It didn't hurt that Sorryman could both afford and appreciate his best efforts.

Cookie had prepared six courses and they were all delicious. Everyone was particularly crazy about the flaming Eisenfang flourless chocolate tortes with raspberry moat. Gwendolyn spent the dinner listening, exclaiming, pointing, gasping in surprise, and laughing. Especially laughing. She was constantly in motion. She was scatterbrained and charming. Everyone loved her.

When the dessert was eaten, the mead was flowing, and the captains of the Rojoriders were breaking into song, Grandkopf gathered the Six Pack and retired to the seestone room with Theobald King for a special meeting. Cookie brought in spiced meat tarts and Gwendolyn flitted around the room checking the supplies of ale, mead, Silverfire, Silverleaf, and cigars. After everyone was settled, Gwendolyn and Cookie took their leave. Grandkopf chose a hand-rolled robusto from the Turino Firento factory in Del Mar; very hard to find since the Bitch Queen returned. When he had it going to his satisfaction, he began.

"The Great Schnoz doubtless knows by now that something is amiss with Sorryman." He pointed at the low table with his cigar. "The seestone has been humming his signal all afternoon." Right on cue, the seestone began humming. "I fear this will cause him to start his attack on Minor Tetons earlier than he had planned."

"Will he empty Soredoor, do you think?" asked Arrowshaft.

"He might. Or he might save his major blow until all his minions are gathered," said Grandkopf.

"He has enough minions right now to overwhelm Minor Tetons, Rojo, and the elves combined," said Beeromir.

"Yes, but the Great Schnoz fears that one of us will claim the Schnozring and use it against him. One of us wielding the full power of the Schnozring would be formidable indeed. It might even be enough to turn the tide of the battle. If he attacks now, I think it will be a feint to test the resolve of Minor Tetons and make us think he is not as strong as we suspect."

"How soon?" asked Theobald.

"We cannot know," Grandkopf said, puffing tensely on his stogie. "But I fear it will be soon. We must bring the full might of Rojo to Minor Tetons as soon as possible."

"Word has gone out to all parts of Rojo. The mustering of the Rojoriders has begun. It will take six days to gather all the riders at Dungdarrow. It can be done no faster," said Theobald.

"And another six to Minor Tetons," said Arrowshaft.

"Let us pray Minor Tetons still stands twelve days hence," said Beeromir.

"Come, let's break up the parties. We ride at first light," said Grandkopf.

—

Grandkopf was sitting in bed in the master bedroom sipping a glass of brandy and reading a wizarding tome, *The Fourteen Uses of Dragon's Blood* by Al P. W. B. Doubledour. He was having trouble concentrating on the text for worrying about the battles to come. His attention was diverted by a soft click that came from the other side of the room. The bookshelf on the opposite wall began to swing open. Grandkopf was reaching for his wizard staff when a froth of brown hair appeared at the end of the bookcase.

Gwendolyn said, "Hi. Can I come in?"

"Of course."

She walked around the bookcase and pushed it shut. It closed with another soft click. She skipped to the bed, jumped up on it, bounced once, and flopped to her knees beside Grandkopf. Her brown hair swirled around her face.

"The passage behind the bookcase goes to my bedroom," she said.

"I see," said Grandkopf.

"Sorryman wanted to me come every night to see if he needed anything. If he didn't want to, you know, do it, then he sent me back."

"I'm not Sorryman."

"I know. You're much nicer. I can tell." She took his hand and played with his fingers. "I wanted to thank you for tonight. I never got to sit with the guests before. He always made me hide."

"That's at an end. You are the Lady of Eisenfang now. I will have to leave soon to go to Minor Tetons and fight the Great Schnoz. You must keep Eisenfang for the King until he returns."

"I… I was hoping you could come back to Eisenfang and be our master." She pouted a little. "Don't you want to live here with us?" she said.

"I do very much."

"Then promise you'll come back after the war."

"If I live, I will come back."

"Goody!" She threw her arms around his neck and crawled on top of him. She buried her face in his chest. "You know, I don't have to go back to my room right now."

"I shouldn't."

She wiggled her hips against him. "Your little wizard wants to. I can feel him."

"You don't have to."

She sat up and pulled her shift over her head, revealing tiny breasts with hard nipples. "I know. But I'm horny." She began to rub insistently against his crotch.

"Oh, taki." He reached for her and she settled into his arms.

The next morning saw the blossoming of many nearly fatal hangovers. Cookie outdid himself with the breakfast buffet and the Silverfire flowed freely. By second breakfast everyone was feeling much better and by elevenses most of the pages were busy saddling horses and preparing the party for departure. They finally left after lunch, the whole group pounding away to the muster at Dungdarrow. Grandkopf looked back to see Gwendolyn in her white dress standing on a low balcony. She was waving a white handkerchief. Grandkopf wondered if he would ever see her again.

TWENTY-TWO

DUNGDARROW

No one returns alive who passes the Door of Dark.
–Theobald King

The Eisenfang party arrived at Dungdale to find the gathering of the Rojoriders well under way. Theobald King led the way. Spirits among the men were high and there was much cheering at his coming. Theobald called to his men by name, giving them words of encouragement.

Arrowshaft was grim. He understood the dangers that lay ahead. He knew how outnumbered they were and how hopeless their cause was based on strength at arms. He knew that their chance of victory hung on a desperate plan. These men would fight for their king and many would die so that the wizard and the little halfbit would have the chance to save the West from the desolation of Schnozmon. The Rojoriders had little choice. They could fight now, or fight later when the servants of the Great Schnoz came for them in their homes.

The king's party continued through the Dungdale encampment and started up the switchback trail to Dungdarrow, a high refuge used by the Rojoriders and by the men of the Whittled Mountains before them.

The king's party rode single file up the path to the summit, exactly as invaders would be forced to do. They made easy targets for any archers stationed above. The heights of Dungdarrow could be long defended. Dungdarrow was a narrow cleft between the Whittled Mountains, the Farradhorn, and the Dimlitbulb. The only other approach was through the Trail of the Croaked, which was guarded by the ghosts of the men of the mountains. No living man had passed that way for three thousand years.

At the top, tents had been prepared for the king and his party. They had a simple meal together in Theobald's tent and afterward most retired to their own tents to rest from their journeys. Grandkopf and Arrowshaft stayed behind to consult with Theobald. They were getting comfortable when a page entered.

"M'lord, the elf says there is a great eagle approaching. It is some ways off but making straight for Dungdarrow at great speed," said the page, who delivered his message and promptly left.

"What does this mean?" asked Theobald.

"It is a message, surely," said Arrowshaft.

"But from whom?" asked Theobald.

"Celerybrains perhaps; he is one of the few who holds the respect of the great eagles," said Grandkopf.

They went out to watch the eagle approach. Sharp-eyed Lededgas pointed into the distance, but it was a minute before the others could see the eagle that was flying rapidly toward them. As he neared the edge of the cliff, the great eagle flared his wings, sloughed off his speed, and settled gently to the grass. He surveyed the group and spotted Grandkopf.

"Celerybrains sends his greetings, Grandkopf," said Airtoground. "I bear a message for Arrowshaft." It sounded like *Ah-a-shat*. Without lips, it was difficult for Airtoground to form all the sounds of common talk. He extended his left leg to Grandkopf. A small tube was strapped to it with a leather belt bearing the silver tree of Lostlorriland. Grandkopf extracted a slim parchment from the tube and handed it to Arrowshaft.

"Celerybrains bid me wait for a reply," said Airtoground.

"A messenger," said Gimmie. "That must be humiliating for the Great Windbreaker."

Airtoground lowered his head until one large dark eye was level with Gimmie. Gimmie took a step back. "I do this because a friend asked it of me," said Airtoground. "Celerybrains would do the same for me had he wings and I not."

"I… I meant no offense," said Gimmie.

"I took none," said Airtoground. "I know of you, Gimmie son of Glowstick. I know you understand the meaning of friendship." Gimmie bowed.

"I thank you, too, old friend," said Grandkopf. Airtoground switched his gaze to Grandkopf, who did not step back. Airtoground nodded once, straightened, and became still.

"There will be a reply," said Arrowshaft, who had finished the note and looked shaken. He ran back to his tent to find a quill. When Arrowshaft returned, he knelt by the great eagle's leg, and placed a small rolled parchment inside the leather tube.

"Fair winds, Airtoground," said Arrowshaft. Airtoground nodded and hopped to the edge of the cliff. He leaned forward and plummeted toward the ground. The great eagle spread his wings and shot out over the plain of Dungdale. Many saw him leave and knew they

had seen something special, something they could tell their grand-
children.

"Friends," said Arrowshaft. "We must talk." The Six Pack and
Theobald retired to Theobald's tent. Arrowshaft addressed the group.
"The message from Celerybrains brings unwelcome tidings. The Cor-
sairs of Ember gather twenty thousand strong at Port o' Gonner.
They intend to sail up Old Man River and join the forces of the
Great Schnoz in the assault on Minor Tetons."

"When?" Beeromir asked.

"Within the week," said Arrowshaft. "Celerybrains reports that
Schnozmon has mobilized only part of his forces. As we guessed, his
first blow will be a test. He will try to overrun Minor Tetons before
the ring can arrive. Failing that, he will see if one of us will claim the
ring and become his rival."

"Minor Tetons is weak. He may carry the day with his initial
attack," said Beeromir, "Especially if the Corsairs aid in the attack."

"All the more reason to hurry," said Grandkopf.

"Friends, there is something else I must tell you." Arrowshaft
paused. "I must take the Trail of the Croaked."

"No one returns alive who passes the Door of Dark," said Theobald.

"The ghosts that guard the Trail of the Croaked were cursed by
Whiskeysour at the end of the second age. They forsook their oath
to fight against Schnozmon. Whiskeysour cursed them to remain
under the mountain without rest until called to serve his heir. I am
the heir of Whiskeysour. I may call them to the Rock of Retch and
there bind them to my will. In this way I can remove the threat of
the corsairs of Ember and bring some men from the south to the aid
of Minor Tetons."

"This is madness!" said Gimmie. "You might not return."

"The Trail of the Croaked has been on my mind for many days. I thought it might come to this in the end, but this news from Celerybrains seals it. We must try to save Minor Tetons and gain some time to execute the plan for the ring. If Minor Tetons falls..." Everyone was quiet for a moment.

"I will go with you," said Lededgas. Gimmie's head jerked toward Lededgas. A moment later Gimmie said, "And I."

"I will go, too," said Froyo.

"As will I," said Grandkopf.

"No, friends, I can ask none to come with me. Besides, Grandkopf, Froyo, and Beeromir must go to Minor Tetons. Grandkopf, you must pretend that you are going to claim the Schnozring. You are the most powerful among us. The Great Schnoz will expect you to have the ambition to replace him. He will expect you to beat the others down and claim the Schnozring for yourself. Froyo alone among us can resist the powers of the Schnozring. He must carry it to Minor Tetons and on to Mount Drool. Beeromir, you must go to fight for your fair city and for Gonner. No one would ask you to lay aside this duty." Beeromir bowed his head.

"I will go with you, Arrowshaft, I do not fear the Croaked," said Lededgas.

"I will go, too," said Gimmie. "I would use my axe on some corsair necks for a change. I'm tired of yucks and wags."

"It is decided then. We must break the Six Pack. Tomorrow I will travel the Trail of the Croaked." Arrowshaft looked off into the distance. He looked uneasy. His hand strayed to the hilt of his sword. His grip tightened and his eyes became hard.

"Tomorrow," he said.

TWENTY-THREE

THE TRAIL OF THE CROAKED

Where is the son of a wag who claims to be the heir of
Whiskeysour?
–Yancy, ghost of a man of the
Whittled Mountains

Arrowshaft, Lededgas, and Gimmie stood outside the Trail of
the Croaked, peering through the Door of Dark to see what
might be inside the mysterious cavern under the mountain
of the Dimlitbulb.

"It's dark," said Gimmie.

"Duh," said Lededgas.

Gimmie kicked Lededgas in the shins. Lededgas smacked Gimmie on top of the helm, causing the helm to slide down over Gimmie's eyes. Gimmie tried to grab Lededgas, but Lededgas danced away and laughed as Gimmie tried to pull off his helm and got his nose stuck in the eye hole.

"Children, let's concentrate on the task at hand," said Arrowshaft. The other two came back to the door, reluctant to give up their feud.

"It's dark in there," said Gimmie.

"Duh, I mean, yes it *is*," said Lededgas.

"What's supposed to be in there?" asked Gimmie.

"The ghosts of the men of the Whittled Mountains dwell here. They swore allegiance to Whiskeysour during the previous partnership of elves and men at the end of the second age. When it came time to fight Schnozmon, they betrayed Whiskeysour. Whiskeysour cursed them to linger as spirits in the Whittled Mountains without peace until his heir came to call them to battle against Schnozmon."

"So?" said Gimmie. Lededgas whacked him on the back of the helmet.

"So Arrowshaft's the heir of Whiskeysour, taki-for-brains, so he can call the ghosts to fight," said Lededgas.

"You know how to do that?" said Gimmie, looking at Arrowshaft.

"Theoretically, I tell them I'm Whiskeysour's heir, call them to the Rock of Retch and they follow us to the fight."

"What if they don't believe you?" asked Gimmie.

"Then I show them Narithil, the Sword That Was Busted—and remade."

"What if they still don't believe you?" asked Gimmie.

"I guess they kill us all then."

"Taki," said Gimmie.

"Time's wasting—we have to go in," said Arrowshaft, who took firm hold of his horse's reins and disappeared through the Door of Dark.

"I do not fear the croaked," said Lededgas. He took the reins of the second horse and followed Arrowshaft through the Door of Dark.

"See you later!" cried Gimmie. "I'll stay here in case someone comes along." He looked around. He was alone in the valley between the Dimlitbulb and the Farradhorn. It was quiet. Very quiet.

Ominously quiet. Only silence came from under the mountain. Gimmie began to feel lonely. Very lonely.

"Maybe I'd better come along," he hollered into the door and then he, too, plunged in.

Within a few steps it was pitch black. In a few more steps he ran into the back of Lededgas, where he and Arrowshaft had stopped to light a torch. Arrowshaft was using a steel to strike sparks into some kindling.

From the depths of the Dimlitbulb, a deep, resonant voice said, "How may I help you?"

"*Aaaaaaahhh.*"

"*Aaaaaaaahh. Aaaaghhhh.*"

Gimmie dropped his axe and ran for the door. Arrowshaft passed him easily and Lededgas passed them both. They all ran back down the trail to the Door of Dark screaming like little girls.

"*Aaaaaaaahh. Aaaaghhhh. Aaaaaaaahh. Aaaaghhhh. Aaaaaaaahh.*"

Back in the daylight, Arrowshaft sat on a rock panting and clutching his chest. Gimmie was sprawled on his back in the dust and Lededgas was busy examining his manicure.

"What in holy green yuck taki was that?" cried Gimmie from the dirt.

"I think that was a ghost," Arrowshaft panted.

"Nothing to be afraid of then," said Lededgas, still examining his manicure.

"I noticed you running out of the cavern," said Arrowshaft. "Screaming like a little girl," he added.

"It took me by surprise," said Lededgas, still examining his manicure.

"Me, too," admitted Arrowshaft.

"Taki," said Gimmie.

"You know, we have to go back in there," said Arrowshaft.

"Yes, especially since we left the horses, all of the supplies, and Gimmie's axe," said Lededgas.

"Taki," said Gimmie.

"Could you ease up on the 'taki' a little and get up? We have to go get the horses," said Lededgas.

"And we have to gather the ghosts of the mountain and go save Minor Tetons," said Arrowshaft.

"Who's going to save me?" asked Gimmie, getting to his feet.

"I am," said Lededgas.

"Great, but who's going to save you?"

"You are."

"It's a bit unsettling that this conversation is beginning to make sense," said Gimmie.

"Let's go," said Arrowshaft

This time they lit a torch before they started. Soon they were all through the door and down the trail. They quickly found Gimmie's axe, the horses, and a few paces beyond the horses, a ticket booth manned, or rather ghosted, by a bearded spirit.

"Welcome to the Trail of the Croaked," said the spirit. "How may I help you?"

"Sorry about running away. We were startled," said Arrowshaft.

"Not to worry—happens all the time. So, do you want the self-service plan or the surprise plan?"

"Who *are* you?" said Arrowshaft.

"I am Kelly, keeper of the kiosk. I help the living choose their plans and I conduct the tours."

"Tours?" said Gimmie.

"Yes, follow me and I'll show you," said Kelly. "We have the most extensive collection of croaking aids in Central Oith."

The three companions followed Kelly into the cavern. After a few steps, Kelly stopped in front of a guillotine. There was a skeleton on the bench, the blade was down, and there was a skull in a basket at the head of the device. He gestured toward it with a transparent hand.

"Here is the most popular method in the self-service plan. Very efficient, very quick."

"Who's that?" said Gimmie, pointing at the bones lying on the guillotine.

"That's Bob Smelderheis, our last customer on the self-service plan. We can't move the bones, you see, being ghosts and all, and the cleaning service hasn't been here in a while. If you want self-service with the guillotine, you will have to shove old Bob's bones out of the way."

"I don't think we want the self-service plan," said Arrowshaft.

"Well, the surprise plan is excellent! You never know when it will happen. You're walking along and wham! A thousand tons of rocks fall on you. Or, whoosh! The floor gives way to a yawning pit and you are skewered on spikes at the bottom. The anticipation is really quite delicious. The customers talk about it for years after they've croaked."

"I don't think we are interested in that plan, either," said Arrowshaft.

"Well, that's a problem because we only have the two plans and once you get past the kiosk you have to choose one plan or the other." Kelly tried to wring his hands, but they passed through each other. He gave up and pointed to a sign that was nailed to the back of the kiosk. The sign was crudely lettered and hung crookedly on its single nail. It read:

Plan 1—Self-Service Croaking

Plan 2—Surprise Croaking

No Substitutions.

No Exceptions.

"Actually, we are here because I am the heir of Whiskeysour and I want to talk to someone about fighting Schnozmon and fulfilling your oath."

"What oath?"

"The oath sworn by the men of the mountains to Whiskeysour at the end of the second age."

"Well that was before my time. I'm new here since they started the business."

"What business?"

"The tired-of-living, throw-off-the-mortal-coil, assisted-croaking business. We are the only ones in the business in Central Oith."

"So people come here to die?" asked Gimmie.

"Plan one, kill yourself. Plan two, we kill you. That's the idea. Come in the Door of Dark and wind up dead."

"If you are all ghosts, who cleans up the mess?" asked Lededgas, gesturing toward the bones on the guillotine.

"We have a contract with the men of the valley. They maintain the equipment and carry off the bodies in exchange for looting the personal effects. We let them come and go without the croaking part, obviously, or no one would come. As it is, there aren't many customers and the cleaning crews don't show up very often, so sometimes we wind up with bones lying around for while, like old Bob Smelderheis back there."

"We really aren't interested in the croaking," said Arrowshaft, sweeping his arm around the self-service area. "Is there someone I can talk to from the old days, from the time of Whiskeysour?"

"Well, there's Yancy but he doesn't much like to be disturbed."

"You should get someone. This is important to those who were cursed."

"Okay, okay, whom shall I say is calling?"

"I am Arrowshaft son of Arrowhead, called Elixir the Elfrock, Westhomey, the heir of Whiskeysour, Ellendale's son of Gonner and bearer of Narithil, the Sword that was Busted—and Remade." said Arrowshaft.

"Wow, that's a long one. I'll tell him Arrowhead is calling and see if he will come."

"*Arrowshaft*, the heir of Whiskeysour."

"Whatever," said Kelly and vanished.

"I thought that went well," said Arrowshaft. They waited patiently in the glow of the single torch. The bones of Bob didn't seem to have anything to say and neither did the others. They peered into the gloom. Vaguely they made out a rope noose hanging from a wooden beam that had a chair underneath it. They saw a curious chair with straps on the arms and legs and a copper cap with wires running up toward the ceiling. They saw a wide selection of swords, a tantō for ritual *seppuku*, and a rack of knives of various sorts that could be used to slit throats or puncture hearts. There was a chair beside a table containing an assortment of bottles and liquors mostly labeled with skulls and crossed bones.

Kelly reappeared with a large ghost who towered over them all.

"Where is the son of a wag who claims to be the heir of Whiskeysour?" boomed the ghost.

"It is I," said Arrowshaft. "I am Arrowshaft son of Arrowhead, called Elixir the Elfrock, Westhomey, the heir of Whiskeysour, Ellendale's son of Gonner and bearer of Narithil, the Sword that was Busted—and Remade. I am here to summon the men of the Whittled Mountains to the Rock of Retch."

"Not so fast, Arrowbutt. Yer not the first to make this claim. How do we know you aren't lying like the others?"

"Here is Narithil, the sword that was remade from the shards of Nasal, Whiskeysour's sword that cut the Schnozring from the schnoz of Schnozmon at the end of the second age."

The large ghost turned to Kelly and said, "Get the Shrimp." There was a faint pop and Kelly was gone. An uncomfortable silence fell. Arrowshaft looked around while Lededgas examined his manicure and Gimmie fidgeted with his axe. After a minute, Arrowshaft said, "It must be peaceful here under the mountain."

"If by 'peaceful' you mean deadly dull, then you'd be right. Darkness and quiet for 3000 years. You try it sometime. I hope you *are* the heir of Whiskeysour for both our sakes. If you are, you can get us out of this hell hole, and if you are not you'll have a chance to join us and see for yourself how peaceful it all is." Gimmie's eyes darted around the cavern. Lededgas looked unconcerned. There was a faint pop and two specters appeared: Kelly and a ghost barely five feet tall.

"Shrimp, you got a good close look at Nasal when Whiskeysour ran it through your middle. Have a look at this sword and see if you recognize it."

Arrowshaft pulled Narithil out of its sheath and held it on open palms for the short ghost to view.

"This here blade ain't right. Nasal didn't have no fancy elf writing on it."

"It has been reforged. The elves put the runes there when it was remade," said Arrowshaft.

"The hilt looks right, though. I got a real good look at the hilt, it being right there above my belt there while Whiskeysour was sticking it into my guts and all," said the Shrimp.

"But you're not sure?" asked Yancy.

"Naw, these kind of hilts were a dime a dozen back then. All them dwarf sword makers were doing the silver pommel and black leather grip back then."

"We will have to do the door test then," said Yancy.

"Door test?" asked Arrowshaft.

"The realm under the mountain is cursed. No living person who passes the kiosk may leave. If the living attempt to leave, they die at the door. The only exceptions are the men of the valley, whom we suffer to pass, and the true heir of Whiskeysour who may come and go as he pleases. So if you can get out alive, then you are the true heir of Whiskeysour and you can release us from this pit of darkness. If not, you die at the Door of Dark and your friends can choose among the toys to ease their passing." Gimmie looked with apprehension at the *toys*. They all trudged back past the kiosk to the Door of Dark. Arrowshaft walked to the threshold and did not pause. He walked right out into the daylight. The ghosts exchanged glances. Then they all went down on one knee.

"Arrowshaft, heir of Whiskeysour, what is your command?" said Yancy.

"Take us through the mountain and follow us to the Rock of Retch, where you will fulfill your oath and be at peace."

"It shall be as you say," said Yancy. He waved his arm in a shooing motion toward Kelly. "Take them through." Then he and the

Shrimp disappeared, leaving the three friends with the Keeper of the Kiosk.

They gathered up their horses and trudged back past the kiosk, the guillotine, and the other self-service paraphernalia. During the trip, Kelly kept up a travel-guide patter.

"The noose. Very popular for unrequited lovers. Poisons. Women like them, leaves a pretty corpse. Of course, the women also go for the dagger to the heart. Occasionally, we get the old soldier who wants to fall on his sword, but they usually bring their own swords, hence the collection. Vat of acid. Don't know why we keep it, really, it has never been very popular. Crossbow and chair. Never saw the appeal myself, but it is surprisingly popular."

They reached a dimly lit section of the trail and Kelly motioned for them to stop. "This is the beginning of the surprise service area. There are five booby-trapped sections: the falling floor dumping into spike-filled pits, the collapsing ceiling, poison darts, the arrow arcade, and the flame roaster. This is the first section, so follow me and stay on the left—about three feet is safe.

"We once had a drunk make it past the falling floor by leaning on the left wall the whole way. Then the falling ceiling jammed and he didn't get crushed. He got hit by a bunch of the poison darts but it had been so long since the darts were serviced that the poison had expired. We got him with the arrows, though. It was a good thing, too—the flame roaster is spectacular when it works but it's hard to keep the pilot lights lit for years on end. Anyway, we've never gotten to actually roast anyone in it."

They trudged onward. At each section, Kelly showed them the safe paths. Hours later they were on a narrow, but booby trap-free path, making steady progress toward the southern door.

TWENTY-FOUR

THE ROCK OF RETCH

I, Arrowshaft son of Arrowhead, ... summon the men of
the Whittled Mountains to the Rock of Retch.
                              –Arrowshaft son of Arrowhead

We're here, ain't we, you brainless git.
                              –the Shrimp, ghost of a man of the
                                        Whittled Mountains

T he companions emerged from the Trail of the Croaked at
noon. Behind them followed the Croaked, pouring through
the southern door. They appeared as a transparent army, the
individuals not quite distinct. Banners and spears waved over them
and the sound they made was like the wind through pines on the
slopes of a high forgotten valley mixed with muffled footsteps. They
traveled quickly through sparsely populated highlands. The farmers and crofters that dwelt in the land knew the legends, knew that
the time of the Croaked had come. They cowered in their hovels,
sensing the army's ominous purpose. All day the ghostly army traveled, and on into the night. The moon peeked over the mountains as they traversed the last slope up to the dell of the Rock of
Retch. The companions dismounted and walked over to the rock.

"Why is this called the Rock of Retch?" Gimmie asked. "Oh, taki!
What is that smell? Gak." He clutched at his throat, his eyes bulged,

and he threw up all over the rock. Arrowshaft looked uncomfortable. Lededgas was unconcerned.

"That's why," said Lededgas. Gimmie, still bending over and retching, gave Lededgas the finger as comment.

Yancy and the Shrimp appeared with a pop.

"So now what?" said Yancy.

"I don't know. I've never done this before," said Arrowshaft.

"No one has ever done this before," said Lededgas.

"I've got it," said Arrowshaft. "I, Arrowshaft son of Arrowhead, called Elixir the Elfrock, Westhomey, the heir of Whiskeysour, Ellendale's son of Gonner and bearer of Narithil, the Sword that was Busted—and Remade, summon the men of the Whittled Mountains to the Rock of Retch."

"We're here, ain't we, you brainless git," said the Shrimp.

"Have some respect—that brainless git can free us from the curse," said Yancy, bending over to speak to the Shrimp and pointing a ghostly finger at Arrowshaft.

"Right you are! Sorry guvna', go right ahead."

"Men of the Mountains..."

"Ghosts, we're ghosts, ain't we."

"Ghosts of the men of the Mountains, I call upon you to fulfill your oaths. What say you?"

"Okay," said Yancy. There was a long pause while everyone looked around.

"That was anticlimactic," said Lededgas.

"I sorta thought we'd get solid or sumptin'," said the Shrimp.

"Are you sure you know what you're doing?" said Yancy.

"The legend says that I summon you to the Rock of Retch," said Arrowshaft, gesturing at the rock.

"You did that," said Yancy.

"I ask you to fulfill your oaths."

"You did that, too."

"Then you go kill whomever I want." Arrowshaft drew his thumb across his throat in emphasis.

"I'm good with that, but considering we're still ghosts, how are we going to kill anybody?" asked Yancy. He passed his arm through Gimmie's head to demonstrate the impotence of Arrowshaft's ghostly army. Gimmie hopped back and shivered.

"Maybe you scare them to death," said Gimmie.

"Naw, that's silly. Who's going to be scared to death by this?" said Yancy gesturing toward the Shrimp.

"He's got a point," said Gimmie, looking to Arrowshaft.

"Maybe you get solid before the battle," said Arrowshaft.

"How many are we fighting?" said Yancy.

"Twenty thousand Corsairs of Ember," said Arrowshaft.

"If we don't get solid, the three of you are going to look awfully silly charging down on those Corsairs," said Yancy.

"No taki," said Gimmie.

"There's no choice. We will find out when we get there," said Arrowshaft.

"Where are we going?" said Yancy.

"To Port o' Gonner."

"You going to ride the whole way?"

"Unless you can carry us."

"We'll go on ahead and meet you there. Which way do we go?"

"Go southeast until you hit the sea or Old Man River. Then turn east," said Arrowshaft, pointing to his left, "and go along the water until you find Port o' Gonner

"See you in three days," said Yancy, as the host of the ghosts of the men of the mountain moved off southeast.

Three days hard riding later, the three companions arrived at the hills overlooking the Port o' Gonner. Illuminated by the setting sun, the white walls of the town below had taken on pinkish hues that were fading quickly to blue as the sun set. It looked almost peaceful except for the swift, black ships of the Corsairs dotting the harbor.

"The Corsairs are still here. We have arrived in time," said Arrowshaft.

"Where are the ghosts?" asked Gimmie.

"Lost, I expect," said Lededgas. Gimmie snorted.

"Since there's nothing we can do without them, we might as well get some sleep," said Arrowshaft. Gimmie and Arrowshaft, who had been dozing atop their horses for three days, were soon asleep. Lededgas let his mind drift into the waking sleep of the elves.

The morning came too early. Still, Arrowshaft and Gimmie had gotten more sleep than they had for the whole of the previous three days. Lededgas shot a brace of rabbits and Gimmie had them turning them on spits when the host of ghosts arrived. Yancy came forward with the Shrimp.

"We got lost," said Yancy.

"Went too far south, din't we? Wound up in Lind-hop. The blighters wouldn't talk to us so we couldn't ask directions," said the Shrimp.

"Big surprise there," said Gimmie.

"So we turned right and went along the river for half a day. We came upon this old blind man sitting in front of a cafe. He didn't know we were ghosts and told us we were going the wrong way," said Yancy.

"East, you were supposed to turn east. That would be left," said Arrowshaft.

"Told ya so," said the Shrimp.

"Shut up," said Yancy.

"No matter, you are here," said Arrowshaft. "Let's get started."

"We ain't solid. How are we going to kill these Corsair takis if we ain't solid?" asked the Shrimp.

"Okay, let's try this again," said Arrowshaft. "Ghosts of the men of the Mountains! Stand ye ready to fulfill your oaths?"

"We do," said Yancy. A murmur arose from the ghosts as they began to solidify. In a minute, the host stood before the city of Port o' Gonner in three solid dimensions and beautiful living color.

"I'm solid!" said Yancy, patting his chest. Then he took out his sword and ran it through the Shrimp in almost the same spot that Whiskeysour had picked three millennia earlier.

"Taki that hurts," said the Shrimp. "What did you do that for, taki-face?"

"I wanted to see what would happen."

"Well it hurt like frozen yuck taki."

"But it didn't kill you."

"I'm already dead, ain't I," said the Shrimp. Yancy grinned.

"Let's go kill the stinking corsair takis and get this over with," he said. He raised his sword. "Follow me!" The host of now-solid ghosts sent up a roar and started off down the hill.

"Wait! Wait!" hollered the Shrimp. All the ghosts came to a stop and everyone turned toward the Shrimp. "What do we do when we get to the water? I can't swim."

"So walk across the water," said Arrowshaft.

"That will work?"

"What does is matter? You're already dead, so you can't drown. Go down there and walk on the bottom if you have to, just kill the stupid Corsairs."

"Okay," said the Shrimp. "I can do that."

Yancy nodded. "Follow me!" he cried, again, and the host started off down the hill toward the port, again. Lededgas stood at Arrowshaft's shoulder and watched them go.

"Do you think it will work, walking on the water?" asked Lededgas.

"I don't know, but they won't kill anybody milling around up here," said Arrowshaft.

"I guess we'd better go, too," said Lededgas. He looked at Gimmie. "Want to go kill some Corsairs?" Gimmie smiled widely and nodded.

—

The now-solid ghosts *could* walk on water so they strolled on out to the boats, clambered up the sides, and started killing Corsairs. It quickly became apparent to the Corsairs that their attackers couldn't be killed, so they decided it was better to run than to fight. Most of them went overboard and started swimming back to the shore. Those that didn't drown or get eaten by sharks kept going until they got back to Ember. That or they stayed in Port o' Gonner, married local girls, and took up work in the sea trade after the war.

Arrowshaft, Lededgas, and Gimmie arrived at the shore to find the ghosts already on the ships, hacking the Corsairs to pieces. Since they couldn't walk on water and since Gimmie was wearing his mail and would sink like a stone (and couldn't swim even if he were without armor) they had to commandeer a rowboat to join the fight. Neither Arrowshaft nor Gimmie had ever rowed before. This left the rowing to Lededgas, who had at least had a modicum of experience in boats on the rivers of his homeland. However, his experience did not specifically include rowing. While he looked graceful rowing, as he did in all things, his course zigzagged rather more than a little and it was the better part of a half hour before they arrived at the nearest ship. Yancy and the Shrimp met them on deck. There were no Corsairs to be seen.

"About time you got here. We've done all the dirty work for you," said Yancy. Gimmie was the only one of the three companions that looked genuinely disappointed. Arrowshaft looked over the gunwale and saw that the rest of the ghosts were now gathering around the ship. Most stood on the water, but some came aboard and perched on the gunwales or climbed the mast and sat on the yard arms. Soon thousands were gathered in and around the ship.

"You should have seen the looks on those takis' faces when they realized that they couldn't kill us. It was hilarious! Of course, that doesn't mean that they couldn't stick us a little. The Shrimp never was a good fighter and got himself run through three or four times," said Yancy.

"An' it hurt like a bitch every time, dinnit," said the Shrimp.

"You have done well; the Corsairs are vanquished," said Arrowshaft.

"I don't know about vanquished, but they're mostly chopped liver or shark bait," said Yancy, leering. This sent a murmur of agreement through the ghosts.

"So 'ow 'bout it then, we done?" asked the Shrimp.

"Yes, you have fought the enemies of the kingdom of Gonner. As the heir of Whiskeysour, I deem that you have fulfilled your oaths. Go and be at rest." Pandemonium broke out. Yancy and the Shrimp began dancing a jig, the ghosts in the rigging broke out into an old drinking song, and the ghosts on the water waved their weapons and began dancing, cavorting, and cheering. Slowly they all became translucent and began to vanish with soft pops. Yancy and the Shrimp were the last. They abandoned their jig, turned together toward Arrowshaft, bowed, and, *pop,* were gone.

The three companions were left standing on the deck. The sea breeze blew softly in their hair and the only sounds were the slap of the waves on the sides of the ship and the lonely cries of the gulls overhead.

"What do you say to lunch?" said Gimmie.

They rowed back to the mainland and found a likely pub, the Lusty Pelican. Lededgas's credit was good and they had a most satisfying lunch. The pub didn't serve mead but Gimmie, who had tasted nothing but water since entering the Door of Dark, found grog much to his liking. He soon passed out and fell off his barstool. Lededgas thoughtfully kicked him under a table where no one would walk on him. Meanwhile, Arrowshaft and Lededgas set up a recruiting center offering free grog, ale, and Silverfire, and soon had the complete attention of a sizable crowd. When everyone was happy, they set about enlisting soldiers, pirates, cutthroats, mercenaries, and sailors to go to the aid of Minor Tetons.

TWENTY-FIVE

KAHN BERRI KAHN

Kah! Me save you ass, Horse Man. You listen Kahn Berri
Kahn.

–Kahn Berri Kahn

On the fourth day of the ride of the Rojoriders to Minor
Tetons, a rider came out of the woods and started down
the road toward the Rojoriders. The rider was Argyle.

"Greetings Grandkopf, Theobald King," said Argyle. "My father,
El Round, sends his greetings."

"He is recovered then?" asked Grandkopf.

"Yes. Not many days after the Six Pack left Clovendell, his nephew heard him say goodbye to the oliphant. He came out of his room,
ate a serving of everything on the breakfast buffet, placed a large
order for mushrooms, and took up business as usual."

"It is well. We shall all need his counsel in the days to come," said
Grandkopf.

"I bring a thousand elf warriors, archers all, from El Round to
honor the Previous Partnership of Elves and Men."

"They are most welcome," said Theobald King.

"Has Lord Arrowshaft taken the Trail of the Croaked?" said Argyle.

"Yes, m'lady. We fear for him," said Theobald King.

"Fear not. He is the true heir of Whiskeysour. The ghosts of the mountain can do him no harm. He will win through and bring help to Minor Tetons," said Argyle.

—

That night, the Rojoriders camped on the edges of a forest that extended east into the misty distance. The leaders sat around Theobald's campfire, discussing the fate of Minor Tetons and the number of yucks they might find surrounding the city. An old man stepped out of the darkness and stood by the fireside. He was a bit short of five feet tall, had spindly arms and legs, and an admirable potbelly. He was bald on top, but his remaining gray hair fell to his shoulders. He wore a breechcloth, a headdress that consisted of feathers of many colors, and several strings of brightly colored beads. He carried in his right hand a spear that had a great eagle feather tied to its shaft. He planted his feet firmly in front of Theobald King and stood with left arm akimbo.

"Ha! Horse Man!" he said. "You ride road. You big surprise. Many yuckos. Ha! Very funny!" He walked to a log and sat down.

"Me Kahn Berri Kahn," he said, tapping his thumb on his chest. "Me head man Kahana! Me save you yuckos! Now give drink. Silverfire." He snapped his fingers to hurry things along. Argyle smiled at this speech and nodded at one of the elves, who produced a bottle of Silverfire. Kahn Berri Kahn broke the seal, pulled the cork out with his teeth, spit the cork into the fire, and took two large swallows.

"Kah!" he said, grinning broadly. "Me save you ass, Horse Man. You listen Kahn Berri Kahn. Price very cheap. One axe, many horse."

"How can you help us, Kahn Berri Kahn?" asked Theobald, glancing at Argyle as if to ask, "Who is this old fat guy kidding?"

"Kahana know many things. Kahana show old road. Sneak up on
yuckos. Kill 'em! Ha! Bring axe now. Tomorrow many horse." Argyle
nodded again, and one of the elves ran to a pack horse and produced
a hand axe that had been used for chopping kindling. It wasn't new
but it was well made and had a lot of life left in it. Kahn Berri Kahn
held it to the firelight, ran his thumb over the blade to test the edge
and, apparently satisfied, tucked the axe into the rope that served as
his belt. He took another swig of Silverfire and began to haggle over
horses in earnest.

Grandkopf, who had been chasing his pipeweed with ale, had
need of the bushes. When he finished his business he stopped to
look at the stars through an opening in the trees. When he looked
back down there was a man in front of him.

"Aaaaah! Taki, you scared me."

"Sorry, sneaking up on visitors is a tradition," said the stranger.
He was five feet four inches tall and wore a buckskin shirt and trou-
sers. A finely woven cloak hung over his shoulders.

"I am Larri Kahn of the Kahana, the people of the forest. You are
Grandkopf the Gray. I would speak with you about the danger on
the road ahead."

"Are you related to..." Grandkopf pointed at Kahn Berri Kahn.

"My grandfather. Take whatever he says with a grain of salt. He
has a tendency toward embellishment."

"Fancy language..."

"For an unlettered savage? Minor Tetons University, class of '11. I
majored in agriculture—seed crops—the better to help my people."

"Is Kahn Berri Kahn the headman?"

"No, I am," said Larri. "And his name is Berri Kahn. He likes to say it like Bond, James Bond."

"Who is that?"

"No idea. But he smokes a lot of pipeweed and eats a lot of mushrooms. He claims he sees a world where people sit around watching talking rocks that make pictures. I'm trying to get him to cut down on the mushrooms."

"Are there really yucks on the road?" asked Grandkopf.

"Yes, he is telling the truth about that. Two or three thousand yuckos swept away the garrison at the gate three days ago. If you go down the main road you will find the gates and wall held against you."

"And the secret road?" said Grandkopf.

"Truth again. There is a road built by the old kings of Gonner. The road is now overgrown but still passable for your riders. If you take it, you can surprise the yuckos from behind."

"And for a price you will show us," said Grandkopf.

"Yes, a kingly price: one axe and one bottle of Silverfire," said Larri, grinning. "Grandfather enjoys being the center of attention. He forgets that he hasn't been headman for twenty years. Promise him all the horses he wants. He will pass out on the Silverfire and our people will carry him off in the night. He won't remember anything in the morning. I wouldn't ask for the axe, but you've already given him one and it will save me a trip into the city to get a new one for him."

"You never intended to charge us," said Grandkopf.

"No, your fight is our fight. We have no love of the Orange Nose or the yuckos he sends out to pillage and conquer. If you lose, the fight will come to us soon enough. My people are hunters, not warriors. We will hunt the yuckos if they come, but they are many and we are few. We will not win that fight."

"Thank you, Larri Kahn."

"Don't mention it. By the way, ask my grandfather how he got that great eagle feather. The truth is remarkable enough. His old feather wore out so he asked the Great Windbreaker for another. Airtoground gave it to him, plucked it right out of his wing. But the story he will tell is worth the price of the Silverfire. Just remember, it is all bull taki."

Grandkopf did ask about the feather and the story *was* worth the price of the Silverfire. Kahn Berri Kahn started another story that was just as fabulous but passed out in the middle of it. In the morning, as promised, there was no sign of Kahn Berri Kahn, not even any footprints. There was a note on the log: *Thanks for the axe. – Larri.*

The Rojoriders were rousted from their beds at daybreak. Larri Kahn came into camp and took first breakfast with Theobald and his party.

"How's your grandfather?" asked Grandkopf.

"He says there is an oliphant stomping around in his head. Worse, he had to suffer a sound tongue lashing from my grandmother. She wasn't pleased when she got up this morning and found him passed out in front of the wickiup in his ceremonial dress."

"Is he in much trouble?"

"No, his daughters and granddaughters all spoil him. He's really a charming old geezer," said Larri.

"How do we do this?" asked Grandkopf.

"I'll lead your party through. I have scouts in the hills watching the yuckos. If the yuckos do anything, we'll know about it. The road is narrow through the foothills. It will take maybe ten hours to bring all your riders through. When you are ready, my people will provide a distraction in front of the wall. Then you strike."

Ten hours later, the Rojoriders were lining up in a shallow valley. Larri Kahn was talking with a scout. When the conversation finished, the scout ran back into the forest and Larri made his report to Theobald King.

"All is quiet," said Larri. "When you are ready we will create the distraction."

When the Rojoriders were assembled behind a low hill, Larri Kahn pulled a white cloth from beneath his cloak and waved it at the mountainside. There was no response that Theobald could see, but in a few minutes all the yucks started running toward the walls.

The Kahana had crawled unseen to within fifty yards of the walls. All at once they stood. They were wearing the traditional loincloth and carrying spears. They stood completely still for thirty seconds before breaking into song. They sang in the ancient language of the Kahana, which was incomprehensible to the yucks, about a maiden that gets carried off by a bear. A young warrior goes to save her but he has body odor and bad breath so the maiden rejects the warrior, marries the bear, and lives happily ever after. It was a song that the Kahana used to teach their young about the importance of personal hygiene, but its message would surely have been lost on the yucks— even had they been able to understand it.

While the yucks enjoyed the serenade, the Rojoriders crested the hill behind them and charged down. A thousand elven bows thrummed and a thousand yucks died. The yucks started down off the ramparts. The ones who made it to the ground were ridden down by the Rojoriders, while those who chose to stay on the walls were felled by arrows or spears. Finally, the Rojoriders charged up the narrow stairs on foot to finish the job with swords. In two hours, the battle for the wall was over.

The celebration that night was muted. The Rojoriders knew that the real battle lay ahead. In the morning, or perhaps the morning after, they would ride to glory, or to the demise of the third age.

TWENTY-SIX

THE FIRST BATTLE OF MINOR TETONS

Taki, that's a lot of yucks.
—Foamier son of Alehouse, Commander
of the Defense of Minor Tetons

Taki, that's a lot of yucks.
—Theobald King of Rojo

Foamier and the prince of Dul Amway stood in the command center on the highest level of the city with their generals, aides, body guards, assorted messengers, and signalmen. They were watching the yucks advance over the field of Picador. Teams of yucks pushed trebuchets and ballistae. Three siege towers higher than the outer walls of Minor Tetons were powered forward by pairs of mountain trolls. Foamier, acting Steward of Gonner and commander of the city, watched them come.

"Taki, that's a lot of yucks," said Foamier.

—

Theobald King sat on his steed in front of his Rojoriders, who stretched in a half-mile long line on the crest of a hill overlooking the field of Picador. The Rojoriders had arrived two hours after the yucks had begun their attack. As they looked on, two siege towers burned while another was about to attain the wall. A covered ram worked on the gates and tens of thousands of yucks sprawled across the field of Picador. Theobald King surveyed the carnage.

"Taki, that's a lot of yucks," said Theobald King. He looked up and down his line of riders. For a long moment he watched the banners blow in the breeze, the sun glint off the armor. He sighed. He raised his sword.

"Ready Rojoriders!" he cried. Horns blew, horses stamped, the Rojoriders drew their swords. Theobald King rode to the fore and shouted the ancient motto of the Rojoriders.

"Ne conjugare nobiscum!" The Rojoriders banged their shields with their swords and chanted the traditional reply. "Kill! Maim! Kick ass! Kill! Maim! Kick ass!"

Theobald King turned toward the yucks, lowered his arm, and spurred his mighty war steed. The Rojoriders accelerated after him, thundering toward the yucks, riding to doom or glory.

Twenty-Seven

Monkeyshines

You have failed us, Alehouse.
> –The Bitch Queen of Del Mar to Alehouse
> son of Brewpub, Steward of Gonner.

As the battle raged before the gates of Minor Tetons, Grandkopf, Beeromir, and Froyo entered the city through a small postern concealed by trees in a section of the north wall near the base of the mountains. They made their way to the main gate where they found Foamier in the thickest of the fighting. Foamier embraced his brother and clasped forearms with Grandkopf. He glanced at Froyo and did a double take.

"Is this the halfbit that bears the Schnozring?" asked Foamier.

"How did you know?"

"My father told me. He much desired to speak with this halfbit."

"That's not good, is it?" Froyo asked. Unconsciously, he touched the ring in his pocket.

"Taki, does everyone in Central frecking Oith know?" said Grandkopf tugging his beard, clearly exasperated.

"Where is Lord Alehouse?" asked Grandkopf.

"He would not leave his study," said Foamier. "He said he was too busy. He said he had a jigsaw puzzle to finish, that he hadn't worked the crossword in the Minor Tetons Gazette, and that his crown needed polishing. I left him and assumed command of the city defense. There is something else you should know. The captain of the guard foiled a plot to open the gates as the enemy came up from the river. We captured two of them. They say that the man who hired them claimed to take his orders from someone in the palace. We have a traitor."

"We must go to your father. I fear he may have been brainwashed by the Great Schnoz. He may be in great danger."

Foamier nodded. "The lift is still working. It will take us directly to the sixth level."

—

Grandkopf and the sons of Alehouse were met on the sixth level by the captain of the guard. The captain was accompanied by soldiers, two carrying ceremonial lances, a squad of swordsmen and a dozen or more archers. It looked as if all the guards of the palace were assembled at the foot of the stairs leading to the courtyard.

"Please come with us to the palace," said Grandkopf. "I fear that Lord Alehouse may not be in his right mind."

"Lord Alehouse ordered all the guards out of the palace," said the captain. "He said he couldn't think with us clanking up and down the halls. He told us not to play croquet on the lawn but to go down the Dragon Bowl and go bowling, but none of us has our bowling shoes with us so we are just milling around here."

Grandkopf rolled his eyes. Before he could compose a proper response, some of the men of the guard pointed at the battle below. "Schnozgoons! Schnozgoons!" they yelled.

Grandkopf leaned over the rampart. Far below, the Schnozgoons wheeled over the field of Picador on their flying monkeys. The war cries of the monkeys, *chee chee cheeeee*, could be heard dimly over the din of the battle. Wherever they flew, the Schnozgoons projected an aura of terror. Men lost heart, horses panicked and bolted. As they turned and dived over the battlefield, the fearsome monkeys hurled watermelon-sized globs of taki at the riders below. Riders were swept from their mounts. The smell was so bad that even the yucks wouldn't approach the afflicted riders. Anyone unfortunate enough to be hit by flying monkey taki was slowly and painfully dissolved, armor and all. The lines of the Rojoriders fell into disarray. The battle was turning in favor of the minions of the Great Schnoz.

Grandkopf caught a hint of motion above. A Schnozgoon was descending toward them. Grandkopf ducked behind the rampart and the others crouched beside him. They looked skyward and saw the flying monkey glide over them to the seventh level.

A wide set of stairs connected the sixth and seventh levels of the city. The stairs opened into the plaza of the dead, previously green tree of Gonner. Grandkopf started up the stairs with Froyo and the brothers close on his heels. Grandkopf peeked over the low wall that bordered the top of the stairs. To the left, the Bitch Queen of Del Mar was bouncing on her flying monkey as it hovered over the courtyard. The monkey was fifteen feet tall and its wings spread nearly forty feet from tip to tip. The monkey wore a red vest with golden edging and a festive red fez with a black tassel. The Bitch Queen sat in a saddle high on his back and held reins that connected to a harness on the monkey's head. She was wearing a black helm with long, black spikes rising vertically from the top and sides. Her eyes flashed neon blue through the eye holes. Her lips were blue against the shimmering ectoplasm of her face. She wore a black leather teddy that was slit down the front. Her navel sported a flashing neon orange ring in the center of which was a metallic nose that glowed orange. Her high-heeled knee boots were black leather except for steel knee covers with six-inch spikes. Over her ensemble she had a black leather duster that billowed in the currents of wind that swirled from the rhythmic strokes of the monkey's wings.

To the right, Lord Alehouse stood beside the dead, once green tree of Gonner wearing his ceremonial robes and the simple steel ring that served as a crown for the ruling stewards. He carried the green wooden rod that was the symbol of his authority. He was struggling to look unconcerned.

Grandkopf jerked his head down.

"It's the Bitch Queen of Del Mar!" said Grandkopf under his breath.

"Listen!" whispered Froyo, pulling on the hem of Grandkopf's robes.

"You have failed us, Alehouse!" said the Bitch Queen. "The gates were supposed to be open."

"I gave the order myself. I don't know what happened," said Alehouse.

"Doddering old fool! You will not fail us again!" The Bitch Queen held a double-edged sword in a gloved hand. She raised the sword and a bolt of lightning jumped from its end. The bobbing of the flying monkey spoiled her aim and the lightning struck the ground beside Alehouse, writhed along the ground for a second, and left a smoking crater. Alehouse stared at the crater for a half second, then swiveled in place and took off like a frightened chihuahua. He dropped his green staff of authority, his crown fell to the ground a few paces later, and his skinny, white legs thrashed beneath him as he sprinted to the relative safety of the palace.

"Taki!" said the Bitch Queen. She fired another bolt. It struck five feet behind the retreating Alehouse and chased him along the ground, sizzling and leaving blackened grass in its wake. It was gaining on him but the Bitch Queen ran out of juice and the lightning stopped. Alehouse reached the entrance of the palace. He heaved open the heavy wooden door and threw himself through the entryway. The door slammed behind him.

"Monkey taki!" said the Bitch Queen, Her monkey tried to look up at her; it just made him cross-eyed. He gave up and gave her the finger instead. She whacked his head below his festive red fez with the flat of her hand.

"Oh, behave!" she said.

"Evita Kraigsdotter!"

"Who dares?" said the Bitch Queen, spinning her bobbing mount to face the voice. She spotted Grandkopf. Her eyes flared blue inside her helmet. Her mouth turned up into a wry smile.

"Grandkopf the Gray," she said. "Go back to your pipe. You are no match for me."

"Evita, as charming as ever, I see. Fly your little monkey home now or you are going to get hurt."

"Fool! No man can kill me." She fired a lightning bolt from her sword. This time her aim was true, but Grandkopf blocked the bolt with his staff. For a long second the bolt crackled between them. Grandkopf gripped his staff with both hands. His staff twisted and bucked. Grandkopf jerked his staff back and the lightning stopped. Grandkopf stood inside a blue aura, the air around him popped and snapped, the smell of ozone wafted on the air. Grandkopf leveled the end of his staff and shot the lightning bolt back toward the Bitch Queen. The monkey dipped and the bolt barely grazed a spike on her helmet, which glowed briefly red.

"Up!" Grandkopf cried to the soldiers waiting on the stairs. "Shoot the monkey! Shoot the monkey!" Foamier and Beeromir charged up the stairs carrying the ceremonial lances they had swiped from the guards. A dozen archers ran at their heels. The brothers ran into the open courtyard and hurled their lances together. Foamier's lance hit the monkey in one of its leathery wings, passed completely through and left a painful but not debilitating rent. Beeromir's lance struck the monkey in the thigh. The monkey screamed, pulled the lance out of its thigh, and flung it spinning back toward the brothers. Foamier dove to the side, Beeromir flopped to the ground on his stomach. The spinning lance flew over Beeromir and swept three of the archers off their feet. The remaining archers began to fire at the monkey. The giant monkey jerked as the arrows struck him. He screamed his displeasure through his fangs, rose on laboring wings, and turned away from the archers. The Bitch Queen was jerking the reins to turn the monkey back to fight, but it paid her no heed; it wanted away from the painful arrows. Grandkopf raised his staff again and a shaft of fire as big around as his fist burst from the end and flew toward the Bitch Queen. The fire passed over her left shoulder and exploded into a fireball a few yards away, doing her no harm. The monkey dove over the rampart and dropped out of sight. Grandkopf, Froyo and the guard ran to the rampart and watched it glide down toward the battlefield.

TWENTY-EIGHT

THE BITCH QUEEN OF DEL MAR

You killed Jo Jo. Now you must die.
          –The Bitch Queen of Del Mar to Elli Mae

Theobald King, Theorug, and Elli Mae reunited on a grassy knoll near the center of the field of Picador. The battle was going badly. They watched the Schnozgoons on their fearsome simian mounts swoop back and forth across the battlefield, spreading fear and disarray. They saw the brave Rojoriders being swept from their horses by globs of flying monkey taki and others trying to stay atop their frightened, gyrating animals. Theobald rose up in his stirrups.

"To me! To me!" he cried, waving his sword. "Rally to the king!"

A shadow passed over them. They looked up to see a flying monkey descending upon them. A bolt of lightning came from above and struck Theorug in the chest. He fell from his horse and lay with empty eyes turned skyward, a gaping hole smoking in his chest. The monkey continued downward, and landed beside Theobald King. The monster monkey plucked Theobald from his horse and sank its fangs into his chest, biting through his steel breastplate. The monkey struck again, ripped out Theobald's throat and hurled him to the ground. Elli Mae's horse reared and threw her. She landed beside the dying Theobald. The horses bolted. The Bitch Queen of Del Mar looked down from her saddle on the back of the huge monkey. She peered at the broken body of Theobald.

"Theobald King," she said. "Ha! King of the stables!" She spat at him.

Elli Mae pushed herself up from the dust of the field of Picador and faced her king's murderer.

"You killed Theobald and Theorug!"

"And now I will kill you," said the Bitch Queen of Del Mar. She looked down at her over-sized simian mount and patted him affectionately beside his fez.

"Kill her," she said.

The monkey moved forward, baring fangs that were half as long as Elli Mae's forearm, and flexing its fingers as if it couldn't wait to wrap them around her throat, sink its teeth into her neck, and drink her blood. Elli Mae reached into a pocket on the thigh of her leather riding pants and pulled out a battered banana. She took it in her left hand and held it before her. The monkey stopped, fixated on the banana. She lifted the banana up. The monkey's head followed the movement. She moved the banana slowly to the right. The monkey followed the motion, staring intently. Eli Mae flicked her wrist and the banana flew off to her left. The monkey's head jerked around, following the flight of the banana. It crouched to leap after the banana. When it crouched, its neck came closer to the ground. Elli Mae swung her elven sword with a two-handed grip and brought it hard against the monkey's neck. Its head popped neatly off, sending a column of blood spurting up. The monkey's body jerked backwards spasmodically and the Bitch Queen of Del Mar tumbled off its back. The monkey's body fell into the dust of the field of Picador, its wings jerked feebly, and it was still.

The Bitch Queen came slowly to her feet. She gazed for a moment at the dead monkey and turned deliberately toward Elli Mae. Her eyes flashed angry blue flames inside her spiked helmet. Her black leather duster billowed in the wind that also stirred the dust of the field of Picador. She stalked slowly toward Elli Mae.

"You killed Jo Jo. Now you must die."

"You named that thing *Jo Jo?*" asked Elli Mae, pointing to the monkey, whose head still displayed an array of gleaming fangs.

"He had to have a name and I liked him. Now you must die."

"You keep saying that. In your dreams."

"Do you know who I am?"

"No, nor much care."

"I am the Bitch Queen of Del Mar." She gave a shallow bow.

"I am Elli Mae, shieldmaiden of Rojo." She gave a mocking curtsy.

"Who are you kidding, you're no maiden. And who the hell dresses you? You look like a barmaid at Knockers™."

"You should talk. You look like an out-of-work dominatrix. Does your mother know you walk around in the daylight looking like that? And those boots! They are so last millennium."

"We Schnozgoons had to lay up for a couple of thousand years. There's not exactly a Demon Markups in Barn Adoor. *Those* are nice boots, are you a size seven?"

"You like them?" Elli Mae turned so the Bitch Queen could see them from all sides. "I got them in a little shop off Craftsman's Square in Minor Tetons last summer. I'd tell you where, but I'm going to kill you now."

"*You* kill *me*? Wench, do you not know the prophecy? No living man may kill me."

"Hello?" said Elli Mae, banging her sword on her ample breast plate. "What do you think these are? These are tits! I am a woman!"

"You know, I don't think that's what the prophecy means. I think it means man, like in the race of men. So you'd be a 'man' as opposed to, say, an elf. I suppose an elf could kill me, unless the prophecy means "man" as in living sentient entity, in which case..."

While the Bitch Queen of Del Mar was musing, Elli Mae thrust her elven sword into the Bitch Queen's ghostly abdomen, an inch above her navel ring.

"...in which case...*Erk*! Oh, taki!" said the Bitch Queen of Del Mar, as the elven-magic-imbued steel of the sword dissolved her ectoplasm. In seconds, all that was left was a black helm, a black sword, a pile of black clothing floating in a pool of steaming goo, and two black boots standing in the sunlight of the field of Picador.

Elli Mae's hand went numb. She looked down and watched the blade of her sword turn gray and fall away as a fine ash. The hilt fell from her hand. She couldn't feel her arm. Her vision grew dim. The last thing she thought before passing out was, *those boots are bitchin' retro! I've got to get me some of those.*

TWENTY-NINE

ALEHOUSE

Too much talk. —Beeromir son of Alehouse

Grandkopf, Beeromir, Foamier, and Froyo walked down the center of the empty throne room. Their footsteps echoed amidst the ornate columns. Midway down on the right was the steward's study, where they hoped to find Lord Alehouse. A serious young man stood outside the door. He held up a hand as the group approached.

"You cannot enter. Lord Alehouse left specific instructions that he was not to be disturbed," said the young man.

"Who are you?" said Grandkopf.

"That's Berolund son of Beron. He is Alehouse's personal assistant," said Foamier.

"What happened to Feneton son of Beneton?" said Beeromir.

"He quit six months ago and left the city for a job in a clothing shop in Lostlorriland. No one has seen or heard from him since," said Foamier.

"How long has Lord Alehouse been in there alone?" said Grand-kopf.

"Since right after the Schnozgoon came, m'lord," said Berolund.

"Berolund, we have desperate need of speaking with my father," said Foamier. "We fear he might not be well. You must let us in."

"I will not. Lord Alehouse was very specific about—" Beeromir punched him in the jaw and Berolund crumpled to the floor. Foamier bowed his head, wrapped his hand around his forehead as if he had a headache, and gently shook his head back and forth. He was unconsciously mimicking a gesture his mother had made a thousand times during their childhood after one of Beeromir's transgressions.

"Too much talk," said Beeromir, shrugging.

"Let's go," said Grandkopf. He pushed the door slowly open and peeked in. There was a desk and chair. Bookshelves lined the room except next to the desk where a map of Central Oith occupied a convenient space. The room was shaped like an L. Grandkopf could see the corner of a tapestry where the room bent to the right. The tapestry was a portrait of the first of the ruling stewards, Martel Volwart (officially known as Martel the Munificent, affectionately known as Marty the Warty), sitting beside the throne in the chair of the ruling stewards.

"Lord Alehouse?" said Grandkopf.

He walked across the room. The others followed behind. He turned the corner and stopped. Lord Alehouse was seated in a chair with his throat cut. Foamier cried out "Father!" and took a step forward. Grandkopf stopped him with an arm. Beeromir put his left hand on Foamier's shoulder to steady his brother. His right hand gripped the hilt of his sword. His knuckles turned white. There was a quill and a note on the table beside Alehouse. Grandkopf looked at the table. The seestone was uncovered and the Great Schnoz was in its window. Grandkopf was hit by a wave of hopelessness. The Great Schnoz spoke in his mind.

"Grandkopf the schemer. So you hope to supplant me. Fool! You are no match for me. Take up the Schnozring and come for me. Take it now, coward."

Desire suddenly swept over Grandkopf, desire to take the Schnozring, to hold it, to worship it, to make it his own. Images sprang to his mind of the great deeds he would do. He saw himself defeating the Bitch Queen, challenging Schnozmon in Soredoor, and standing triumphant on the rubble of the tower of Barn Adoor. He also saw the consequences of not taking up the Schnozring. He saw the Plateau of Googolplex teaming with yucks and men; saw yucks swarming the streets of Minor Tetons, killing and raping; saw the heads of Arrowshaft and Argyle on spikes on the wall of the city.

"It is hopeless without the Schnozring, Grandkopf. Take up the Schnozring and save your friends. Take up the Schnozring, coward."

"No!" cried Grandkopf. He strode to the seestone and tapped it three times. The image of the Great Schnoz faded. Grandkopf reached into his sleeve and pulled out a hand towel, which he placed over the seestone. Grandkopf's heart was beating hard and his breathing was heavy. He turned to the others. They were holding weapons, except Froyo, who had backed against the wall and was clutching the Schnozring in a fist. Grandkopf looked at Beeromir.

"What did you feel?"

"Despair, mixed with desire to take the Schnozring. He spoke my name, called me coward," said Beeromir.

"Me, too," said Foamier. Froyo looked warily at Grandkopf but said nothing.

"He wanted us to kill each other.," said Grandkopf.

Grandkopf picked up Alehouse's note and read aloud. "Alehouse the Fool writes for me. Behold what happens to servants who fail the Great Schnoz. When you read this Grandkopf, realize that I know that the halfbit carries the Schnozring. I know all your plans. I am coming for you Grandkopf. I am coming for you all."

"Is that true? Can he know all our plans?" said Froyo.

"I think not," said Grandkopf. "Sorryman undoubtedly told Schnozmon about the ring, using the seestone at Eisenfang. That's how Alehouse and Foamier knew,."

"What of the rest?" said Froyo.

"No one in the city could know our whole plan. Not even Lord Foamier," said Grandkopf.

"Know what?" said Foamier.

"The Great Schnoz thinks that one of us will take up the Schnozring because that's what he would do," said Grandkopf. "He must continue to think this. We must continue with our plan."

"Wait, what plan?" said Foamier.

"We must not despair," said Grandkopf.

"What?" said Foamier.

"It is paramount that no one comes near the seestone," said Grandkopf. "Anyone who uses the stone is in danger of falling under the sway of the Great Schnoz and giving away our plans."

"What plans?" said Foamier.

"Your most trusted guards must be set on the door," said Grandkopf to Foamier. "But now, I think we should get back to the battle." He strode toward the door of the study. Beeromir and Froyo followed.

"*What* plan?" said Foamier to their backs, scratching his head.

THIRTY

CONFERENCE IN MINOR TETONS

I thought she'd never shut the freck up, so I stuck my
sword into her guts right above that stupid navel ring.
—Elli Mae, Shieldmaiden of Rojo, referring to the
Bitch Queen of Del Mar

In the palace, behind the ornate throne, is the King's conference
room. Its door opens into the center of the room. To the left
and right are fireplaces. The walls are adorned with tapestries
that depict the history of Gonner and Minor Tetons. During the
day the room is awash in light from high, thin windows that are
set into the wall opposite the door. Oil lamps are set at intervals
between the tapestries to provide illumination at night. The room is
filled by a long table made of thick planks of dark wood polished to
a high gloss. Around the table are twenty chairs with thick armrests
and high backs into which are carved a silhouette of the green tree
of Gonner with the three frogs of Gonner in an arc above the tree.

On this, the day after the first battle of Minor Tetons, only eight
of the chairs were occupied. The group had gathered at the end of
the table on the left side of the room. A small fire burning cheerily
in the left-hand fireplace dissipated the chill of the stone walls. The

chair at the end of the table had been left empty for Grandkopf. To the left of the empty chair was Beeromir, then his brother Foamier, followed by Lededgas, Gimmie, and Froyo. On the right, Jethro, the newly crowned king of Rojo, Arrowshaft, and Argyle. They had just finished lunch except, of course, for Froyo, who was happily building his fourth sandwich. They were waiting for Grandkopf and discussing the previous day's battle.

"It all went to taki when the Schnozgoons came up on those flying monkeys," said Jethro King. "The Rojoriders couldn't control their horses and we lost cohesion in our lines."

"Our knights had the same problem," said Foamier. "They went out to help the Rojoriders retreat to the city, but the Schnozgoons wrought havoc among their horses as well."

"The elves might have been able to drive the Schnozgoons off by shooting at the monkeys," said Argyle, "but at that point in the battle we were out of arrows. We were plucking them out of dead yucks to use again."

"Then, just when we thought it couldn't get any worse, the Haragrim came charging up from the river on their giant war hippos," said Jethro King.

"I thought it was over right there," said Beeromir.

"Even from the walls of Minor Tetons, the charge of those hippos was terrifying," said Foamier.

"It's a good thing Argyle thought to use fire," said Jethro King.

"We were able to make torches, some burning spears, and a few fire arrows," said Argyle. "It was enough to break up the charge and scare most of the hippos back to the river."

"I can't figure out why the war hippos were wearing pink tutus," said Jethro King.

"I know the answer to that," said Foamier. "After the battle we captured a wounded hippo driver. He told us that the hippos were tired of the war business and wanted to break into the entertainment industry. They wore the tutus to an audition and got back too late to change into their armor and war paint."

"An audition?" asked Argyle, the incredulity apparent in her voice.

"Yes, Wilt Dizzy is putting together a new act for the main stage at Barn Adoor," said Foamier. "It involves ballet dancing hippos, greased penguins, and a jar of pickles."

"Kinky," said Elli Mae.

The conversation stopped as the room filled with smacking and grunting. Froyo was in a halfbit feeding frenzy over a serving of bread pudding and was face down in his plate, which caused the plate to scoot across the table as Froyo crawled after it. Gimmie smacked his hand down on the table with a loud thwack.

"Ahem," said Gimmie loudly. The slurping sounds ceased. Froyo's eyes swiveled to the group at the head of the table. Everyone was staring at him. The room was silent. Froyo raised his eyebrows and grinned. He quickly crawled backwards to his chair and dragged his plate after him. When he was seated again, he hastily wiped his face with a napkin, thereby removing most of the bread pudding. He folded his hands in his lap and lowered his head.

"Sorry," he said.

"Then we saw the black ships sail up," said Beeromir. "We thought the Corsairs of Ember had arrived."

"We *wanted* everyone to think it was the Corsairs until we had time to get to the docks," said Arrowshaft. "The yucks near the docks were surprised when we jumped off the ships and attacked them."

"I'll bet," said Beeromir.

"Fortunately, we brought a bunch of archers with us and they had enough arrows to drive the flying monkeys off," said Arrowshaft.

"The war hippos retreated and the Schnozgoons flew back to Oshgosh," said Jethro King. "The Rojoriders and the Knights of Gonner were able to organize their lines, and the yucks were flanked by the men from the ships. Suddenly it didn't look so good for the yucks. They all retreated back across the river and the battle was over."

"Until the Great Schnoz sends reinforcements and they attack again, only in larger numbers," said Arrowshaft. Everyone was silent for a moment while they contemplated the next assault.

The door opened and Grandkopf entered. He walked to the head of the table, but instead of sitting he leaned against the mantle and fiddled with his pipe. At length he spoke.

"I have news," he said. "We have word from Celerybrains that Gack has escaped."

"How?" said Arrowshaft.

"The guards tied him up while they were cleaning his cage. The elf guarding him was keeping his distance because of the spitting. Gack chewed through his rope and was up a tree and gone before the guard could get to him. Celerybrains is pissed. He had half the elves in Lostlorriland looking for him all night, but Gack gave them the slip," said Grandkopf.

"What matter? Let the little taki go," said Gimmie.

"Gack wants the Schnozring. It's his *snooky ookums*. He'll try to steal it from Froyo if he can. We must all be wary," said Grandkopf.

"Maybe we will get it into the fire pit of Mount Drool before he can get here from Lostlorriland," said Gimmie.

"Let us hope, but Froyo must be wary. Gack will take back the Schnozring if he can," said Grandkopf. "I've also had a report from

Airtoground. Nothing stirs in Soredoor. All the troops are encamp-ed. None of the Schnozgoons is abroad."

"What's the surveillance costing us?" asked Gimmie.

"Nothing. Airtoground is a bit embarrassed about holding us hostage on the last deal. Besides, if we lose, all the eagles will likely perish with us. The great eagles overfly Soredoor twice a day at great height. There is nothing the Great Schnoz can do about it even if he sees them," said Grandkopf.

"Likely he doesn't care. When he empties Soredoor and sends forth the Schnozgoons, there will be little we can do to stop him," said Arrowshaft.

"How many does he have?" said Jethro King.

"Airtoground isn't very good at counting. He says lots more than we have. Given the number we killed on the field of Picador during the first battle, I estimate one hundred twenty-five thousand against our twenty-five thousand," said Grandkopf.

"He could take us now," said Foamier.

"I think he is waiting for a last contingent from the south," said Grandkopf.

"Schnozmon can overrun us now," said Foamier. "No need to let him wait for reinforcements."

"Why *not* fly now?" said Gimmie.

"Because of the yucks camped around Mount Drool and because of the Schnozgoons," said Arrowshaft. "Even if the troops leave the Plateau of Googolplex, if the Schnozgoons defend the Door of Drool, it will be very difficult to gain access to the fire pit. We might be able to overwhelm the Schnozgoons if we could get a couple of dozen warriors to Mount Drool, but only Grandkopf could counter the Bitch Queen of Del Mar."

"I have just spoken with Elli Mae in the Mansion of Medicine," said Grandkopf. "She says she killed the Bitch Queen of Del Mar and her monkey, Jo Jo, on the field of Picador."

"Can this be true?" asked Beeromir.

"I believe Elli Mae did fight the Bitch Queen," said Grandkopf. "The Schnozgoon that Elli Mae fought *said* she was the Bitch Queen. Elli Mae isn't the sort to make up stuff like this. The clothing that Elli Mae described matches the clothing we found beside her and the clothing that the Bitch Queen was wearing when she attacked Alehouse in the courtyard of the tree of Gonner."

"How did *you* know it was the Bitch Queen?" said Gimmie.

"I knew her before she became a Schnozgoon and I called her by name," said Grandkopf.

"You knew her *before?*" said Foamier.

"Yes, her name was Evita Kraigsdotter and she was quite the beauty. Her father, Kraig Baradsson, was the last King of Del Mar and a good man. She also had a brother, Brad Kraigsson, who was in line for the throne. Evita began to dabble in magic at a young age and by the time she was a young woman had become quite adept at it. Schnozmon came to her, played on her ambition, and seduced her into taking one of the rings of men. A few months after she claimed the ring, her father was poisoned and her brother had a fatal accident while cleaning his crossbow. No one could ever prove anything. She assumed the rule of Del Mar. She put down all opposition ruthlessly and Del Mar became a living hell—until Whiskeysour cut the Schnozring from Schnozmon's schnoz at the end of the second age. Then the Bitch Queen and the rest of the Schnozgoons were disembodied for three millennia."

"What happened to Del Mar?" asked Lededgas.

"With the King's line ended and the Bitch Queen gone, they needed a new government. So they elected a prime minister and a parliament and squabbled happily until the Bitch Queen showed up a few years ago, fried the prime minister, burned down the parliament building with most of the parliament inside and declared herself queen again. The people were not pleased."

"But did Elli Mae kill the Bitch Queen or only dissolve her temporarily?" asked Arrowshaft. "You blew up the Bitch Queen on Whithertop but she was put back together for the battle yesterday."

"That's the important question, isn't it?" said Grandkopf. "There is a chance that Elli Mae did kill the Bitch Queen. The prophecy of Barnabas says that no man may kill her. The fact that Elli Mae isn't a man…"

"No taki," said Beeromir.

"…combined with the magic of Elli Mae's elven sword may have done the trick. However, if the Bitch Queen is merely dissolved, then the Great Schnoz can put her back together."

"Never underestimate the power of prophecy," said Arrowshaft. "I think the Bitch Queen is toast."

"So do I," said Argyle.

"And I," said Lededgas.

"How can we know for sure?" asked Foamier.

"We won't be sure until we destroy the Schnozring in the fire pit of Mount Drool, which will finish *all* the Schnozgoons," said Grandkopf. "Or she flies up on a giant monkey and starts blasting people."

"What shall we do?" said Foamier.

"We stick to the plan. We must wait until Schnozmon empties the Plain of Googolplex and the Schnozgoons are attacking Minor

Tetons. *Then* we fly the Schnozring to Mount Drool and destroy it in the fire pit," said Grandkopf.

"What if the Bitch Queen lives?" said Gimmie.

"Then she and I fight and we all pray for luck," said Grandkopf.

THIRTY-ONE

ARGYLE AND ELLI MAE

Girl talk...with swords. –Argyle daughter of El Round

Elli Mae sat fuming in her bed at the Mansion of Medicine. She felt fine. The healers wanted her to stay in bed for another week. Well, freck that taki! Elli Mae was going to make a break for it. The only problem was clothes. These Mansion of Medicine gowns were very drafty, especially in the rear. It was almost 11:30 in the morning. The geezer down the hall started ringing his bell at precisely 11:30 every single day. This morning, she was planning a little jailbreak during the excitement.

Ring. Ring. Riiiiiiiing. Right on time. She peeked out her door and saw all the assistant healers running down the hall as they did every day. She stepped into the hallway and padded down to the assistant healer station. There was a door behind the station. Maybe they kept the clothes in there. She pushed the door open slowly and scanned the room. Nobody home. She spotted a door that opened to a bathroom. Another door—lockers! Some of the lockers had name plates and she recognized the names of several healers. There were more lockers that were labeled only with numbers. She opened number one. Bingo! Clothes. Unfortunately, not her clothes. Her clothes appeared in number six. It was her battle gear and someone had cleaned it all, thank goodness. It had been covered in blood, mostly yuck blood, but a little of men, wags, trolls, and even some war hippo blood. It had been a target-rich environment. She smiled at the memory as she searched for her sword—after all, she couldn't convincingly walk around in battle gear without a sword. Then she remembered that hers had dissolved when she killed the Bitch Queen. No matter, the sword in locker number two looked like it was about the right size.

She dressed quickly and buckled her borrowed sword over her leather riding pants. Now, if she could just make it to the main hallway without being spotted. Dressed in this gear no one would think her a patient. If she got out of the Mansion of Medicine, no one was going to get her back in. She walked swiftly to the door at the end of the hall and slipped through. She was nearly running and quickly reached the other end, where she peeked out the door to the main hall. She waited until an assistant healer pushed a rollingchair by and she followed as if she were a friend of the patient. Soon she was out the front door and off down the lane.

Beeromir had been to the Mansion of Medicine every day to see her. She wanted to see him soon, but even more she wanted to go look for the Bitch Queen's boots. She started for the lower levels.

—

Argyle was on the field of Picador working with the elven archers, but she was thinking about Arrowshaft. He was always up in the Mansion of Medicine healing someone or off doing war stuff; too busy to come visit her, she supposed. She sighed. Still, she was horny and needed a few personal minutes with him, king or not. She decided to find the skinny son of a wag and haul him off to bed.

She walked through the gates of the city and started for the upper levels. Her path intersected Elli Mae's near Craftsman's Square on the third level.

"You!" said Elli Mae.

"Me?" said Argyle.

"You stole my man."

"I don't think so. He was never *your* man."

"I wanted him."

"I'm sorry."

Elli Mae went for her sword and slashed at Argyle. Argyle was taken by surprise but was able to draw her sword and parry the blow. Acting on reflex, she executed a counter that would have severed Elli Mae's carotid had she not aborted. Elli Mae pressed her attack but Argyle had no desire to kill her so she retreated and parried all the blows and thrusts. She realized that Elli Mae had attacked her with a perfect Fermi. Argyle stepped back in surprise.

"You're pretty good with that sword," said Argyle.

"You're not too bad, either."

"Do you know Fabonacci?"

"Yes!" Elli Mae attacked with a very creditable Fabonacci. A small crowd had gathered at the sight of two women having a sword fight in the middle of the day.

"Curie?" Elli Mae attacked with a Curie that was very precise. Argyle responded perfectly.

"Do you know Mendeleev?" said Elli Mae, and Argyle attacked with a perfect Mendeleev.

"Taki, you *are* good," said Elli Mae. "How about Turing?" Now it had become a game. Argyle executed a Turing; Elli Mae made the proper defense.

"Helmholtz!"

"Schrödinger!"

"Is your sword master Master Brahe?" asked Argyle.

"Yes! How did you know?"

"I recognized your technique. It's very good. But you're using a borrowed sword, aren't you?"

"How in the taki can you tell that?" asked Elli Mae.

"You move as if you are used to a lighter sword. But you are very good with this one," said Argyle.

"Thank you! Leibig!" said Elli Mae and their swords flashed.

Elli Mae was winded. To her credit, she had been near death and had spent the last week in the Mansion of Medicine flat on her back.

"Do you know the reverse-Oppenheimer?" said Argyle.

"No." Elli Mae looked disappointed.

"If we survive the coming weeks, I would be happy to show you."

"I'd like that," said Elli Mae. She slid her borrowed sword back into its scabbard and threw her arm over Argyle's shoulders. "Let's save the swords for the yucks. I think we should go get drunk and bitch about men." She tugged Argyle toward the second level.

Argyle was taken aback for a moment. She wasn't used to being touched with such familiarity, but she decided that Elli Mae meant no harm. Besides, Argyle didn't have that many friends and maybe it was time to make a new one.

"Okay," said Argyle. She sheathed her sword and they set off to find a bar. The crowd that had gathered dissipated, impressed by the swordsmanship but disappointed that there was no bloodshed.

They found a bar to Elli Mae's liking: The Dirty Dog, on the first level. It had a sign that pictured two dogs doing the dirty. The male dog's tongue hung out of its mouth through an exaggerated smile. As the two women made their way to a table, Argyle looked around in the dim light. The whole place was uniformly gray, as if it had been assembled out of weathered cedar fence pickets. The bartender had one ear, an eye patch, and a face that was a mask of scars. *A fighter* Argyle thought, *though perhaps not a very good one given all the missing bits.* The clientèle of The Dog struck her as cut from the same cloth—mercenaries and footpads, a grimy, desperate lot.

Elli Mae got a pitcher of mead and Argyle a bottle of Silverfire, seal unbroken. The waitress brought Argyle a shot glass that looked as if it had been rinsed in pond scum and dried with a greasy cloth. Argyle thanked the waitress, but when the waitress left she took a small silver cup out of the pouch she wore at her waist. This attracted some attention. The silver in that little cup would keep any of the customers in ale for a month. If they had known it was not silver but vargentum, they might have tried to snatch it despite the formidable swords worn by the two ladies. Good thing no one tried; they would have died in the attempt.

Two hours later, Elli Mae passed out on the table. She had only consumed a pitcher and a half of mead, but she had forgotten her weakened condition. Argyle decided to sit with her new friend until the mead wore off and she woke up. She stared off into space and let her mind wander into the waking dreams of the elves. She became unnaturally still. She might have been mistaken for a wax figure if not for the almost imperceptible motion of her breathing. She sat thus for a little more than an hour until a large ruffian, emboldened by ale, disturbed her dreams. He placed both his hands on the table and leaned toward her. His dirty hair framed a face that bore a broken nose and many scars, evidence of previous brawls.

"You ladies look lonely," he said. His breath smelled of mead and pepper sausage. His smile was interrupted by missing teeth. "You'd be wanting some company, I reckon?" Before he could blink, Argyle's knife fixed his left hand to the table.

"*Aaaaaaaaaaaa*. Taki!"

Argyle stood and pressed the knife against his throat.

"What is your name, knave?" said Argyle.

"Boris?"

"Boris, my friend here is a noble lady."

Boris glanced at Elli Mae. Her head and bare arms were on the table and one hand still grasped the handle of her mug. Her mouth was open and she was snoring softly. He looked as if he were having a difficult time getting his mind around the noble part.

"Clearly she does not want to be disturbed. Yes?" Boris was a beat too slow to answer so Argyle emphasized her question with a little twist of the knife blade against his jugular. It left a tiny trace of blood.

"Yes!"

"There are those in the city who would take it badly if she were to be discomforted in any way."

"Yes, m'lady."

"I am one of those," she said and gave her blade another little twist.

"*Yes*, m'lady."

"Boris, I would consider it a great personal favor if you would be so kind as to discourage any of your *acquaintances* from disturbing our conversation." Boris cast a furtive glance at Elli Mae, who lay as if comatose. He was more than a little dubious about the conversation part, too. He frowned, but was in no position to argue.

"Yes, m'lady."

"Thank you. Tell the bartender to put your ale on my tab."

"Thank you, m'lady." She removed the knife from his throat and wiped the blade on his pants.

"That will be all for now, Boris." He backed away from her, bowing and holding his bleeding hand. Argyle watched until the bartender delivered his ale and went back to her meditations.

She sat undisturbed for another hour until Beeromir and Arrowshaft entered the bar. They spotted Argyle and headed toward her. As they approached, Boris stepped in front of them with his right hand on the handle of his knife. His left hand was wrapped in a greasy gray bar towel that was decorated with a red splotch.

"Wait just a minute, bub," said Boris. Arrowshaft looked at him and then raised his eyebrows at Argyle.

"Boris?" said Argyle.

"Yes, m'lady?" said Boris without removing his eyes from Arrowshaft or his hand from his knife.

"These gentlemen are my friends. Please allow them to pass."

"Yes, m'lady." Boris stepped aside. Arrowshaft cast him an inquisitive glance as he sat beside Argyle. Beeromir took the seat across from Arrowshaft.

"What the freck was that about?" said Arrowshaft, nodding at Boris, who had reclaimed his spot at the bar.

"A new acquaintance. Very protective of young ladies," Argyle said, smiling.

"A knight in shining armor. Right here in The Dirty Dog. Who'd have thought?" said Arrowshaft. "What happened to his hand?"

"He accidentally cut it on my knife." Argyle's eyes sparkled.

"Riiiiight."

"What's wrong with Elli Mae?" Beeromir asked, as he helped himself to the last of her mead.

"She was overly optimistic about her mead capacity," said Argyle.

"We've been looking for Elli Mae since a little after noon, when we got a message from the healers saying that she had escaped from the Mansion of Medicine," said Arrowshaft.

"Escaped! Good for her."

"We were setting out to find her when we heard that two women were having a sword fight in broad daylight in Craftsman's Square. Naturally, we thought of you," said Arrowshaft.

Argyle smiled. "More like practice. So what took you so long?"

Arrowshaft smiled back at her. "We started looking on the higher levels, in the classier bars."

"Ah," said Argyle, laughing.

"Elli Mae isn't well," said Beeromir, brushing her hair lightly, "The healers want her back for another week at least. She shouldn't have been playing with swords or drinking."

"She looked pretty healthy when she tried to run me through this afternoon."

"Practice?" said Arrowshaft.

"Girl talk," said Argyle. "With swords. By the way, where did Elli Mae get a sword in the Mansion of Medicine?"

"She stole it from the locker of another patient. It is the beloved sidearm of Count Monte Crispo of Dul Amway who, by the way, is really ticked off. Beeromir and I had to swear on the green grass, the three green frogs, *and* the green tree of Gonner that we would get it back," said Arrowshaft.

"I've sent for a carriage," said Beeromir. "When it arrives we can take her back to the palace. I've had a room prepared for her. She will be well attended."

"Good, she deserves it," said Argyle.

"Let's get her breastplate off. It's murder to carry someone wearing steel," said Beeromir. They undid the fastenings and pulled the steel breastplate over her head. Apparently, Elli Mae's blouse and bra hadn't returned from the cleaners because her ample breasts flopped naked onto the table. Arrowshaft looked embarrassed and Argyle covered her mouth and giggled. Beeromir sighed, unfastened his cloak, and wrapped it around Elli Mae.

"I hear the carriage. Let's go," said Beeromir. He tossed the limp Elli Mae over his shoulder as easily as he would a pillow and started for the door. Arrowshaft picked up the breastplate and the sword. He wrapped his arm around Argyle as they walked toward the door.

"I like her, she's tough," said Argyle.

"I like her, too," said Arrowshaft. Argyle looked at him and raised her eyebrows.

"I *love* you," he said.

"Hold that thought," Argyle said, putting her arm around his waist and bumping her hip against his.

THIRTY-TWO

PRELUDE TO BATTLE

Did you pack your shorts? –Gimmie to Froyo

A month after the first battle of Minor Tetons, the Six Pack and their allies once again gathered in the king's conference room. It was mid-afternoon. Smokestacks atop the twin towers of Barn Adoor had been pouring forth dark, acrid fumes for days. The menacing cloud filtered through the peaks of the Shady Mountains and covered the field of Picador and Minor Tetons. The clouds blocked the sun, and scant light came in through the tall windows of the conference room. Small fires burned in both fireplaces to cut the chill, and oil lamps burned to augment the dim light that filtered through the haze outside. There was a buffet set out. Froyo was loading a plate when Grandkopf came into the room puffing steadily on his pipe, the last to arrive.

Grandkopf sat down at the head of the table where there was a small porcelain cup and a bottle of Silverfire. He filled the cup and took a sip of the Silverfire before he spoke.

"The armies of the Great Schnoz are moving," said Grandkopf. "Airtoground reports that the armies on the Plain of Googolplex are moving toward the Bleak Gate of Soredoor. The forward units are in the Valley of Undone.

"How long do we have?" asked Foamier.

"It will take the Schnoz at least six days to march his armies to Oshgosh and another two to get them across Old Man River in any numbers. We can expect them to attack in eight to ten days," said Grandkopf.

"Is he leaving a guard on Mount Drool?" asked Arrowshaft.

"Airtoground says all the armies are moving toward the Bleak Gate," said Grandkopf. "There's nothing moving around Mount Drool."

"What of the Schnozgoons?" asked Lededgas, sipping his Silverfire from a small silver cup.

"The Schnozgoons have not been sighted since the battle," said Grandkopf. "Not a single report from any of our watchers or the great eagles."

"It worries me that we don't know where they are or what they're doing," said Arrowshaft.

"They are likely just holed up in Barn Adoor, watching the gladiator fights and playing twenty-two," said Foamier.

"Plain of Googolplex empty, Schnozgoons in Barn Adoor, why not take the Schnozring to Mount Drool now?" asked Gimmie.

"The flying monkeys can fly to Mount Drool from Barn Adoor in only an hour," said Grandkopf. "If the Great Schnoz sees us coming over the Shady Mountains, the Schnozgoons will block the Door of Drool and we'll need all my powers and a small army to get past them. Better that they aren't there at all. That's why we want them attacking Minor Tetons when we fly the ring to Mount Drool. If we start from the Shady Mountains southwest of Mount Drool, the Schnozgoons won't have time to fly back from Minor Tetons and stop us."

"How can make sure that the Schnozgoons attack at the same time as the yuck armies?" asked Gimmie.

"I know!" said Elli Mae. "Get in his face."

"He doesn't have a face, he's a nose," said Beeromir.

"Get in his nose," said Gimmie.

"Ew!" said Elli Mae.

"No, that's a good idea," said Grandkopf, holding up a finger and shaking his hand excitedly. "Six days from now, as the armies of the Great and Powerful Schnoz gather by the river, we will use the seestone to taunt him. We'll tell him that I'm gong to claim the Schnozring and supplant him."

"He'll send the Schnozgoons after Grandkopf for sure," said Beeromir.

"After we taunt him, we will wait until nightfall and the great eagles will fly Froyo and me to a base camp in the Shady Mountains," said Grandkopf. There was a choking sound. Everyone looked at Froyo. He held a fresh sandwich in his hands and there was a slice of ham hanging out of his mouth. His eyebrows were up and his eyes bulged. Apparently, he was in deep denial about his role in the destruction of the Schnozring. His eyes flicked from side to side. He stood in his chair, reached across Gimmie, grabbed Lededgas's bottle of Silverfire and tipped it up. He took two swallows, coughed, pounded his chest several times, and sat down heavily in his chair, still grasping the bottle. He stared across the room blankly, eyes unfocused, and hiccupped.

"What if the Schnozgoons don't attack with the Schnoz's armies?" asked Arrowshaft. "Minor Tetons can't hold out for long against those numbers."

"We will have to fly soon after the attack starts, even if the Schnozgoons aren't there," said Grandkopf. "We will just have to fight our way through if the Schnozgoons defend the Door of Drool." More loud swallows came from Froyo's seat. He lowered the Silverfire bottle, burped, looked up at Grandkopf, and smiled wanly.

"In six days, dress for war and gather in the steward's study. We will tweak the Schnoz," said Grandkopf.

—

Six days later, just after lunch, Froyo was in Gimmie and Lededgas's suite in the guest tower of the palace. Froyo's room was in the back of the tower and had a close-up view of the sheer cliff just a few feet away. There would be absolutely nothing to look at but rock if it weren't for the pair of cliff swallows building a nest across from his window. Once the nest building was over and the egg sitting started, there wasn't much going on. So Froyo spent a lot of time in Grandkopf's room, which had a great view, or with Gimmie and Lededgas in their suite. This day, Froyo was in a tizzy trying to decide how to dress for the coming confrontation with the Great Schnoz.

"What do I wear?" he asked. "Halfbits don't have armies."

"How do you go to war?" said Gimmie.

"We don't *go* to war, we only fight when we have to."

"Don't you have a militia or police or something? What do they wear?" asked Lededgas.

"We have marshals. They wear normal clothes, but they put a feather in their hats."

"What about the head marshal?" asked Gimmie.

"Two feathers."

"Terrifying," said Gimmie. "Not much to work with there."

"Wear your vargentum vest over a leather shirt and strap on Sticker," said Lededgas. "You'll be fine."

"Can't go wrong with vargentum—it's always stylish," said Gimmie.

"I'll feel like a bog eel in a sandbox," said Froyo.

"It doesn't matter," said Lededgas. "This is Grandkopf's show. You only have to stand, look serious, and pull the ring out of your shirt on cue. It's important that we, the peoples of Central Oith, stand together."

"I'm scared," said Froyo.

"If you pee your pants don't let on until Grandkopf finishes," said Gimmie.

"He won't pee his pants, he's got more guts than you, you tactless dwarf moron," said Lededgas.

"Moron! Those pants must be pinching your brains again, you skinny elf son of a cross-eyed fire lizard. I'm braver *and* smarter than you," said Gimmie. "And better looking."

"Fine, but your shirt tail is hanging out in back, your beard still has lunch in it, and your fly is undone, styleless dwarf," said Lededgas.

Froyo had heard this before, so he headed for the bathroom. Better to pee now than in front of the Great Schnoz. He could hear the pair bickering like a couple of dwarf mothers-in-law, even through the thick wooden door.

—

A few minutes before the third bell in the afternoon, all were assembled in the steward's study. They wore battle gear and carried an impressive array of cutlery. The room was narrow near the seestone table and they were bumping and jostling each other. Grandkopf was trying to get them into a line.

"Arrowshaft in the middle. Jethro King on his right, then Elli Mae, Argyle, and Lededgas. To the left of Arrowshaft: Beeromir, Foamier, and Gimmie. Froyo, stand on this chair beside me." Froyo clambered up on the chair. Grandkopf faced the group.

"The seestone communicates through thoughts, but if we speak into it, our thoughts will be communicated as well. When I open the seestone the Schnoz ad will appear. When it fades to black, do like we rehearsed. I will throw down our challenge. Froyo, you must take the ring out when the Schnoz appears. Do not falter," said Grandkopf, putting a steadying hand to Froyo's shoulder. Froyo nodded.

Grandkopf sat in the chair and Froyo took his place, standing on the chair next to Grandkopf. Grandkopf tapped the stone four times and sat up very straight with his hands crossed in front of him.

The orange oval appeared followed by the orange schnoz. The Schnoz ad started, "Need a vacation? Come to Barn Adoor… "

"Wait for it..." said Grandkopf. The advertisement drew to a close and the Schnoz appeared.

"I smell you there. Who is it? What do you want?" The words came into their minds. Behind Grandkopf, the group began to chant, "Boom! Doom! Ba Da Boom! Barn Adoor Go Boom!" After the first round, they put their arms over each others shoulders and began to dance and kick like a chorus line, left-right-left, right kick, right-left-right, left kick, repeat. There was some swearing as the various swords and axes smacked into various shins and calves. In a universe far, far away, Ziegfeld was spinning in his grave. Lededgas and Argyle were in perfect time and looked great, smiling as they high kicked. Gimmie kept turning the wrong way and couldn't remember the *Ba Da Boom* part. The chanting was accompanied by the clanking of armor, the rattling of chain mail, and the smacking together of sheathed swords.

"Hi Schnozzie," said Grandkopf. "Look what we have." Froyo grabbed the gold chain at his throat and pulled the Schnozring out of his shirt. He leaned over the table and put one hand down to steady himself. Froyo held the golden ring before the image of the Great Schnoz. The ring swung toward the seestone. The image of the Great Schnoz twisted toward the ring and glided forward as if it were trying to win free of the seestone window.

"We've got it. You want it. Nya, nya, nya…" said Grandkopf, putting his thumb to his nose and blowing the Schnoz a raspberry. The chant continued behind him.

"Listen, Schnozzie," said Grandkopf. He crossed his arms and leaned in on his elbows. He raised his right hand and extended his forefinger. "You know I'm the most powerful wizard in Central Oith, right? So, I'll give you some free advice." …*Ba Da Boom. Barn Adoor Go…*

"If you send your little yucky army to Minor Tetons, I'll claim the Schnozring for my own. I'll make yuck pie out of your army. I'll turn the Schnozgoons into Grandkopf groupies and send them back to scare all the customers out of that stupid casino of yours and then we'll show up with a dwarf wrecking crew and raze Barn Adoor to the ground. While you watch, of course," said Grandkopf. The chorus continued in the background.

"Listen," thought the Schnoz. "Perhaps I have been hasty. We can make a deal. What do you want: money, girls, a line of credit, a seat on the board?"

"No deals, Schnozzie," said Grandkopf. "We're coming to settle your account." ...*Boom! Doom! Ba Da Boom...* Grandkopf reached up to turn off the seestone.

"No taxation without representation!" yelled Elli Mai. She threw up her right arm, her hand in a fist. Grandkopf tapped the seestone three times and the image of the Great Schnoz faded. The Schnozring swung loose in Froyo's hand and the chorus line stopped chanting. Lededgas and Argyle exchanged high fives. Arrowshaft and Foamier clasped forearms and slapped each other on the back. Beeromir stepped over and gave Elli Mae a hug; their steel breastplates made a squealing sound as they ground together.

"That wasn't so bad," said Arrowshaft, pounding Grandkopf on the back. Gimmie tapped Froyo on the shoulder.

"Did you pack your shorts?"

"No, but this seestone taki makes a body hungry." said Froyo. "Is it time for tea?"

THIRTY-THREE

ZERO DARK 03

Chicken-fried yuck taki, I'm going to be late.

—Grandkopf

Just before midnight on the day that they tweaked the Schnoz, Arrowshaft and Lededgas stood together at the rampart of the courtyard of the dead, formerly green, tree of Gonner. They looked toward the river and the ruins of Oshgosh. Schnozmon's army of yucks had lit thousands of campfires that twinkled in the distance. Gimmie walked up and stood on a rock to see over the rampart.

"Taki, that's a lot of yucks!" said Gimmie.

"And they'll be here in the morning," said Lededgas.

"Tell me again why we are sending the halfbit to Mount Drool," said Gimmie.

"Stone-headed dwarf," said Lededgas. "Froyo's the only one who can handle the ring without claiming it for his own and trying to conquer the world."

"Oh! Right!" said Gimmie. "I think someone mentioned that once in one of the meetings."

"You should drink less mead at the meetings and listen more," said Lededgas.

"Mead will get you through meetings better than meetings will get you through times of no mead," said Gimmie.

"A philosopher," said Argyle, walking up to the rampart.

"There's the palace chime. It's midnight. Everyone else is here, where's Grandkopf?" asked Arrowshaft.

—

Grandkopf jerked awake when the palace chime struck midnight. *Chicken-fried yuck taki, I'm going to be late*, he thought. Then he remembered that Airtoground couldn't tell time. So "middle of the night" plus or minus an hour or two was probably all the same to him. Nonetheless, he made full use of his long legs, striding to the courtyard of the dead, formerly green, tree of Gonner. He arrived at three minutes after midnight.

The Great Schnoz had been pumping dark, acrid fumes out of smokestacks atop the twin towers of Barn Adoor for days. The fumes obscured the moon and stars, leaving it dark enough to trouble the weak eyes of the humans and the halfbit.

"Who has the lantern?" Grandkopf asked.

"I do," said Foamier.

"Please make the signal, Lord Foamier," said Grandkopf. Foamier turned to the south and opened the dark lantern twice. He repeated the signal twice more, turning a little to his right each time.

"Do you think they will see it?" said Beeromir.

"We will know in a few minutes," said Lededgas.

"Airtoground will be here as it pleases him," said Grandkopf. "He is one of the great leaders of Central Oith, not a pet. We will do well to remember it."

"Not to mention that we are all flattened yuck taki without him," said Gimmie. They had not long to wait.

Ten minutes later, Argyle pointed to the South. "Two eagles are coming," she said.

"I see them," said Lededgas. "They are moving fast."

"Two eagles?" asked Froyo, squinting into the darkness, unable to see anything but darkness.

"I think the large one is Airtoground, I don't recognize the smaller one," said Lededgas.

Within minutes, both eagles were on the ground. Grandkopf went to Airtoground and touched the great eagle on the wing.

"It is good to see you my old friend. Many thanks for coming," said Grandkopf.

"No thanks are needed. The orange nose is our enemy, too," said Airtoground.

"Where are the others?" asked Lededgas.

"Perched on ledges south of the city. There's no need for us all to fly down and back up," said Airtoground. "They will join us when we fly out."

"Who is this?" said Argyle, looking at the second eagle, who stood a head shorter than Airtoground.

"This is my grandson, Airtoair, son of Aireffect. He will carry the passengers."

"Why not you?" asked Gimmie.

"Airtoair is young and strong. He is the fastest of us," said Airtoground.

Gimmie looked at Airtoair. "Does he speak?"

"Yes, master dwarf. I can speak and I do speak,when I have something to say," said Aireffect.

"Grandson, these are the lords of Central Oith. Be polite. We are all in this together." Airtoair nodded and was silent. "I would introduce you all, but it would take forever to say all the titles. If we live, I will let Grandkopf do it."

"It would be my privilege," said Grandkopf.

"What of the fumes? Will they hinder you?" asked Foamier.

"No, they stink, but we will fly above them most of the way," said Airtoground.

"We can find the Shady Mountains in the dark, have no fear," said Airtoair.

"Bring the harness," said Grandkopf.

Foamier brought a leather contraption of saddles and straps over to Airtoair, and with the help of Lededgas began to fit it onto the great eagle. When they were done, Airtoair carried two high-backed saddles, a small one in front of a large one. Behind the saddles there were two saddlebags. Grandkopf loaded the seestone into one saddlebag and followed it with the rest of his gear. Froyo had a sleeping bag and a small backpack, lumpy with what a halfbit thought would be useful on a dangerous mission—food. When all was packed, Grandkopf hoisted himself into the larger saddle and lifted Froyo into the smaller one. Foamier handed them both a pair of goggles to protect their eyes in flight.

"Soredoor has many watchers in the mountains from the pass of Serious Ugly north. So we have scouted a camp further south, high in the Shady Mountains," said Airtoground.

"It will be an hour or a little more to get to Mount Drool from the base camp," said Grandkopf. "If the Schnozgoons are attacking Minor Tetons when we start, they will be hard pressed to arrive in time to stop us."

"Away!" said Arrowshaft. "Tailwinds, Airtoair, Airtoground."

"Please fasten your seat straps," announced Airtoair. "Keep your arms and legs out of the way of the wings. Wear your goggles at all times. There is no food service for economy class. Flying time to the base camp is two hours and twenty-three minutes."

The great eagles hopped to the rampart and dove off the side.

Lededgas and Argyle could see in the darkness, thanks to their elven eyes. They watched the two great eagles fly to the southwest. In a few minutes the other great eagles joined up with Airtoair and Airtoground. They formed a large V to break the wind for each other and make the best time.

"Good luck," whispered Argyle and the others murmured their agreement.

In the darkness of the courtyard, none saw the watcher in the third story window. Against the rustling sounds of their movements no one heard the faint squeak as Berolund closed the window. After the death of Alehouse, Berolund had become the personal secretary to Foamier. Foamier and the others did not know that the curious Berolund had gazed into the seestone when Alehouse wasn't around. The Great Schnoz had brainwashed him. *So they mean to destroy the ring,* thought Berolund. *The seestone is guarded at all times. How can I warn the Great Schnoz?*

THIRTY-FOUR

MOUNT DROOL

Fool of a halfbit! The Schnozgoons attack Minor Tetons.
Get up now. It is time to fly!

—Grandkopf the Gray

F royo woke to a sky filled with the hovering gloom of Soredoor. The sun was an orange streak between the mountains and the fumes that spread above the Plateau of Googolplex like a huge umbrella. Froyo was cold. His sleeping bag had seemed warm when he went to sleep beside the small fire, but after the warmth of the fire had faded, the cold crept over him as the mist seeping up from the stone heart of the mountain found its way through the fabric and chilled his skin through his clothing. He was tired, too. He had spent the night waking with starts, gazing at a starless, moonless sky as if the stars could bring hope or the moon help. He looked east over the plateau, now devoid of living things; all the yucks and men had gone to destroy the city of Minor Tetons and the kingdoms of men. He was hungry. He looked wistfully at the unlit fire and imagined a fat rabbit turning on a spit, a skillet with a nice mess of bog eels sizzling merrily, biscuits baking in a dutch oven, and a coffee pot perking brightly with its stimulatory promise. His reverie was interrupted by Grandkopf, who strode past and dropped a pouch by Froyo's head.

"Breakfast," said Grandkopf. "Get ready, we leave when we get the word."

Froyo grimaced. The pouch contained jerky. Poor fare for one who might not survive the day, he thought. He wriggled his upper half out of his bag and reached for his backpack. Fortunately, it was full of food. Bagels and cream cheese, cinnamon rolls (a little stale, but still edible), dried sausage links, three kinds of hard cheese, a round loaf of sturdy bread baked in the style of Dul Amway (quite similar to the pumpernickel baked in the Mire), an insulated flask of coffee laced with Goldenwasser, and a bottle of Silverfire, a purely medicinal protection against the chill of the mountains.

—

Arrowshaft stood on the battlements of the seventh level of Minor Tetons watching the armies of the Great Schnoz approach the city. *Taki, that's a lot of yucks*, he thought. Above him, the green banner of the King of Gonner, showing the green tree and the three green frogs of Gonner—which nobody could actually make out against the green field representing the green grass of Gonner, an ancient design flaw—rippled in the morning air. Other standards fluttered beside it: the standard of the Stewards of Gonner (a very serious waiter wearing a tuxedo and holding in his right hand a tray with a wine bottle and a wine glass, and in his left hand a wicked-looking corkscrew with the motto *Dum Vivimus Servimus* or *While we live, We Serve)*; the standard of the Prince of Dul Amway (a dunce cap over crossed lances and the motto *Quid, Me Anxius?* or *What, Me Worry?)*; and the standard of the King of Rojo (a red horse, rampant, on a white field with the inscription *Ne Conjugare Nobiscum* or *Don't*

Freck with Us). The standards of the free peoples of the west stood defiant before the oncoming of the minions of the Great Schnoz.

The armies of Soredoor surged up from the river at dawn. They carried the banner of the Great Schnoz: an orange, hooked nose surrounded by an oval in neon orange on a black field. On they marched, more than one hundred fifty thousand strong, driven by the will of the Great Schnoz, and confident of ultimate victory. Opposing them behind the walls of Minor Tetons were twenty-five thousand defenders of the kingdoms of the West.

The servants of Soredoor broke on the walls of Minor Tetons like a wave against a lighthouse. Many died. But this was a sea of enemies and there were always more: more yucks, more men, more swords, more bloodlust. The attackers died by the hundreds, and hundreds more took their places. The men of Minor Tetons settled into a rhythm: kill yucks, rotate out, rest, rotate in, kill yucks—like a day of harvesting except that the harvest was heads and the crops were trying to kill them. The men of Minor Tetons knew they could not win, but they denied their doom and continued to fight. They fought for their families, their city and for the slim hope that lay on the shoulders of a gray wizard and a perpetually hungry halfbit.

Beside Arrowshaft stood Vidar son of Voland, a tall man of the city guard dressed in gray robes and a gray hat. He wore a false white beard and carried a white staff. On his right ring finger was an oversized gold ring. From a distance, he looked like Grandkopf. He wasn't happy about it.

"What happens when the Schnozgoons show up?" said Vidar. "They're going to be on me like a hog on corn. They're going to think I'm Grandkopf and come after me with everything they've got. I'm going to get my ass fried to taki."

"Don't worry," said Lededgas. "They'll probably get you on the first shot, you won't feel a thing."

"If they miss, they can always feed you to their monkeys," said Gimmie.

"Well, they are going to have to chase me down to do it. As soon as there is any hint of a Schnozgoon I'm running for the palace. I'm going to find the deepest, darkest cellar, lock myself in, and curl up like a frightened hedgehog. What are you going to do?"

"We're going to wait until the Schnozgoons are chasing you across the courtyard, then attack them from behind," said Lededgas.

"You're kidding," said Vidar.

"Nope," said Gimmie.

"Taki," said Vidar.

"Schnozgoons! Schnozgoons!" came the cry from below. Arrowshaft glanced over the rampart then turned to Vidar.

"Stay here," he said, but Vidar was gone. Instead, Arrowshaft was looking at Lededgas, who shrugged. Gimmie was looking at something behind them, so Arrowshaft turned as well.

"Who pinned the target to his back?" said Arrowshaft. Without looking up Gimmie jerked a thumb at Lededgas.

"I thought it would provide a moment of levity," said Lededgas.

"It did," chuckled Gimmie, as the hem of a gray robe disappeared into the palace.

Arrowshaft pulled a far-seeing tube from his pouch and scanned the battlefield.

"Lededgas, do you see them?" said Arrowshaft, scanning the field of Picador for the Schnozgoons.

"Yes, about one o'clock halfway across the field. They are flying low in two V formations of four."

"Only eight?"

"Only eight. I guess Elli May really did kill the Bitch Queen," said Lededgas.

"They'll either attack the walls or fly up here to deal with Grandkopf…and me," said Arrowshaft.

"What if they come up here?" said Gimmie.

"Then Lededgas will kill their little monkeys with well-placed arrows, I'll call Grandkopf on the seestone, and then we will all run for the cellars in the palace and curl up like hedgehogs," said Arrowshaft.

"Good plan," said Gimmie.

"The Schnozgoons are all attacking the wall of the first level. The men are running before them," said Lededgas. "There is little hope now but for Froyo."

"I'll tell Grandkopf," said Arrowshaft, and ran for the palace.

Arrowshaft nodded to the guards as he slammed through the door to the Steward's office. He ran to the seestone table and sat in the waiting chair. He tapped the seestone twice to open Grandkopf's channel. In a few seconds he could see Grandkopf sitting with the acrid fumes of Soredoor covering the sky behind him and a thin streak of light where the sun had tried to rise. Then he felt pressure in his mind and saw Grandkopf wince. The Great Schnoz was trying to break in. It was all he could do to resist. Grandkopf wore a strained expression as if he too were in a mental struggle.

"Eight Schnozgoons assault the walls of Minor Tetons," thought Arrowshaft.

"What of the Bitch Queen of Del Mar?" the thought formed in his mind.

"No sign," he thought. "Told you so! Fly now!" Arrowshaft felt annoyance, affirmation, and resolution in roughly equal proportions. Grandkopf nodded, raised his hand toward his seestone, and the view went black. Arrowshaft tapped his own stone three times to be sure it was off and covered it with its cloth. He left it on the table and walked to the door of the study.

"Lock the door behind me," he said to the guards. "Let no one in but myself, Lord Beeromir or Lord Foamier." Arrowshaft watched while the guards locked the door and took their positions on either side. He strode down the long throne room toward the doors and the courtyard of the tree of Gonner. When the doors shut behind him, Berolund appeared out of the shadows bearing a tray with a pot and two cups.

"Lord Foamier sends his regards and ordered me to bring hot coffee to those who guard the seestone," said Berolund, smiling.

Arrowshaft joined Lededgas and Gimmie at the rampart and looked down on the battle.

"Where are the Schnozgoons?" he asked.

"As you walked out, they turned and started back toward Soredoor at high speed," said Lededgas. "You might just be able to make them out there." He pointed to the southwest. "They fly in a single V to make the best time."

"Taki!" said Arrowshaft, He turned and ran back to the palace and the seestone.

Outside the Steward's office, the two guards lay with cups by their hands. Arrowshaft drew his sword as he flew through the open door. He rounded the corner to find Berolund dead at the table, his throat cut. A wave of hopelessness hit Arrowshaft. The Great Schnoz was in the seestone.

"Despair, King of Nothing! I know all your plans. The Schnozgoons fly to Mount Drool. In an hour I will take the Schnozring from the cold dead finger of that halfwit halfbit and in two hours more my yucks will come for you." Images appeared in Arrowshaft's mind: Minor Tetons burning; yucks running through the garden; Argyle borne down by a dozen attackers; Arrowshaft, Lededgas, and Gimmie, the last defenders of the White Town, overwhelmed on the steps of the palace.

"Not while I draw breath!" exclaimed Arrowshaft. He crossed to the seestone and raised his sword before him as if in a salute.

"Behold Narithil, Nasal remade! The sword that cut the Schnoz-ring from your schnoz at the end of the second age. *I* am coming for *you*. I bear Schnozmon's bane. Be afraid," said Arrowshaft. He tapped the seestone off and leaned against the wall, breathing hard from the effort. In a moment he recovered and tapped the seestone for Grandkopf. There was no answer. He felt the pressure of the Great Schnoz trying to break in. Arrowshaft turned the seestone off and covered it. He found the key in the pocket of one of the dead guards, locked the door and returned to the courtyard.

"Berolund poisoned the guards," said Arrowshaft. "He is dead in the Steward's office. He has betrayed us. The Great Schnoz knows we mean to destroy the Schnozring. The Schnozgoons fly to inter-cept Froyo."

—

Froyo sat in his sleeping bag. Only his arms and head were exposed to the cold morning air. He had finished off the bagels, the cinnamon rolls, and half the coffee. He had a mouthful of sausages and pumpernickel and was feeling very pleased with himself when Grandkopf strode up. Grandkopf stood over Froyo with his hands on his hips and gave Froyo a scowl powerful enough to snuff out the flames of a full-grown fire lizard.

"Fool of a halfbit!" he said, glaring down at Froyo. "The Schnoz-goons attack Minor Tetons. Get up now. It is time to fly!"

As Froyo struggled out of his bag, Grandkopf reached into his sleeve and pulled out a serrated bread knife. He sliced off two thick slices of pumpernickel and made himself a sausage and cheese sandwich before striding off toward Airtoair, munching happily.

Grandkopf was standing beside Airtoair wrapping the seestone in a soft cloth as Froyo ran up, buttoning his fly. Grandkopf put the seestone in a saddlebag, fastened the strap securely, took up his staff, and hoisted himself into his saddle. He extended an arm down to Froyo and hauled the halfbit into his smaller saddle in front.

"Please fasten your seat straps," announced Airtoair. "Keep your arms and legs…"

"Yeah, yeah," said Grandkopf. "We know, we know. Wear our goggles."

"No food service…" said Froyo, adjusting his goggles and glancing wistfully over his shoulder at his backpack.

"Just so you know," said Airtoair. Airtoair took two hops to the edge of the cliff. The effect on his passengers was that of being on a horse that suddenly decided to take umbrage at his riders. Airtoair dived over the side and plunged a hundred feet toward the plain below. Soon, the other great eagles joined them.

They flew into the V formation, with Airtoair serving as the anchor in the second position in the right arm of the V. The other eagles cycled into and out of the point position, which Airtoground had explained allowed them to fly faster and with less effort. Airtoair would conserve his strength for the last desperate rush to Mount Drool. When they were twenty minutes out, Airtoair would split off and fly around Mount Drool on the southeast side while the others flew northwest to intercept the Schnozgoons if they came. They all settled into their business. There was no chatter amongst the eagles. Even the young ones were serious, focused.

After an hour, there was some activity on the left wing. Airtoground flew to the point and screeched at the lead eagle. He flew back over the formation and screeched to Airtoair. Airtoair translated.

"The Schnozgoons have flown over the Musty Mountains at the pass of Serious Ugly." Grandkopf looked toward the northwest.

"Your eyes are not sharp enough, you cannot see them. They cannot see us."

"How did they know?" said Grandkopf.

"No matter, new plan," said Airtoair. Grandkopf nodded.

"I will split from the formation soon and drive for Mount Drool. We should be minutes ahead of them. The other eagles will fly up and swoop down upon the Schnozgoons and their silly monkeys from above. We will kill them all or at least buy a few more minutes."

"What of the Bitch Queen?"

"They will attack regardless. My grandsire bids me to show you the meaning of speed. Tighten your straps, we begin in a moment." No sooner had Grandkopf and Froyo tightened their seat straps than Airtoground screeched. Airtoair folded his wings and dove. When he pulled out of the dive he shot out over the Plateau of Googolplex. His wings beat out a steady rhythm. They were going half again as fast as they had been flying in formation. The cold morning air buffeted the passengers, who clung to their seats with trepidation.

—

Twenty-five minutes later, they approached Mount Drool. Airtoair hurtled at the side of the mountain. He flew only feet from the side, his wingtip almost touching the rocks. Froyo was wide eyed as he watched the side of the mountain roar past. He imagined a small tree or an errant branch, but he needn't have worried. Airtoair knew his business. Seconds later, the twin towers of Barn Adoor came into view. Between the towers they could see the orange nose surrounded by its blinking neon circle. The glowing orange nose swiveled toward them. A wave of malice swept over Froyo. Airtoair began to say something. They only caught snatches through the roaring wind, *"seat backs up... tray tables something something..."* Then his voice rose. "And if either of you were stupid enough to take off your seat straps, now would be a frecking good time to fasten them back! We are coming in hard!" Grandkopf and Froyo began to yank on their seat straps. They dove for the Door of Drool. Airtoair came in fast, flaring his wings at the last instant and hopped three times to kill his speed. Froyo felt as if his guts were churned to pudding by the time they stopped. Grandkopf undid Froyo's seat strap, lifted him out of his seat and practically threw him to the ground. Froyo lay on his back, trying to catch his breath, and wondering if the stars he was seeing were the same ones that Darren, the great king of the dwarves, saw at Mudomirror. Grandkopf's boots appeared before his face and he was jerked to his feet.

"Run to the fire pit! Destroy the Schnozring! There is the door! Run!" said Grandkopf, pointing.

Froyo shook his head to banish the last of Darren's stars and set off at a dead run. He paused at the Door of Drool. Ahead was a long unlit tunnel with an orange glow at the end. He ran into the tunnel but tripped on some bones and sprawled in the dirt. He scrambled to his feet and glanced behind him. Eyes! Gack had escaped from the elves. Had he made his way to Mount Drool, somehow sensing that Froyo would bring the ring to its origin? Froyo knew he must go on. He put his hand on the hilt of Stinger, lowered his head, and ran toward the fire pit.

—

"Do you see them?" asked Grandkopf. He squinted toward the west.

"They are west-northwest and moving fast," said Airtoair. "For monkeys."

"How long?"

"On their own, they'd be here in ten minutes. But they won't make it. My grandfather is preparing the attack."

"There is no need to take the chance. If Froyo tosses the Schnoz-ring into the fire pit of Mount Drool, the Schnozgoons will all evaporate."

"If he tosses it soon! My brethren have their bloodlust up. They *will* attack the stupid monkeys. They are preparing to dive. One on each monkey. Three in reserve in case the first wave doesn't kill them."

"What of the Bitch Queen?" asked Grandkopf.

"If she is there, then eagles will die. Ten minutes after that, she's your problem, *wizard*."

"I hope Froyo hurries," said Grandkopf.

"No taki."

—

Froyo stood before the fire pit of Mount Drool. He glanced over his shoulder, looking for trouble. Bad luck if Gack were to jump him now, when he was so close. He saw nothing.

Froyo peered down at the churning, glowing cauldron of liquid rock below. He wondered idly about the temperature of the seething mass. It hardly mattered—it was hotter than chicken fried yuck taki.

If Grandkopf said it would destroy the Schnozring, then it would destroy the Schnozring.

He grasped the chain he wore around his neck and pulled it over his head. The Schnozring came out of his shirt. It glowed in the light of the molten rock. Red writing appeared on its side. *Property of the Great and Powerful Schnoz...* and all that yadda yadda. He dangled it in front of his eyes. A wave of desire swept over Froyo. His deepest wish was to keep the Schnozring, to put it on his finger, to make it his own. He gazed at the gleaming gold. Such a pretty thing. A shame, really, to pitch it into the fire pit of Mount Drool. Why not keep it? He undid the clasp of the chain and slipped the Schnozring free. He saw Grandkopf, Arrowshaft, Beeromir all on one knee before him. He saw himself rebuilding Minor Tetons, restoring the kingdom of Gonner to its former glory, and draining the Mire. He was kind, benevolent, a great ruler. He held the Schnozring up. Silhouetted against the dark of the cavern wall, it glowed in a perfect golden circle. It called to him, it sang. Froyo moved it toward the ring finger of his right hand. Closer. Froyo's stomach rumbled. He hadn't finished his breakfast. The thought crossed his mind that he could go get a proper breakfast if he could just get rid of the stupid Schnozring.

"Well, taki, I came all this way to throw it in the fire pit of Mount Drool," he thought. "Might as well toss it in."

He flipped it into the air over the fire pit with his thumb as if he were flipping a bronze chicken. He watched it sink toward the glowing rock. Down it fell, spinning slowly, silhouetted against the light of the fire pit. It seemed to float. After a drop that seemed to last minutes, it hit the surface of the molten rock.

Bloop.

"Huh," thought Froyo. "I sort of expected a gout of flame, or an oithquake or something." He drew Sticker and turned to the tunnel. Woe be unto Gack or any other creature that stood between *this* halfbit and a proper breakfast.

—

"Here they come," said Airtoair. "The Schnozgoons are clueless."

"What's happening?"

"Seven down on the first pass. The eighth is injured. It is spiraling down."

"I saw no bolts of lightning."

"There were none. Now the eighth is down. All the stupid monkeys are dead. The Schnozgoons are on the ground," said Airtoair.

"They can't stop us now!" said Grandkopf.

"Airtoground is coming toward us," said Airtoair. "He is not flying right. Something is wrong."

Airtoground hit the ledge hard and fell onto his back. Grandkopf and Airtoair rushed over to him.

"Grandfather! What is wrong?" asked Airtoair.

"Archer. Lucky shot. Heart," said Airtoground. "What of the ring?"

"Froyo went into the fire pit of Mount Drool. He has not returned," said Grandkopf.

"Yes I have," said Froyo, standing at his elbow.

"Aahhhh! Taki, you scared me!" said Grandkopf. "Where's the Schnozring?"

"In the fire pit."

"You threw it in?"

"Yup."

"What happened?"

"It went bloop."

"Bloop?"

"Bloop."

"Turn out your pockets!"

"No need. Look," said Froyo, and pointed at Barn Adoor. The neon light around the Great Schnoz flickered and went out. The twin towers began to crumble on either side of the Schnoz. Twin clouds of dust billowed upward from their collapse. The Schnoz swiveled back and forth between them. The building beneath the Schnoz fell apart and the sign, *Barn Adoor Hotel and Casino*, tumbled to the ground. The Schnoz and the unlit neon bulb were suspended in mid-air above the rubble of the casino. The neon bulb tilted forward from the top and crashed into the ground. The Schnoz strained upward, struggling to stay suspended. The now ash-gray Schnoz began to crumble from the tip. In a few seconds all that remained of the Great and Powerful Schnoz was gray dust that hung in the air and floated downward toward the remains of the casino.

Two clouds of dust mushroomed over the debris of the twin towers of Barn Adoor. Froyo's stomach gave a twinge at the thought of a plate of mushrooms sautéed in butter and a little Westermire sauce.

"Grandson! Grandson!" Airtoground cried.

"Yes, Grandfather," said Airtoair, hopping to the side of his grandsire.

"Take care of your mother," said Airtoground.

"Yes, grandfather," said Airtoair.

"Airtoair, listen!"

Yes, grandfather."

"Always dive out of the sun."

"Yes, grandfather, I will."

"Airtoair?"

"I am here, grandfather."

"May the wind be always at your back."

"Thank you grandfather."

"Airtoair?"

"I am still here grandfather."

"This is important. Gasp. Always remember, never… never… no, *always… Ahhhhhh. Uk.*"

"Well, that was cryptic," said Airtoair to no one in particular.

"That 'dive out of the sun' thing sounded like good advice," said Grandkopf.

"Eagle tactics 101. Nice of him to mention it, though," said Airtoair. He turned from his grandfather and looked west over the Plain of Googolplex.

"There are eight columns of dust rising above the plain," said Airtoair.

"The Schnozgoons!" said Grandkopf.

Mount Drool began to rumble. A plume of smoke rose from its crater and the ground shook violently. Grandkopf looked with apprehension at the top of the mountain.

"Grandkopf, there's lava coming out of the Door of Drool," said Froyo, pointing.

"Hammered yuck taki! Let's get out of here." Grandkopf threw Froyo into his saddle and climbed up behind him.

"Please fasten your seat straps," announced Airtoair. "Keep your arms and legs…"

"WE KNOW! WE KNOW," shouted Grandkopf and Froyo together. They began frantically jerking their seat straps and fumbling with their goggles.

Airtoair took two bone-jarring hops to the edge of the mountain and launched himself into the void. He rocketed down to gain momentum and flapped his wings furiously as he rose to the meet the other eagles. The rest of the eagles surrounded Airtoair, forming their traveling V. They said nothing as they set out for Minor Tetons.

Behind them Mount Drool erupted in earnest, spraying clouds of smoke and globs of molten rock hundreds of feet into the air.

"The flying time to Minor Tetons is two hours and thirty-three minutes. Enjoy your flight," said Airtoair.

Much to his chagrin, Froyo realized that he was going to miss first breakfast, second breakfast, and elevenses entirely. He sincerely regretted that there was no in-flight food service.

THIRTY-FIVE

MEANWHILE, BACK IN MINOR TETONS

You are one hundred and thirty-seven yucks behind.
—Lededgas to Gimmie

Arrowshaft, Gimmie, and Lededgas fought together on the second level of Minor Tetons. The yucks had not been able to breach the gates or reduce the outer walls, but they had swarmed up siege ladders in such numbers that the defenders could not stem the tide. The walls of the second level were not as high, but the yucks had to get their ladders through the gates or over the walls and then up the narrow streets, all the while being pelted with rocks and skewered with arrows from above. The yucks were working a ram on the gates to the second level but they did not know that the defenders had collapsed the city walls behind the gates. Once they broke through the gates, the yucks would face a wall of stone. They would clear it eventually, but it would cost them time and numbers.

"Six levels to go before we're toast," thought Arrowshaft, as he stretched his back during a momentary lull in the fighting. He looked toward the east and Soredoor. He thought of Grandkopf ,

Froyo, and their desperate mission. He sent a wish for safety and success.

"They are fine; I feel it," said Lededgas, also looking east.

"Where are all the yucks?" said Gimmie.

"There'll be more along in a minute," said Lededgas.

"Good. I have to catch up," said Gimmie.

"You are one hundred and thirty-seven yucks behind," said Lededgas.

"There are lots of yucks. I can catch up," said Gimmie.

The companions heard a distant boom. The walls of the White Town moved beneath their feet. Arrowshaft and Lededgas were almost thrown off the allure but regained their balance. Gimmie, who was less fortunate, was thrown to one side and was teetering on the edge, windmilling his arms to regain his balance when Lededgas grabbed him by the beard and pulled him back up.

"Son of a Wag!" said Gimmie.

Lededgas looked over the edge of the allure at the street below and then back at Gimmie.

"Uh, thanks," said Gimmie, rubbing his chin. Lededgas patted him on the helm.

"Lededgas, look to the East. There are clouds rising from Soredoor. What can you see?" said Arrowshaft.

"The clouds on the left are dust. Perhaps from the twin towers of Barn Adoor," said Lededgas. "To the right, I see flames and rocks flying in the cloud. I think it is Mount Drool erupting."

"Holy freckin' chunks of green steaming yuck taki! Do you think Froyo and Grandkopf succeeded?" said Gimmie.

"Looks that way," said Lededgas, "But did they survive?"

"We'll know soon enough," said Arrowshaft.

On the first level of the city all motion had stopped. The yucks stood perfectly still and looked to the East as if waiting for a signal or command. They began to mill around aimlessly as if they weren't quite sure what they were doing.

"Fire!" roared Arrowshaft. Up and down the city's walls the cry was echoed. A rain of arrows began afresh. The yucks awoke and started for the open gates. Their exodus turned into a stampede. The yucks were fighting at the gates to get out. In a few minutes there were no living yucks left in the city. Outside the city gates, the field of Picador was still covered with yucks and men. The yucks were fighting with the men and with yucks of different clans. The whole mass began to recede from the city walls. Arrowshaft set in motion a plan to secure the first level and the gates. He set out with Gimmie and Lededgas to form a welcoming party for the Froyo and Grandkopf.

Arrowshaft assembled the welcoming party in the courtyard of the dead, formerly green, tree of Gonner. The rest of the Six Pack, plus Argyle, Foamier, and Elli Mae were waiting. Lededgas was the first to spot the great eagles approaching.

"The eagles are coming over the pass of Serious Ugly. There are only eleven," said Lededgas.

"What of Froyo and Grandkopf? Do you see them?" asked Gimmie.

"Yes, Airtoair flies in the second position. Froyo and Grandkopf are with him," said Lededgas.

"Thank goodness," said Gimmie.

A half-mile out, Airtoair broke from the others and started his descent to the courtyard. The other eagles rose to perch on ledges above the city. Airtoair flared and hopped to a stop.

Grandkopf swung down from his saddle and lifted Froyo gently to the ground. They turned to face the party. Grandkopf placed his hand on Froyo's shoulder. All of the gathered friends went down on one knee and bowed their heads before the pair.

"What's for lunch?" said Froyo.

THIRTY-SIX

AFTERMATH

It went bloop. —Froyo

F royo got his lunch: chicken limone with artichokes and capers, roast beef, pulled pork a la Ember, twice-baked duck with orange sauce, five-flavor stir-fried vegetables with rice noodles, ceviche with assorted Del Mar fish and chopped bog eels fillets, rolls, loaves of sourdough and pumpernickel bread, a fruit plate, a five-cheese potato mountain, red wines from Del Mar and white wines from North Gonner and Dul Amway, a white-chocolate dessert shaped like Minor Tetons, and a licorice cake shaped like Barn Adoor topped with an orange hard candy circle and an orange slice in place of the Schnoz. It was served in the king's conference room. After everyone but Froyo was finished eating, Grandkopf stood before the gathered royalty of Central Oith and made his report. Froyo was "filling in the corners" with a few roast beef sandwiches.

"The Schnozring is destroyed," said Grandkopf. "Its effect on Froyo has always been weak, so he was able to overcome the siren song of the ring and summon the will to pitch it into the molten inferno of the fire pit of Mount Drool."

"It went bloop," said Froyo with his mouth full of sandwich.

"Bloop?" said Arrowshaft. Froyo swallowed.

"Bloop," said Froyo. "I made it through the tunnel to the edge of the fire pit. I pulled the Schnozring out of my shirt on its chain. I could feel it calling to me. The Schnozring wanted me to put it on. I could see all the great things I could do with the Schnozring: be a great king, drain the Mire."

"The Schnozring was trying to seduce you even in those last moments," said Grandkopf.

"I almost put the Schnozring on. I had it an inch from my finger when my stomach rumbled and I remembered that I didn't get to finish breakfast. I thought, if I pitch this stupid, freckin' ring in the pit I can go back to Minor Tetons and get a proper lunch. So I flipped it in. It went bloop."

"Saved by a halfbit's stomach," said Gimmie

"The Great Schnoz and the Schnozgoons are undone? This is certain?" asked Beeromir.

"Right after Froyo tossed the Schnozring into the fire pit of Mount Drool, I watched the Great Schnoz crumble and the twin towers of Barn Adoor collapse," said Grandkopf. "Airtoair saw eight columns of dust rise to the west of Mount Drool where the Schnozgoons had fallen. We also checked the seestones; the channel of the Great Schnoz is gone."

"What of the Bitch Queen of Del Mar?" asked Arrowshaft.

She was not with the others, either at Minor Tetons or later, in the skies above Soredoor. Elli Mae must have truly undone her on the Field of Picador."

"Yes!" said Elli Mae, clenching her fist. Beeromir put his arm around her shoulders and squeezed her. She kissed his cheek.

"Told ya so!" said Arrowshaft. Everyone took this opportunity to jeer and throw rolls at Grandkopf who fended them off with a wry smile and even zapped a few with minibolts from his staff just to show there were no hard feelings.

"With the Bitch Queen gone, the great eagles were more than a match for the giant flying monkeys," said Grandkopf. "Once the Schnozgoons were on the ground, they couldn't get to Mt. Drool in time to stop Froyo."

"So the Schnozring is destroyed, the Schnozgoons are toast, the Great Schnoz is finally undone, and the yuck armies are fleeing into the mountains," said Arrowshaft.

"So what do *we* do now?" asked Elli Mae.

"I guess we live happily ever after," said Grandkopf.

"We can do that?" asked Elli Mae.

THIRTY-SEVEN

OF TREES, SHOES, CAVERNS, AND WOODS

I have to meet Elli Mae at Demon Markups in an hour to pick out shoes.

—Grandkopf to Froyo

What are you doing?" asked Argyle, coming into the living room of the king's tower in the palace of Minor Tetons. Arrowshaft was lying on his back on the largest couch with a book propped open on his chest.

"I'm looking at a catalog from Anne's Arbor, Inc. in Del Mar"

"Why?"

"Well, now that the threat of the Great Schnoz is ended forever and the Bitch Queen is gone, the people of Del Mar have elected a new parliament and prime minister," said Arrowshaft

"So?"

"So now we can order a new green tree of Gonner."

"From Del Mar?"

"They have great nurseries down there. It's the climate and all."

"Why don't you just man up and go pluck one out of the mountains?" asked Argyle.

"We can get a full grown one from Del Mar. It'll look great in the courtyard for the wedding," said Arrowshaft.

"That will cost plenty."

"One goose, eighteen pigs, and sixteen chickens plus shipping. Cheap."

"Two golden geese! For a stinking green tree. That's outrageous!"

"Did I mention that it was full grown?" asked Arrowshaft.

"Still…"

"Installation is included!" said Arrowshaft.

"Well..."

"Replacement guaranteed if it dies in the first year."

"Still that's a lot to pay for a yuck lovin' green tree," said Argyle.

"Look, I am the freckin' king of Gonner and this is a symbol for my people. If I say we buy a freckin' green tree of Gonner then we sure as stinkin' green yuck taki are going buy a freckin' green tree of Gonner!"

"I love it when you get all bossy," said Argyle.

"You do?"

"Arrowshaft?"

"Yes?"

"I think we should go upstairs and practice being married right now," said Argyle

"We practiced twice last night and again this morning."

"But I'm horny."

"You're half-elf; you're always horny," said Arrowshaft

Argyle sighed. "I suppose Elli Mae would kill me if I did it with Beeromir. Maybe Foamier is available?"

"Foamier is dating the daughter of the Duke of Dul Amway."

"So?"

"So just go get Elli Mae and sword fight for a couple of hours."

"Sword fighting makes me horny," said Argyle.

"Taki."

"I love it when you talk dirty."

"Argyle?"

"Yes?"

"Let's go upstairs."

—

While Arrowshaft and Argyle were talking in the king's tower, Grandkopf and Froyo were in Grandkopf's suite in the guest tower of the palace. They were sitting on the balcony, enjoying a sunny afternoon now that the fumes of the Great Schnoz had finally cleared. They were both smoking pipes filled with Gonner Gold and sharing a bottle of fortified wine from Dul Amway.

"Are you coming with me to the Mire?" asked Froyo.

"No, I'll only go as far as Eisenfang," said Grandkopf. "I'll have a lot to do to put things in order there. Besides, we'll have to stop at Eddyroost in Rojo first. Jethro King and Elli Mae will want to feast you in Metamucil, the great hall of Rojo, before you return to the Mire. I dare say that Gwendolyn will want to host you in Eisenfang for a while as well. I fear you will be some months getting home."

"When are the weddings?"

"It will take a month, at least. These things take time."

"Even in the Mire, it seems to take the halfbit women an age to choose a dress," said Froyo.

"Yes, and here in the civilized world the women have to choose shoes, too, which seems to be an even bigger problem," said Grandkopf. "Speaking of shoes, I have to meet Elli Mae at Demon Markups in an hour to pick out shoes."

"*You* are picking out shoes with *Elli Mae?*"

"For Gwendolyn. She likes shoes."

"But she never wears shoes."

"Women, go figure."

"I hear you."

—

Elli Mae had thrown open a window in a tower room in Minor Tetons. She was standing naked before it, her breasts trying to smother the windowsill. She looked over the White Town and the field of Picador to the ruins of Oshgosh in the distance. She sighed.

"Can we have a tower like this when we are married?" she asked. Beeromir lay in bed enjoying the view. Beeromir liked women with some figure. Argyle, for instance, was beautiful, sure, but too skinny for his taste. Elli Mae was gorgeous from all over. Beeromir was watching her ass and legs as she swayed back at forth at the window. His little soldier stirred.

"We will build a beautiful keep in Oshgosh. Our bedchamber will be in a high tower with windows looking east and west. You will have a view of the White Town on one side and a view of the river and mountains on the other."

"Promise?" she looked at him over her shoulder.

He crossed his heart and held up three fingers.

"By the three green frogs of Gonner, I swear," he said solemnly.

"Good!" she skipped back to the bed and straddled Beeromir.

"I have to get dressed. I have to go shoe shopping at Demon Markups with Grandkopf."

"Grandkopf buys shoes at Demon Markups?"

"No, silly, he's buying shoes for Gwendolyn."

"Why?"

"Because he loves her."

"Grandkopf loves Gwendolyn?"

"Men are so stupid! I can't wait to tell Argyle," she said. "Every time someone says her name he goes all mushy. He's been in love with her since he first met her in Eisenfang."

"I'm in love with you," said Beeromir.

"You'd better be."

"My little soldier is in love right now."

"Taki, are you up again? I can take care of that," she said, grinding against him.

"You have to go shoe shopping," said Beeromir.

"I've got a minute."

—

Lededgas and Gimmie were in their suite. Lededgas was sitting at the table near the window reading a book in the good light and smoking his pipe. He had a bottle of Silverfire and a silver cup in front of him. Gimmie was sitting on a stool by the bed playing dwarf-peg, a game in which one used a variety of techniques to stick a miniature battle axe (the size of a hatchet, but with an elaborately ornate head and a spike at the top) in the floor by the blade or the spike. Gimmie had an empty pitcher of mead and an empty mug on the floor beside him. He had just completed thirty-one different throws when he missed attempting a double spin twist and a half from a back of the forearm start.

"Taki!" said Gimmie. Lededgas looked up.

"What?" said Lededgas

"*What* is right. What are we going to do now?" said Gimmie.

"We have lots to do: the weddings, parties, mopping up yucks," said Lededgas.

"You know what I mean."

"I thought we were going to travel around and see the caverns and woods."

"We could settle down. The Twinkling Caves at Heimie's Dip are spectacular," said Gimmie.

"It's a cave."

"It's a beautiful cave."

"It's still a hole in the ground. I can't live underground. We could go live in Ye Olde Woode, and be neighbors with old Thom Bombardier and Boysenberry," said Lededgas

"Live in the trees? Eat roots and berries?" Gimmie shuddered.

"What's wrong with trees?"

"Well, you can fall out of a tree," said Gimmie

"You fall off barstools all the time."

"It's not the same thing."

"We should travel around first and then decide," said Lededgas. "Maybe we could just travel around all the time. We could have a place in Heimie's Dip, a cottage in Ye Olde Woode and just stay in inns or with our friends. It could be fun."

"You have friends?" asked Gimmie.

"Very funny," said Lededgas

"Well, I promised to go see all the yuck-taki woods with you so I suppose we'll have to travel around for a while, anyway," said Gimmie.

"We've been doing it for years. Now we can do it without all the wag and yuck fighting and stay in inns instead of sleeping on the ground. Did I mention that the inns all have mead and that you don't have to kill your own food? It will be fun. You'll see," said Lededgas.

THIRTY-EIGHT

NEW BEGINNINGS

The Six Pack is broken forever. –Arrowshaft

I'm going to miss you soooo much," said Elli Mae. Elli Mae and Beeromir stood before the gates of Minor Tetons. Elli Mae was dressed for the road. She wore her steel breastplate and her sword. She pressed the breastplate hard against Beeromir's ribcage. Beeromir winced.

"And I you," said Beeromir. "But you must bury Theobald King and Theorug and help Jethro King set things right in Rojo. I must begin to hunt the yucks out of Soredoor."

"I know. Duty. But I'll miss you." She kissed him. "I'll be back soon." She turned and mounted her horse.

Jethro King, Grandkopf, Froyo, Gimmie, Lededgas, retainers, and Rojoriders were waiting for Elli May to mount up so they could begin the journey to Eddyroost. Jethro King raised his gloved hand and motioned forward. The long train of riders and wagons began to lurch forward. Harnesses groaned, armor, swords, and axes clanked, hoof beats echoed from the walls of the White Town, and the wheels of the supply wagons squeaked to life. The King of Rojo was going home.

Argyle, Arrowshaft, Foamier, and Beeromir waved from beneath the city gates.

"I miss them already," said Arrowshaft.

"They'll be back," said Argyle.

"Not all at once. The Six Pack is broken forever," said Arrowshaft.

"So have a reunion every five years," said Argyle.

"A Six Pack reunion?" said Arrowshaft.

"Yeah, you can all sit around and drink and make up stories about what heroes you were during the war," said Argyle. "It will be fun."

"We can get Gimmie and Lededgas to try to count up all the yucks they killed," said Arrowshaft.

"We can get Elli Mae to tell about killing the Bitch Queen of Del Mar…again," said Beeromir.

"Elli Mae's not Six Pack," said Foamier.

"Neither is she," said Arrowshaft, nodding toward Argyle. "But I'm not going to be the one to tell either of them they can't come."

"Besides, I never get tired of hearing Argyle tell about attacking the war hippos," said Foamier.

"And fighting the Corsairs of Ember," said Argyle.

"And all the farm girls we banged," said Beeromir. Argyle shot him a look.

"It's the armor," said Beeromir. He shrugged.

Argyle narrowed her eyes, turned toward Arrowshaft, and gave him a look that would have killed a lesser man.

"Don't look at me," said Arrowshaft. "I have a lover who's half elf. I can barely walk."

—

In Metamucil Jethro King honored the members of the Six Pack with much pomp and ceremony, along with much food and wine. The friends spent two weeks basking in the praise and bounty of Rojo before they felt that they simply must get on the road. Grandkopf was clearly anxious to return to Eisenfang to get things in order, he said, but everyone knew it was because he wanted to see Gwendolyn. Gimmie and Lededgas were to begin their grand tour of the caverns and woods of Central Oith—first stop, Heimie's Dip and the Twinkling Caves. Gimmie was dancing with excitement but Lededgas was a little less enthusiastic about seeing, as he called it, a musty old cave. Froyo, although enjoying the feasting in Rojo, was beginning to miss the Mire and the peace of his comfortable home.

The friends finally set out one morning after second breakfast. Gimmie and Lededgas shared a proud warhorse given to them by Jethro King; Froyo and Grandkopf rode in a new horse cart. Grandkopf had refused offers for a variety of ostentatiously decorated carriages and instead asked for a plain horse cart with bench seating for two and a small open back for supplies. Then Froyo had his say. After missing more than a few meals during his adventures, Froyo had vowed never to set out again without proper supplies. So the central section of the horse cart became an icebox and pantry. The pantry had sliding compartments for the food and dishes. There was a stove, complete with oven. The cart carried a ten-gallon supply of oil for the stove, a twenty-gallon water barrel and, most importantly, a cask of ale. In short, everything a halfbit might need for a camping trip or a quest.

Jethro King commanded the construction of the horse cart to Froyo's specifications; it was built of the finest woods and the best steel and bronze fittings. The cart was assembled by the most accomplished craftsmen; no joint was accepted unless it was perfect. It was finished with oils and hand rubbed until the wood seemed to glow from its own internal light. It turned heads with its beautiful simplicity, starting a fashion, first in Rojo and then in Gonner, that lasted five hundred years.

On the road that morning, Grandkopf and Froyo did not know that they were trend setters—they only knew that the wheels didn't squeak, the cart didn't rattle, it was a beautiful morning, and they had plenty of pipeweed and strong Rojo ale for their journey. Swiftmane pulled the cart, which was so beautiful that the majestic steed hardly looked out of place. Jethro King had also provided a pony so Froyo would have transportation for the last leg of the journey, from Eisenfang to Boggy End. The pony, whose name was Heppin, or Lucky in commontalk, had a reddish-brown coat and a long white mane. Lost in its pony thoughts, it plodded along silently behind the cart. The back of the horse cart also contained a dozen pairs of shoes in various styles and colors, size six. These were packed in small boxes labeled Demon Markups and wrapped in paper in a variety of festive colors.

On the third day, Lededgas and Gimmie took their leave and turned south toward Heimie's Dip. Grandkopf and Froyo continued to the ford of the Eisen River and then up the river road toward Eisenfang.

"What are you going to do now?" asked Grandkopf.

"I'm going to write a book about the war. I'm going to call it *The Green Book of the Great War with the Great Schnoz*," said Froyo. "I've also got an order from Arrowshaft, I mean, King Telecom, to hire engineers and drain the Mire. I've gotten used to living without mosquitoes so I'm not sure I can cope with the ravenous swarms at Boggy End."

"So don't. You are welcome in any kingdom in Central Oith. Travel around and live off the fat."

"I don't want to be a freeloader."

"Don't be silly. You are a hero of the Great War. You've paid in advance."

"Still, there is a lot to be done in the Mire."

"Thinking of settling down and marrying Primrose, or maybe Tulip?"

"I've had enough adventure for a while. I think I'll put off the adventure of marriage. I could do worse than being a bachelor at Boggy End. Especially if the Westbog gets drained and the mosquitoes thin out."

—

Grandkopf and Froyo traveled at a leisurely pace, and on the evening of the seventh day came within sight of Eisenfang. From a distance, they could see a small red spot in the doorway and a patch of white bobbing up and down. The bobbing patch was Gwendolyn in her white dress, jumping up and down and waving a white handkerchief. The red spot was Cookie in his red vest, which he only wore on important occasions. The final hundred yards was passing very slowly indeed until Grandkopf pulled his buggy whip from his sleeve and cracked it over the withers of his mighty steed. Swiftmane responded to the sound of the whip and the excitement of his passengers by putting on a burst of speed that could only be imagined by most horses. Lucky's rein broke, which was lucky for Lucky since it saved him from being dragged the last hundred yards and arriving on his stomach. The cart careened down the road. The springs of good Rojo steel launched the cart into the air with each bump. The thought flashed through Froyo's mind that, after surviving Schnozgoons, a wag attack, a balfrog in Mordia, a desperate flight on a great eagle, and the fire pit of Mount Drool, it would be a shame to break his neck being thrown from a horse cart, especially right before dinner.

Grandkopf reined Swiftmane to a halt at the bottom of the stairs and ran up to Gwendolyn. Froyo followed at a more leisurely pace. When Grandkopf crossed the threshold, Gwendolyn jumped up, threw her arms around Grandkopf's neck, wrapped her legs around his middle and began showering him with kisses.

"I missed you," she said.

"I *mmmmf*," said Grandkopf.

"We should..."

Mmmmf

"...go to your bedchamber."

Mmmmmf

"M'lord."

Mmmmmmmf

Grandkopf carried her into the lift and Gwendolyn pulled out the stop with her toes. The lift doors closed around them.

Cookie watched the lift doors close on the couple then turned and shook Froyo's hand in greeting as Froyo gained the top of the stairs.

"When the lift comes back down, I'll fix you some dinner," said Cookie.

"Thanks, I'm famished."

"You're always famished," said Cookie.

"I'm always a halfbit."

THIRTY-NINE

BRIE REDUX

Would you be the nephew of old Bobo Bagpants of Boggy End what disappeared into the wilds never to be heard from again?

—Baldiman Butterbutt to Froyo

Froyo stood before the door of the Dancing Donkey and knocked. This time, the door wasn't locked and it swung open at his touch. There was no one behind the counter. From the sound of it, the bar was doing an active business. Froyo supposed that Mr. Butterbutt was off on an errand. He spotted a bell. He had to jump up but he managed to hit the ringer on three out of four jumps. The bell made a pleasant ding that sounded almost happy.

Butterbutt's face appeared over the counter.

"Welcome Master Halfbit. You look as if you could use a room and some dinner."

"That would be welcome. I'll also need to stable my pony."

"Won't be a minute. Ed! Ed! Confound you, dimlitbulb, get your worthless rear outside and take care of this good halfbit's pony." Ed appeared out the kitchen wearing an apron and hustled out the front door. Butterbutt watched him pass.

He turned his attention back to Froyo. "And what would be your name, little master?"

"Froyo Bagpants of the Mire."

"Would you be the nephew of crazy old Bobo Bagpants of Boggy End what disappeared into the wilds never to be heard from again?"

"The same," said Froyo.

"Well, welcome, good sir. It is a pleasure to have a Bagpants of the Mire with us again." He paused, his eyes rolling to the ceiling while he stroked his chin with his thumb and forefinger. "But it seems like there is something I'm supposed to tell you." He frowned. He squinted. He scrunched up his face as if thinking were as much effort as lifting an anvil. Finally, his eyebrows shot toward the roof.

"Nope. Nothing. I'll tell you later, if I remember."

—

Three hours later, Froyo was seated at the very table where, months before, he had first met Arrowshaft. He had eaten well, even for a halfbit. He had a pint of good brown ale in front of him and his pipe was loaded with Silverleaf (he had a little left of the small stash that the elves had given him in Minor Tetons). He was ready to settle in for two or three pints when a strange halfbit carrying a pint of his own approached the table.

"Not many halfbits tonight. Mind if I join you? Name's Zachariah Riversmuck late of Smuckland, now of Brie. I run the feed store. Call me Rye." He sat down without waiting for an invitation.

"I'm Froyo Bagpants of the Mire."

"*The* Froyo Bagpants of Boggy End?"

"Yes."

"Well, I swear! I never thought I'd meet you!"

"Well, I've been away," said Froyo, not really knowing what to say.

"Well, I hope so. Some months back, everyone was looking for you. All these Haragrims, black riders, and who knows whatnot. Then the Mire marshals put out an all-bogs bulletin that you were wanted for molestation, abandonment, non-payment of debts, and fleeing from the law. There were wanted posters up all over the Mire. They were looking for you from Boggy End to Brie, but I guess they didn't find you or you'd be in the lock up, wouldn't you?"

"I... I had no idea."

"Then, about a month ago, here come the constable of Brie into the Dancing Donkey and takes down all the wanted posters. Says it's all a big misunderstanding, that you ain't wanted no more. Mighty suspicious, if you ask me."

Another halfbit walked up to the table.

"Howdy, Rye. Who's your friend?" He invited himself to be seated.

"Wimpy! You'll never believe it, this here is Master Froyo Bagpants of the Mire. *The* Froyo Bagpants what everyone's been looking for these last months."

"I'm Wimpy Webfoot of Wimpy's Wonderful Wine Emporium," said the newcomer. Froyo's eyes widened.

"I was looking for you meself a few months back. A matter of a little bill that you hadn't paid."

"I was called away suddenly; an *emergency*," said Froyo, "but I can pay you now."

"No matter, I ran into these elf friends of yours and they traded me a bag of Silverleaf big enough to choke a brace of oxen. I figured I could sell it here in Brie and turn a tidy profit."

"Well, I'm glad that it worked out," said Froyo.

"The strangest thing though, was that about a week after I sobered up and got back to Brie, this old dude comes into the shop right after dark. 'I am told you have Silverleaf,' says he. I couldn't see his face because of his hood. He was wearing these ugly pink, white, and green robes."

Froyo gasped. "Sorryman," he said, his voice shaky.

"I have thirty-one shot—a shot is a little more than an ounce," says I. "How much do you want?"

"All of it," says he.

"You could get it cheaper in Lostlorriland," says I.

"For political reasons, it is inadvisable for me to visit Lostlorriland at this time. I will pay four golden geese," says he.

"Well, one doesn't usually find Silverleaf in the Mire," says I.

"Six geese," says he.

"The transportation costs from Lostlorriland were considerable," says I.

"Seven geese. And not a bronze chicken more," says he.

"Sold! says I. He paid me right there and left quickly. When I looked out the door, I couldn't see hide nor hair of him. Like he had vanished or something. His gold was real enough, though."

Froyo finished his pint and went straight to his room. He didn't want to risk anyone showing up who hadn't heard about the wanted poster recall. He made a mental note to get an early start in the morning.

FORTY

HOMECOMING

Froyo was gone? –Poupon Roak

Lucky's hooves squelched in the muck along the winding trail of so-called high ground that led through the Westbog toward Boggy End. Froyo dozed as Lucky swayed. On either side of him he was vaguely aware of the squish-pop of halfbit feet as the Westbog halfbits harvested bog fruit and gathered bog eels. Froyo slapped absently at mosquitoes. When he had ridden through Halfbittowne a half hour earlier, he had come almost to tears at the familiar sights of shops and eateries. He hadn't realized he had been homesick.

Froyo had thought of stopping for an ale at one of the inns back in Halfbittowne, but had decided that he wasn't up to telling his story a dozen times. He certainly wasn't interested in telling his story to the marshals. Besides, he was anxious to get back to Boggy End. He had a saddlebag full of Brie sausages, hard cheese, crusty bread baked fresh that morning, bog fruit muffins, and two quarts of good strong ale from the Dancing Donkey. He was imagining a picnic for one. At his own table. In his own hole. In the peace and quiet. He smiled at the prospect.

The ground was rising. The path was going up to the high ground of Boggy End. Soon. Very soon now. Froyo's heartbeat quickened with anticipation. He stopped Lucky in front of his door and swung his leg over the broad withers of the Rojopony. When he turned to his traditional hexagonal door, painted with traditional cheap red paint, he gave a start. The door was ajar. Worse, he could hear voices inside. Happy voices. As if there were a party going on. For a second Froyo imagined a troop of yucks of the White Finger, come to Boggy End for revenge and now drinking his ale and eating his food while they waited to gut him. Then he remembered that the yucks of the White Finger had all perished at the battle of Eisenfang. Treemoss and Theobald King had seen to that. He thought of Theobald King sitting on his mighty warhorse before the first battle of Minor Tetons. So strong. So many good beings gone from Central Oith.

He straightened and put his hand to the hilt of his sword. Probably a family of Muckfeet from the Westbog squatting until his return, he told himself. Well, he had returned.

He pushed open the door and saw carnage in his hall. There were empty ale bottles, empty pizza boxes, empty Silverfire bottles, used rubbers, a single pair of lacy pink panties, and assorted chicken bones. It looked a little like Whithertop but without the Schnozgoons. The voices were coming from the kitchen. He stepped into the doorway and saw his erstwhile friends in various stages of undress playing strip poker around his kitchen table. Marty, Poupon, Sammy, Rosalie, Fatso, and two female halfbits that looked like the Highwater sisters, Mum and Daffy, from Laketowne in the Northbog, were all seated at the table. Primrose sat in Poupon's lap. Her lipstick was smudged and Poupon's face was covered with lip prints. Tulip appeared in the doorway with a baby at her breast. She gave Froyo an incandescent smile. Froyo winced. He was met by a chorus of voices.

"Froyo! Froyo!"

"Froyo, you're out of ale!" said Fatso.

"Welcome back!" said Marty.

"Froyo was gone?" said Poupon.

"You're just in time for the wedding!" said Rosalie.

"Fatso's getting married!" said Primrose.

"Tulip's baby came out with red hair!" said Poupon.

Fatso blushed a shade of crimson that almost made his face disappear into his bushy red hair. Tulip shared her incandescent smile with the whole room.

FORTY-ONE

THE CONTINUING SAGA

I Climbed the Big Tree in Lostlorriland.
—Souvenir T-shirt

Arrowshaft son of Arrowhead, called Elixir the Elfrock, Westhomey, the heir of Whiskeysour, Ellendale's son of Gonner and bearer of Narithil, the Sword that was Busted—and Remade, was crowned King Telecom of Gonner. His new name, which meant Skywalker, literally, "one who walks with the stars" in elvish, had a nice ring to it and was much easier to say than his previous moniker. Kahn Berri Kahn began to call King Telecom "Luke" and cackle hysterically whenever he did it but no one else could figure out what that was all about so the nickname didn't catch on. Larri is still trying to get him to cut down on the mushrooms.

Argyle and Arrowshaft were married in a double ceremony with Elli Mae and Beeromir two months after the end of the Great War with the Great Schnoz. Arrowshaft and Argyle loved well, lived long, and made beautiful babies. They threw lavish parties when any of the Six Packers were in town. Their reign was marked by a level of prosperity and peace not seen in Central Oith for three thousand years.

Beeromir and Foamier were confirmed as costewards of Gonner, the right hands of the newly crowned King Telecom. Beeromir's first job was to clean the yucks out of the tower of Minor Icky, the pass of Serious Ugly, and the Plateau of Googolplex. This was right up Beeromir's alley. After two years of almost continuous fighting, the task was accomplished except for isolated pockets of yucks that had fled deep into the shady mountains. Beeromir became the head of a five thousand-man search and destroy unit. He wound up sitting behind a desk all day reading reports and approving logistics. Beeromir quickly tired of his administrative duties but figured out that he could delegate almost all of the administrative work. He then turned to his favorite pursuit, being a man's man. He wound up spending most of his time hunting, fishing, riding, drinking, and fighting.

Except for sex that was so good she was embarrassed to tell her mother, Ellie Mae was left to her own devices. She went to night school and began to dabble in clothing design. She designed a line of clothing called Bitch-Queen™ that was picked up by Demon Markups in Minor Tetons. This became a big hit. She followed up with Shieldmaiden™ and for girls, Bit-Queen™ and Shield-Girl™. However, her crowning glory was the line she designed for the full-figured woman called, When the Helmet Lady Sings™.

Foamier was assigned the rebuilding and rule of Oshgosh. Foamier cleared the rubble, rebuilt the port, and built the Steward's Palace. The construction attracted workers and businesses to support them. Within a decade, Oshgosh was a thriving city and well on its way to becoming the major city of commerce in Gonner. Foamier excelled at running the city and became know as Foamier the Fair.

Foamier son of Alehouse married Cynthia daughter of Arthur, the duke of Dul Amway. Cynthia's father and her brother, Borre, thought she was marrying down. However, when Foamier became the de facto ruler of the spectacularly rebuilt Oshgosh and the true right hand to King Telecom, they became less displeased—enthusiastic, even. Cynthia truly loved him and didn't give round chunks of flying yuck taki what anyone else thought. Cynthia, although raised in the court of Dul Amway, was really a simple girl and ran a tight ship at home. Foamier and Cynthia prospered. They took ballroom dancing lessons and became known at court as Cyndy and Foamy the dancing duo, but only behind their backs.

Telecom, king of Gonner, entrusted Grandkopf with the management of Eisenfang. Grandkopf settled in with Gwendolyn and Cookie. Grandkopf quickly determined that Gwendolyn was not cursed to stay in Eisenfang but that Sorryman only told her that to keep her around. She was so thrilled that she gave him a big kiss and departed for Lostlorriland to visit her relatives. Grandkopf and Cookie were brokenhearted. Cookie refused to cook anything but macaroni and cheese and Grandkopf spent his days locked in his room, coming out only to restock his supply of pipeweed and Silverfire and eat macaroni and cheese.

After a tour that included visits to Minor Tetons and the major elven hangouts of Lostlorriland, Smirkwood, and Clovendell, Gwendolyn returned to Eisenfang because, "I missed the old fart." She gave Grandkopf and Cookie souvenir T-shirts that said *Have a Grand Bon Temp in Minor Tetons* and *I Climbed the Big Tree in Lostlorriland*. Grandkopf and Cookie were overjoyed at her return. Cookie prepared an eleven-course dinner, and Grandkopf took a much-needed bath, combed his beard, and put on his best robes.

They had a reunion dinner that lasted six hours. Mac and cheese was not served at Eisenfang for ten years, until the tourist business kicked in and the dwarves demanded it be served on the buffet.

Unlike Sorryman, who had a head for business, Grandkopf had always been a wandering wizard and hence poor. Grandkopf quickly discovered that keeping an elf, a dwarf, and a wizard in food, booze, and pipeweed was no mean feat when you have to pay for it yourself. Grandkopf planted a little garden of pipeweed to ensure a steady supply. Treemoss, who loved all living things including pipeweed bushes, took an interest. Treemoss not only landscaped Eisenfang but helped Grandkopf hybridize some new varieties of pipeweed. They settled on one they named Eisenweed™. It was acclaimed the equal of Silverleaf and soon they had thousands of acres of it under cultivation. Gwendolyn, whom everyone had assumed to be a total space case, proved to have learned a thing or two about business from her time with Sorryman. She ran the whole thing while Grandkopf dabbled in farming, brewing, and occasionally, wizard work.

Unfortunately, as a result of Grandkopf's adventures in agriculture, the price of Rojo Red plummeted, putting a big dent in the economy of Rojo. Jethro King threatened to declare war on Eisenfang. Grandkopf and Treemoss developed a strain of Eisenweed™ suitable for cultivation in the rocky soils of Rojo and Gwendolyn licensed it to Jethro King for the majestic price of one bronze chicken. This became the famous Rojo Red Rider™ brand. Gwendolyn cut a distribution deal with Jethro King and marketed Eisenweed™ and Rojo Red Rider™ all over Central Oith. War with Rojo was averted, prosperity reigned, and Grandkopf and Gwendolyn were invited to dine often at Metamucil.

The elves caught Gack two weeks after he escaped. After the destruction of the Schnozring, the elves saw little use in keeping Gack imprisoned. Besides, what with the swearing, the spitting, and the poor personal hygiene, the elves were really, really tired of putting up with him. So they fashioned a golden ring and gave it to him on a chain. Gack called it his *snooky ookums* and never let it out of his sight. The elves hauled him down the Silverwash to a swamp on the banks of Old Man River and pitched him in. Gack was last seen there, happy as a pig in mud, eating raw fish, strangling small furry creatures and mumbling "My snooky ookums, my snooky ookums."

Froyo wrote the now-famous *Green Book of the Great War with the Great Schnoz*. Published by Clovendell Press, LLC, it became an instant bestseller. This made Froyo filthy rich. He became so famous that he couldn't buy his own food or drink anywhere in the more desirable parts of Central Oith. He retired to be a country gentleman and philanthropist. He split his time between Boggy End and Eisenfang, where he hung out with Grandkopf and sometimes accompanied him on his travels. For Froyo, traveling entailed a lot of book signings, but that's what kept the geese rolling in.

What with the pipeweed business and tourists flocking to see the tower, the gardens, and the forests, Eisenfang became a melting pot of the races of Central Oith and a small city grew up. Gwendolyn and Grandkopf turned Eisenfang into a first-class hotel with thirty-five hundred guest rooms, all with a view. Cookie had to hire a sous chef and an army of cooks. The twins got bored with Clovendell and decided to visit Eisenfang for a few decades, much to the delight of Froyo, who began to spend even more time there.

When the twins moved out of Clovendell, Bobo, who had effectively retired there, got the urge to go visit his old buddy Arrowshaft in Minor Tetons. Once in Minor Tetons he proceeded to get himself thrown out of every drinking establishment and most of the whorehouses in the city.

After the Great War with the Great Schnoz, Lededgas and Gimmie commenced a tour of the caverns and woods of Central Oith. The resulting travel guide, *The Caverns and Woods of Central Oith*, made them famous and rich. They, too, went on the signing circuit. As Lededgas already suspected of Gimmie, you can make him bathe, you can dress him up, but you can't make him civilized. Gimmie's book signings were often quite a bit more exciting than the usual book affair. Things calmed down after the organizers forbade Gimmie to bring his axe and started to water down his mead. Their book made the Twinkling Caves of Heimie's Dip a major attraction and the tourist business brought prosperity to an otherwise blighted part of Rojo. A downside of their book was that it made Thom Bombardier's house on the Writhytrinkle a tourist destination, and crowds were gathering to watch Boysenberry hang the wash. Thom was pissed at them for that for a few decades. Finally, Boysenberry had the good sense to open the Writhytrinkle Vegetarian Inn, Brew Pub, and Olde Souvenir Shoppe. The Olde Souvenir Shoppe carried tie-dyed souvenir T-shirts, Elfenstock™ sandals, pipeweed paraphernalia, and the largest selection of custom blended, Herb-Kissed™ flavored pipeweed varieties in Central Oith (*Does your pipeweed taste like weeds? Try Herb-Kissed Eisenweed by Boysenberry, guaranteed completely organic!*). The Olde Souvenir Shoppe brought extreme prosperity to Boysenberry and Thom, thus keeping Thom supplied with cigars, ale, and pipeweed. Thom eventually forgave Lededgas and Gimmie. They became honored guests and were invited often to speak about tourism in Central Oith.

The elves of Central Oith forged new rings of power which, although not as strong as the old rings, did serve to maintain Lostlorriland and elven power in Central Oith. Glenda continued to take the precaution of putting hers in her shoe during recreational activities. The elves decided not to depart for the Watery Islands and continued to smoke Silverleaf, drink Silverfire, and have lots of sex.

The kingdoms of Ember and Del Mar declared war over use of the slogan "Seaside Paradise of Central Oith." Before hostilities could break out, emissaries of King Telecom of Gonner arrived to mediate the dispute. An agreement was reached after a three-day meeting in which a long-standing Central Oith record for the largest per capita consumption of Silverfire at a diplomatic affair was broken. It was decided that Ember would continue to use "Ember, Seaside Paradise of Central Oith" while Del Mar would use the slogan "Del Mar, Paradise by the Sea," which the Del Mar delegation thought had a better ring to it, anyway. The morning after the meeting, neither side remembered what they had agreed upon but both sides remembered that they had happily toasted the outcome several times. Fortunately, the head scribe of the Gonner delegation stayed sober and wrote everything down. Crisis averted. The head scribe, who came up with the Del Mar slogan, went on to have a successful advertising career in Minor Tetons, eventually managing both the Bit-Queen™ and Shieldgirl™ campaigns.

FORTY-TWO

BUSINESS AS USUAL

Bring another batch of Gwendolyn's magic brownies.
—Badgrass the Brown to Grandkopf the Gray

April 17, Year Two, Fourth Age

From: Badgrass the Brown, Smirkwood

To: Grandkopf the Gray, Eisenfang

My Good Friend Grandkopf,

Don't forget the 4717th Annual Convention of the Ouestari in Minor Tetons, May 15-17. The general membership meeting, vendor fair, and seminars will all take place in the Majestic Buzzard Inn, 842 Tinker's Street, two sections above Craftsman's Square on the third level of Minor Tetons. Here is the agenda for the business meeting:

Agenda

1) On 12 April, Gornast the Merciless assumed leadership of the Long Tooth clan of the Musty Mountain yucks by removing the head of the previous leader, Snazbub the Ruthless. He accomplished this while Snazbub was sleeping. Gornast is not expected to last long in his new leadership position. We will discuss containment strategies in light of any new information.

2) Glenda has her panties in a wad about the party, I mean, the training retreat that the northern Rojo section of the Ouestari held on the border of Lostlorriland. Apparently the novices got drunk and held a blasting contest that got a little out of hand. Romeo the Blue went to Lostlorriland to try to calm her down and she turned him into a fire lizard. I hope to have him restored in time for the convention. We will discuss appeasement, but the Smirkwood brothers feel you ought to go see her yourself because A) she likes you and B) you are the most likely to survive the visit.

3) Bobo was found taki-faced drunk and naked behind the Elegant Elf Tavern and Whorehouse again. He was under a wagon singing, badly according to eyewitnesses, an elven ballad about the unrequited love between an elf and an oliphant, waving an empty ale stein, and soliciting the trash men for money to buy more booze. The City Council of Minor Tetons has voted to have him neutered or, at the very least, sent away to Clovendell or the Mire. If you don't want him at Eisenfang, then we need to talk El Round into taking him back because we doubt the Mire can handle him.

4) Loholt the Blue writes that some wags have set up a colony in the Whither Hills north of Whithertop. They are believed to be escapees from the Battle of Eisenfang. Loholt requests some elven archers and some wizards to go root them out. He also received a letter from some dwarf named Gimmie who says that if we don't do anything before he gets back from his vacation at the Golden Nuggie™ in Ember, the Seaside Paradise, that he will "take his axe and do it himself." Should we take him seriously?

5) Balfrog sightings continue in Mordia.

Other announcements

1) Only ale and wine will be available until after the conclusion of the business meeting. No exceptions. Buffet breakfast and lunch for 1c, buffet dinner for 2c. Special prix fixe dinner, including four courses and wine, for 5c. Saturday's banquet is included in the registration fee. Guest tickets for 10c.

2) The Smirkwood brothers have requested that I beg you to bring another batch of Gwendolyn's magic brownies.

See you soon. Please give my love to Gwendolyn.

BtB

FORTY-THREE

DINNERTIME

Beeromir found the rings of men in the ruins of Barn
Adoor. Nothing good can come of that.

—Froyo Bagpants

Froyo was sitting down to a nice halfbit dinner. It was a fine
soft evening in the Mire with just a nip of coolness. The
window was open and Froyo could hear the birds singing
their final songs of the evening. Rosalie had just set his dinner in
front of him. After the Great War with the Great Schnoz, Sammy
had married Rosalie and they had moved into one of comfortable halfbit holes at Boggy End. Froyo, in a fit of inspiration, had
hired Rosalie as the head cook. Froyo leaned over his trough and
inhaled deeply. Ahhh. Hiring Rosalie was one of his best decisions.

Froyo glanced down in anticipation at the letter in the green
envelope beside his knife. It was year two of the fourth age. King
Telecom had gotten the post working all the way from Del Mar to
the Mire. Now letters arrived regularly from Eisenfang and Minor
Tetons. He had just received this letter from King Telecom. As was
his wont, he would read it while he enjoyed his dinner. Tonight, his

trough held some roast beef, a mound of potatoes Anna, their tops cooked to crispy brown goodness, some dirty rice, and three pork chops in Rosalie's special deglazing sauce. Three more troughs to come. Froyo had a mug of good brown ale from the Red Flagon Inn. There was a fresh keg in the cellar, so no worries about running out tonight.

Froyo cut a nice chunk of roast beef and shoveled it into his mouth. Then some potatoes and a dollop of the dirty rice. *Hm, still room. Maybe a pork chop. Well, maybe a half a pork chop.* When Froyo had his mouth loaded and was chewing happily, he reached for his letter. The usual greetings. Argyle sends her best. Beeromir and Ellie Mae had a fight, but they made up. Foamier and Cynthia are building a palace in Oshgosh. *Hmm, this is interesting. Beeromir found the rings of men in the ruins of Barn Adoor. Nothing good can come of that.* Arrowshaft is inviting the six-pack for a reunion in six months. *That sounds like fun. Oops, there's some room in the mouth now. More pork chop, a little more potatoes, and some dirty rice. Just right.*

Froyo was happy in the Mire, but sometimes he was struck by a touch of wanderlust. So far, the feeling had only carried him as far as Eisenfang. But with the Six Pack reunion coming up, it would look as if a trip to Minor Tetons was in his future. This news about the rings of men bothered him, though. *The next thing I know they'll be wanting me to carry them all to Mt. Drool and toss them in.* But that was a worry for the future. Right now, this dinner needed his attention. He was happy to give it.

OF HALFBITS AND THE MIRE

There's nothing better than a mess of fried bog eels in the morning.

—Froyo Bagpants

The origin of the halfbits is much debated amongst the scholars of Central Oith. Some think the halfbits are slender dwarves. Others think they are fat elves. There are some scholars who maintain that halfbits are diminished men, and yet others who believe the halfbits are not descended from any of the peoples of Central Oith but arose separately, perhaps from pigs. What is certain is that the halfbits colonized the area now known as the Mire, a soggy, mosquito- and snake-infested region considered uninhabitable by all the other races of Central Oith, sometime during the First Age.

According to their oral history, the halfbits, being small and always hungry, were considered vermin by many of the peoples of Central Oith and were persecuted as such. They traveled from place to place, always looking for a land of their own, while always being forced to move on. When they stumbled upon the Mire, the halfbits found their home at last.

The Mire was created thousands of years earlier by the impact of a long-forgotten meteor. The resulting crater served as a basin for several streams that flowed out of the surrounding mountains. The Mire was a bowl of mostly shallow water covering muck: basically a swamp. The water from the mountain streams percolated through the Mire and eventually emerged from a low spot on the southern side, forming the headwaters of Smuck Creek. Smuck Creek flowed south and a little east to its conjunction with the Makewater River in Smuckland.

The Mire was divided into quarters (or bogs) known as the Northbog, Southbog, Eastbog, and Westbog. Inside the Mire were three areas of relatively dry ground. Two of these areas were rocky islands, Halfbittowne and Boggy End, which were considered part of the Westbog. The third was a large piece of soggy ground in the Southbog called the South Mound. The Northbog had a large lake that was imaginatively called Mire Lake, or simply The Lake. Mire Lake supported a fishing industry that mainly dealt in the fishing and processing of mirecats, a fish resembling a catfish that grew to be larger than most halfbits, sometimes reaching a weight of seventy-five pounds.

Adjacent to the Mire proper, though traditionally considered part of the Mire, was Smuckland, an area around the confluence of Smuck Creek and the Makewater River. Like the Mire, it was uniformly soggy.

Halfbits divided themselves into loose groups based upon where they lived. The Highbog halfbits lived in the so-called dry parts of the Mire: Halfbittowne, Boggy End, or the South Mound. Halfbittowne consisted of the town proper—a collection of wooden dwellings and commercial buildings at the bottom of Mire Hill—and

Mire Hill, a rocky upwelling that rose a hundred feet above the surrounding marshes. The halfbits of Mire Hill had the privilege of
dwelling in dry, secure halfbit holes that were cut into the rock of
the hill itself. Boggy End was a separate, small island a little west of
Halfbittowne that rose approximately twenty feet above the Mire.
An extensive halfbit hole had been cut into the rock for the current
owner, along with several small holes for the servants. It was considered one of the premier addresses of the Mire. The other Highbog
neighborhood was the South Mound, which rose a foot or so over
the Southbog. Roakland occupied the west end, and a series of small
farms covered the east side. To keep their homes dry in the spring,
when the snow melt caused the water level to rise a foot or more,
the South Mound halfbits built their wooden houses approximately
three feet above the ground on wooden pilings.

The Lowbog halfbits lived in stilt houses built six to eight feet
over the water. The Lowbog halfbits simply walked through the
muck where the water was shallow and used small skiffs propelled
by poles or oars where the water was deeper.

The Lake halfbits lived in houseboats on Mire Lake or in Laketowne, which comprised a group of stilt houses on the edges of the
lake, mirecat processing plants, and the piers where the fishing boats
offloaded their catches. Laketowne also contained a large marina
where wealthy halfbits from Halfbittowne kept their sailboats.

The Smuckland halfbits were similarly divided into the
Banksmucks, Riversmucks, and Marshsmucks or Marshers. The
Banksmucks lived on the relatively dry river banks and farmed corn,
wheat, and vegetables. The Riversmucks lived in boats on the river
itself and were fishermen. The Marshsmucks made a living raising
pigs and harvesting bog eels.

As a race that was widely regarded as inferior by most of Central Oith's inhabitants, one might imagine that halfbits would embrace the notion of equality among themselves. The opposite was in fact true: all classes of halfbits considered themselves the best and looked down on all the others, causing much petty bickering among the residents of the Mire.

At the start of our story, Froyo Bagpants was the owner of Boggy End. As one of the prime pieces of real estate in the Mire, its owner was generally regarded as minor nobility. The only fancier addresses were the dwellings at the top of Mire Hill in Halfbittowne (towering one hundred feet over the bog) and the tenth-story penthouse suite of Halfbit Tower, a posh condo in the center of Halfbittowne.

Boggy End had been owned by a number of families though the years and it had always turned out badly for them. The Halfbittowne Mercantile Bank nearly always emerged the winner, as family after family defaulted on its mortgages and the bank repeatedly sold the property to social-climbing halfbits.

The Bagpants family name came from lowly origins. The name of Bagpants was attached to the profession of plumber. Plumbers in the Mire carried a lot of their gear in special overalls that were at least lumpy, if not actually baggy, with tools and parts. Bagpants remains a regional term for plumber, as in "The commode is backed up again so I'll have to fetch the bagpants." A number of Froyo's forebears were well known plumbers, including his grandfather and father. Bobo's father, Nobo, made a good living as a plumber in Halfbittowne, but the turning point for his fortunes came when he invested in a small pipeweed plantation on the South Mound, which subsequently allowed him to make further investments that grew into a small empire. Nobo became so wealthy that he fell into the Boggy End trap, buying it at the height of his prosperity. Unfortunately, soon after he purchased Boggy End, Rojo Red became available in the Mire (imported through Brie) and the demand for Southbog weed plummeted. It looked as if Boggy End would prove to be Nobo's undoing (as it had been for many others) but before he could suffer the ignominy of defaulting on his mortgage, he managed to drown on a sport fishing trip when he became tangled in the tackle and the mirecat he was trying to land dragged him over the side of the boat.

After Bobo inherited Boggy End it continued to suck all the profits out of his father's businesses. Then Grandkopf and the dwarves came and spirited Bobo off on the Dragon Mountain adventure. When Bobo returned from Dragon Mountain he found his beloved Boggy End in foreclosure proceedings. Much to the dismay of the Halfbittowne Mercantile Bank, Bobo paid off the mortgage with good dwarf gold and became the first owner in a millennium to own Boggy End outright. When Bobo departed for Clovendell he signed Boggy End and all of his business interests over to Froyo, who became the lord of the manor. Froyo's businesses allowed him to live quite comfortably and to support the halfbit family (the Gimchees), seven generations of whom had lived on Boggy End and had functioned as its caretakers. The Gimchees had five small halfbit holes at their disposal. At the time of the story only two were occupied—one by Froyo's friend Sammy and one by Sammy's father, Spud.

Poupon Roak was a member of the powerful South Mound family whose name was taken from the sound a frog makes. They owned the western half of the South Mound, an area the locals called Roakland. The seat of the family's power was Roaktowne, at the western edge of the island. While many of the extended family members were responsible for individual businesses, the patriarch of the family traditionally oversaw all the family interests and ruled Roakland as if it were his own soggy kingdom. Poupon's father, Crepaud Roak, was the manager of the family's frog-leg packing business, the Roak Frog Products plant on the southern side of Roaktowne, where Poupon was employed as a frog processor. However, Poupon's major skill was slacking off, and he spent most of his time hanging out with any friend who had money in his pocket.

Marty was a Banksmuck, one of the most influential families of Smuckland. The Banksmucks farmed the bottom land around the confluence of Smuck Creek and the Makewater river. The land there benefited from the regular spring floods of the Makewater and thus they supplied the Mire and Brie with corn and wheat.

The Banksmucks built their houses on barges in order to float through the spring floods. Every spring several houses would break loose from their moorings and the inhabitants would, as the Banksmucks called it, go boating. The community banded together to find the families' homes and would either return them to their original locations or help build new ones if they had floated too far downstream to retrieve. The possibility of going boating resulted in approximately half of the inhabitants of Smuckland suddenly visiting their friends, relatives, and acquaintances in the Mire proper during the spring floods. This phenomenon was known locally as the Smuck migration.

The Riversmucks main occupation was fishing and they lived in houseboats on the Makewater River. The Marshsmucks lived in stilt houses like their lowbog brethren from the Mire proper. Their main occupation was gathering the local population of bog eels (the only ones outside the Mire). Because the residents of the Mire preferred the Smuckland bog eels, while the Smuckland halfbits preferred the flavor of the eels from the bogs, several families of halfbits made a good living shuffling barrels of eels up and down Smuckland Road and selling them at a premium.

The ravenous nature of the halfbits practically guaranteed that the major industry of the Mire was food production, particularly rice, pork products, bog eels, and bog fruit. Rice was cultivated extensively throughout the Mire, with the majority coming from the rather lightly inhabited Eastbog. The Mire's famous swimming pigs adapted to their boggy surroundings by swimming as a means of foraging. They traveled in loose groups called swerds, tended by pigboys who used shallow boats to swerd the pigs to the processing stations.

When the Mire was first settled, snakes were numerous, including the dangerous bog viper, the bog rat snake, and the beautifully striped bog hoop snake. By the end of the Second Age all varieties of snakes were extinct. The halfbits had eaten them.

Unlike the snakes, bog eels breed prodigiously and were thus saved from extinction. Considered a delicacy by the locals, they are prominently featured in many of the Mire's most beloved dishes, the best known of which was fried breakfast eels. Bog eels were breaded with secret spice mixtures, fried, and smothered in white gravy. Each region of the Mire had its own spice mixture and each not only considered the others to be inferior but to be downright wrong. Many a tavern brawl had started over the proper way to prepare bog eels.

Bog eels were exported to only a few establishments, most of which catered to halfbits in nearby Brie. After the Great War with the Great Schnoz, Froyo Bagpants began to spend a lot of time with Grandkopf the Gray in Eisenfang, so salted bog eels from the Mire were brought in on a regular basis. Some dwarves tried them at the breakfast buffet one day, liked them, and soon bog eels were exported in small quantities to places with significant dwarf populations. However, the other races of Central Oith never grew to appreciate them. After all, it was the general consensus that halfbits (and dwarves) would eat anything.

Bogfruit grew only in the Mire. Its flavor was described as a cross between a strawberry and a cranberry, and the fruit was made into jams, jellies, spreads, and other condiments that were widely distributed. Until fried bog eels caught on with the dwarves, bogfruit products were the only Mire-made foods deemed edible by anyone outside the Mire.

Halfbits ate six meals a day—if they could get them. First breakfast occurred immediately upon awakening and second breakfast two hours later. Elevenses were, as one might expect, a light repast at eleven o'clock sharp intended to tide one over until lunch, which was served at noon and usually lasted for two or three hours. Four o'clock tea tended toward the lighter side (lighter by halfbit standards, meaning only three courses) and dinner could be served at any time in the evening—rural halfbits generally ate earlier and their more sophisticated city counterparts rather later. Working halfbits usually took first breakfast and dinner as sit-down meals. The remaining meals, in the interest of actually working at least part of the day, they took with them, carrying large food boxes decorated with the traditional patterns of their home bog.

For sit-down meals, halfbits used rectangular plates four thumbs by sixteen thumbs (approximately six by twenty-four inches) called troughs. The plates had a raised rim all around, and the short sides had curved handles to provide a good grip on the food while it was being carried to the table. The handles were decorated with colorful leather straps. The straps were used to secure the troughs to the table by tying them to metal eyes set in the table tops. This kept the troughs from sliding away when the feeding became too energetic. Halfbits often ate communally, emitting loud smacking, chewing, burping, grunting, and snorting noises which, to one unfamiliar with halfbit gustatory culture, sounded almost exactly like slopping time at a pigsty. Halfbits prided themselves on their noisy eating habits; indeed, a too-quiet meal implied a lack of enthusiasm for the food to one's host. Talking with a full mouth was considered normal because, well, there wouldn't have been any conversation otherwise. On occasions where a state of ecstasy was achieved during the meal and a fork seemed inadequate to the task of conveying food to one's mouth, halfbits were known to abandon their utensils altogether in favor of plunging face-down into their troughs. Reaching for rolls, salt, or butter while at a table full of halfbits in a trough frenzy could prove a dangerous proposition; missing digits in the halfbit population were far more often acquired at the table than in farming or industrial accidents.

APPENDIX II

MONEY AND MEASURES OF CENTRAL OITH

Don't take any wooden chickens. –Spud Gimchee

In the time of Darren the Great, the dwarf chieftains gathered in the halls of Krazi-dumb to standardize their money. The problem was that the gold coins from the different dwarf kingdoms contained different amounts of gold and each dwarf kingdom advocated for its coinage to the exclusion of the others. After much argument, Darren the Great sent for his head smith, Howa, known as the Hammerhead, to hear his advice.

Howa Hammerhead was in the midst of shoeing a horse when he was summoned. He was annoyed to be interrupted, so he threw down the horse shoe he had been working on and said, "Here, use that." Offending all of the dwarf chieftains at once could have proved to be a fatal mistake, but the dwarf lords were too busy to be offended: they were squabbling among themselves over whose idea it was and who was to keep the standard shoe. The Hammerhead's insult was overlooked and he returned to his work in peace.

Because the weight of the dwarf coins mandated by the shoe was different from all of the existing coins, all of the dwarves were equally pissed off, a sign of a good compromise, but at the same time each was smugly satisfied that the others were as cheesed-off as they were.

The standard of weight became the shoe—2.47 pounds or 1.12 kg by our world's measure. One thirty-seventh of a shoe was named a shot after the common-sized lead shot used in the dwarves' slings for hunting small animals. In our world measure, one shot equals 1.069 ounce avoirdupois or 30.32 grams. One-sixth of a shot is a pat (5.053 g), approximately the weight of a pat of butter or a U.S. nickel.

Dwarves, elves, and men all mint gold coins that weigh one shot. The dwarves call them the Darren because of the portraits of Darren the Great on both sides. The Clovendell mint and the mint of Gonner produce coins called golden geese that have a goose on the obverse and an egg on the reverse. Both sides are marked 1G. The Del Mar mint produces a coin called the golden tuna. Both sides show a swimming tuna and are marked 1T. The tuna on the obverse faces left and the one on the reverse faces right so that the heads of the tunas point to the same edge of the coin. The tuna can therefore be used for decision making because the tuna will face either right or left after the flip.

One-shot silver coins are minted with a value of one-nineteenth of a goose. The dwarves put the Dragon Mountain on theirs, complete with dragon perched on top. These coins are called, unsurprisingly, dragons. Men and elves use the smiling face of a pig on the obverse and a pig's curly tailed butt on the reverse. Both sides are marked 1P. The Del Mar mint uses a scallop shell on both sides. These coins are called either the scallop or the shell, depending upon local custom. The shell is generally considered the prettiest of the silver coins.

Men and elves mint bronze coins called chickens that are exchanged at the rate of seventeen bronze chickens per silver pig. The coins have a chicken on the obverse and an egg on the reverse. Both sides are marked 1C. The bronze chickens are approximately the size of U.S. dollar coins, approximately two-thirds of a thumb (for thumb as a unit of measure, see below). The Del Mar mint uses a seahorse on both sides. This coin is properly called a seahorse but most of the population refers to it as simply a horse. The dwarves do not consider bronze to be real money, so they mint small coins that contain one-seventeenth of a shot of silver (1.78 g). These coins have fire-lizards on both sides and are called lizards, which are approximately three-quarters the weight of a U.S. dime. One rarely saw the lizards in general circulation for they were too easy to misplace. Most of the peoples of Central Oith preferred the heft of the chickens and seahorses.

Most of the localities of Central Oith issue smaller coins called bits, worth a twenty-ninth of a bronze chicken. Bits are issued by local banks and businesses, and their designs, sizes, and weights vary. Dwarves, of course, do not recognize these as money. While most localities use one another's coins interchangeably, a merchant in a large city such as Minor Tetons might balk at taking a coin marked First Fireman's Credit Union, Halfbittowne.

Central Oith money is based on gold and therefore the exchange rate between our world and Central Oith fluctuates, depending upon the price of gold. At the time of writing, golden geese are worth USD 1220.25, silver pigs USD 64.22, bronze chickens USD 3.78, and bits approximately USD 0.13.

The basic unit of length in Central Oith is the thumb, determined by the length of a dwarf's thumb from tip to first knuckle. The thumb is 1.525 inches or 3.874 cm. All the races of Central Oith use a unit called the foot, which differs according to race. Men use a foot of 7 thumbs, elves use 6 thumbs, dwarves use 5 thumbs, and halfbits use 8 thumbs. For the purposes of commerce in Central Oith, the foot of men (called a manfoot) is used, which measures 10.68 inches, 0.89 U.S. feet, or 27.13 cm. Be aware when traveling that the tradesmen use the local foot, so a foot-long hot dog may vary from seven to twelve inches depending upon the place of purchase. Note that sausages are generally ordered in thumbs.

The height of beings is given in thumbs rather than in feet because the notion of feet varies so widely. For example, Froyo measures 28 thumbs, Gwendolyn stands 43 thumbs, and Arrowshaft stands 49 thumbs.

A stride is the length of a man's stride from right heel mark to right heel mark. This is standardized to 5 manfeet. A thousand strides equals a mile. This makes the Central Oith mile approximately 4451 U.S. feet or 0.84 statute miles. A league is three miles, 15,000 manfeet, or 2.53 U.S. miles.

Liquid measure is also based on the shoe. A shoe of water weighs as much as the shoe, the unit of weight. Therefore, a shoe is 1.19 quarts or 1.12 liters. Froyo didn't actually have a pint of beer in Brie as he was returning from his labors; he had a stein, which is 0.5 shoe, 0.593 quarts, or 1.19 pints. A pitcher is 2 shoes or 4 steins. A pail is 4 shoes or 1.185 gallons. A keg is 13 pails.

Throughout the Schnoz of the Rings, Central Oith units have been converted to U.S. inches, feet, and miles to aid comprehension.